Desperate Pursuit In Rio de Janeiro

Karynne Summars

For permission requests, write to the publisher, addressed "Attention: Permissions Coordinator," at the address below. ksek711@gmail.com

Publisher's Note:
This is a work of fiction. Names, characters, places, and incidents are a product of the author's imagination. Locales and public names are sometimes used for atmospheric purposes. Any resemblance to actual people, living or dead, or to businesses, companies, events, institutions, or locales is completely coincidental.

Desperate Pursuit in Rio de Janeiro /Karynne Summars
1st Edition.
ISBN 978-0-9893910-2-3
All rights reserved.

Library of Congress Control Number: 2014920174

Printed in the United States of America

Cover Design by Sean Strong

Books by Karynne Summars

Desperate Pursuit in Venice

Desperate Pursuit in Rio de Janeiro

What Readers Say About The Award-Winning Prequel
DESPERATE PURSUIT IN VENICE

"A first class thriller! Eloquently written. A captivating, emotional, seductive and thought-provoking read".
-PopImpressKA Journal

"This read was an exhilarating roller coaster ride that kept me turning the pages to see what would come next. Karynne Summars has a sophisticated writing style, yet one that is easy to follow and one that keeps you fully engaged in the characters' intricate game of life."
-Pam Evans-Author of RingExchange

"This was not the predictable romance story one reads, so I was impressed with the author. I felt that I had also traveled to Europe and was part of the unfolding story."
-Book Reviewer for Readers Favorite

"Wow. This book really surprised me. I was sad when it ended."
-Book Reviewer on Goodreads

"The author writes in a ravishing imaginative style and with a lot of suspense."
-Book Reviewer on Amazon

"Summars mixes romance with adult occupations and troubles to create a thought-provoking, pulse-accelerating work."
-Pure Jonel-Book Reviewer

"This would be a great movie."
-Book Reviewer

ACKNOWLEDGMENTS

I would like to thank Shuj Datoo for being so generous with his free time to proofread my work. A truly altruistic person and close friend.

Thank you also to my family, and especially to my sister, for the continued support.

A special thank you goes to Olga Papkovitch for featuring my creative projects in her inspiring and unique magazine PopImpressKA Journal.

My gratitude also goes to my friends and creative collaborators in the filmmaking space, Nakkeeran and Yegavaani. I believed in you and your creative talents when I saw the trailer of your movie Disturbed as well as Nakkeeran's music videos. Your commitment and passion made it easy for me to join you as one of the Executive Producers for Disturbed. Doing so opened another world for me I absolutely love, which allowed me to meet more amazing new friends and extremely talented people.

Since writing and publishing the prequel Desperate Pursuit in Venice, I met many inspiring people who I call friends now. I wish you all the success in the world.

Dedicated to the indigenous tribes in the Amazon
rain forests and their quest to preserve our green planet

ONE

Vincente Barone is recalling his life-changing dinner meeting with Luca Romano. What a small world. Luca's fiancée Kataryna Taylor is his adopted son's biological sister. What are the odds that she would have ever found out that Francesco is her brother and that they would ever meet? Yet the impossible has now occurred when Luca presented the adoption paper and explained that Francesco's biological family wants him to know. How is Francesco going to react when he finds out that the only parents he has known are not his biological parents and that this fact was kept a secret for 33 years?

His wife will be devastated when she finds out that Francesco's biological family managed to track them down and insists that he be told. Francesco was born in Germany where they had lived for several years before moving to Italy. They had adopted him the minute he was born and decided that no one needed to know that he was not their biological child. Everything had worked out perfectly until now. How will their families react when they find out? The inevitable conversation he will have to have with his son is running through his mind. The thought scares him.

◆ ◆ ◆

Kataryna is awake, tossing and turning. Why hasn't Vincente spoken to Francesco, she is wondering?

Here it is two days before her and Luca's trip to New York and they are no closer yet to telling Francesco that he was adopted and that Kataryna and Aleksandra are his biological siblings. She had made the point that she wanted this settled before they leave for their trip to New York.

With the acquisition and the move to Milan behind her and a wedding date scheduled, her life was finally perfect. She was so happy when she learned that Francesco Barone was her biological brother, but was then stopped cold from moving forward and telling him the exciting news. Her patience is dwindling fast. They have been sitting on this news for weeks now. How much longer can she bear with not starting her brother/sister relationship with Francesco? It is getting more difficult every day because they are bound together in every walk of life. There has to be a way to speed this up. She will have to convince Vincente to get it over with and tell his wife that Francesco's biological family insists on revealing this important information to him immediately. Life is too uncertain to procrastinate.

"What's the matter, Principessa?" Luca wakes up.

"I can't sleep. My mind is racing. I want Francesco to know that he is my brother before we leave for New York."

Luca takes her hand. "You agreed you would give Vincente time to discuss it with his wife first."

"Yes, but that was weeks ago. I also said I wanted this settled before we leave. What if we die on the trip? I will never have had the opportunity to tell him that I am his sister."

Luca sighs and pulls her closer to him.

"We are not going to die on this trip. Please relax and be patient. You know that Sylvia is quite sick and Vincente has to deal with that right now."

"So are you saying that if she doesn't get well he won't reveal it at all? What if this drags on for months? When I look at Francesco all kinds of emotions well up. I go from elated that he is my brother to upset that he is unaware of what is going on behind his back. Don't try to talk me out of it, but I am going to call Vincente tomorrow to discuss it with him."

"I am not even going to attempt to stop you. I know that this situation is unbearable. All I am asking is that you try to understand his side, too. It's going to be a major shock for Francesco when he finds out that he is not who he thought he was, that neither his mother nor his father is his biological parent. Have you ever wondered how you would feel if someone told you that your entire life was a lie?"

"Well, in a way it was, too. I should have grown up with a brother and only in November last year did I find out that I had one."

"Yes, of course but it doesn't change your identity. The parents who raised you are your biological parents and you grew up with your biological sister. So this is not the same situation Francesco will be going through once he is told that he was adopted. At this time all he knows is that he is half Italian and half German and the Barones are his parents."

"This is not the issue at hand, though. We will deal with that and I will help Francesco through it. Right now this doesn't go any further because of Sylvia's illness. He could drag this out for quite some time. And don't you think Patrizia should know more about the ancestry of her future husband? They are getting married in about three months."

"Patrizia will love and marry Francesco regardless of his ancestry, but sure, it would be good to make it known soon."

"I am still stunned by the fact that you and Patrizia will marry into the same family almost without ever knowing. If my father hadn't said anything, Francesco and I would have lived next to each other our entire lives as in-laws. This is unreal."

"Can we go back to sleep now for a while? I promise all will be well soon."

"Thank you for your support, darling. You have no idea how difficult it is for me to look at my brother and not being able to tell him."

"Dr. Barone is in surgery," the assistant advises Luca when he calls Vincente's office the next morning. "I don't expect him back here until midafternoon."

"Please have him call me as soon as he gets in," Luca requests.

"What should I tell him this is in reference to?" she probes.

"It's a personal call. He will know," Luca responds. "Please tell him it is urgent."

◆ ◆ ◆

While sipping her morning tea, Kataryna stares at the computer screen. Nothing seems to register right now. She is entirely preoccupied. Not even the view of Lake Como from the villa's home office can quiet her mind. The sound of her cellphone ringing brings her back into the moment.

"Good morning, Kataryna," she hears Francesco's soft voice. "Are you ready for your trip to New York?"

She is startled. "Yes, pretty much," she hears her own voice saying in an almost trance, "but I don't even feel like going."

"Why is that?" Francesco enquires. "Don't you trust me alone here with the company?"

"Of course I trust you, Francesco. We are cut from the same cloth," she responds, immediately alarmed by her choice of words.

"Are we?" Francesco says amused. "Well, I take that as a compliment. You are a very accomplished business woman."

Kataryna is relieved. Thank God he didn't pick up on anything, but why would he? He has no clue what's going on.

"I just filed the name change of the company you requested with the lawyers. As of tomorrow, the company will be known as BioMedyca. I was wondering if we can schedule at least one of the interviews for the CFO position before you leave?" Francesco asks. "The recruiter just called to see what our next step is."

"Sure, we can do that tomorrow. I am not coming to Milan today. So why don't you arrange one of the interviews in the morning and one late afternoon."

"Yes, Signora," he says jokingly, "I will do so. Thank you for taking the time. I know you have a full plate but at least you will get a first impression of the candidates and can communicate that to Stephen when you see him in New York before we invite them for the second round."

"Exactly. We need to move on this so you can focus on the CEO responsibilities. We've got a lot to do on that front. When I get back we have to sit down with the R&D guys to see what new products they have in the pipeline. You know that I have been asked for interviews by the international financial news media when I get to New York. They have featured my private equity firm prominently right after the BioMedyca acquisition."

"Yes, I know. I read the article. As far as our R&D is concerned, I am hoping we can come up with some bio-identical products to fight some of the nasty diseases in this world without destroying healthy tissue in the process.

Needless to say, the pharmaceutical companies will fight us tooth and nail along the way."

"Speaking of diseases, how is your mother doing?" Kataryna dares to ask.

"She has good days and bad days. We are still waiting for the final results from the clinic."

"Any idea of what is going on with her?"

"One of the specialists said it could be some autoimmune disorder where certain cells are attacking her body. Wouldn't it be great if BioMedyca could develop something to make her well?"

"Yes, but before we can think in that direction, we would need to know what exactly is the matter with her."

"I know. I hope she will be better for my wedding, which is creeping up fast here. Can you believe it, it's less than three months away?"

"Unbelievable how time flies. Please give my regards to your mother and tell her I wish her a speedy recovery."

"Thank you. Let me call the recruiter quickly and arrange the interviews for tomorrow so we will have a CFO in place before my big day."

"You do that. I will see you tomorrow at your office. Why don't you email me the interview agenda with the questions you intend to ask."

"Coming up in a few minutes. Ciao."

Kataryna reviews the CVs of the candidates. All of them have an impeccable professional background but one of them stands out in her opinion. She wonders if Stephen and Francesco feel the same way. Francesco's email with the interview agenda and questions arrives. Pretty close to the questions she came up with. "Well, great minds think alike, my dear brother," she says out loud.

Mariya enters the home office after a light knock.

"Would you like me to prepare lunch for you, Signora?"

"Yes, thank you Mariya. I will be right up."

"I made veal Milanese with an arugula salad for you." Mariya smiles, knowing it is one of Kataryna's favorite meat dishes.

"You are the best," Kataryna exclaims while shutting off her computer.

As she gets ready to head upstairs for lunch her cellphone rings. She looks at the screen with the intention of letting it go to voice mail but then sees that Francesco is calling her again.

"Wow, Francesco." she laughs into the phone, "twice within a few hours. I hope this isn't a bad sign."

"I just got the most unbelievable news," Francesco says excitedly. "We have to meet as soon as possible. I don't want to do this over the phone."

Kataryna's heart starts racing. "Really? Can you be a little more specific?"

"Not right now. Let's meet early tomorrow morning before the first interview," he suggests, "but please don't say anything to Luca yet."

"I wouldn't know what to say. You are not telling me anything but you really got me curious now. See you tomorrow."

Vincente must have finally told him, goes through her mind. "Well, it's about time," she says out loud elated.

TWO

Larissa Dos Santos is getting ready for her interview with the BioMedyca top management. After some final touches on her resumé, she runs through her professional background in her mind again. This CFO position would be a perfect fit for her. She has been following BioMedyca for the past few years but so far the company did not have any openings at her level. When she saw the press release in February announcing Roberto Silvestri's departure, she had hoped that an executive management position would become available. Reviewing Kataryna Taylor's bio, she wonders what it would take to impress a woman like that. You never get a second chance to make a first impression, she reminds herself. Getting slightly nervous about the interview, she decides better not to have any more caffeine. It would just increase the jitters she is feeling already. She leaves her house earlier than necessary, just in case.

"Good luck with the interview, mamma," her daughter Eliana shouts after her. "You got this."

"Thank you, sweetie. I know I have the credentials for this position. I just need a lucky break," Larissa replies. "I am certain they will invite quite a few qualifying candidates."

◆◆◆

"Good morning, Francesco. So what's the unbelievable news you have?" Kataryna hugs him a little tighter than usual when she walks into his office.

"You are early," he says smiling broadly. "Let's have some coffee and talk."

"I could hardly sleep," she responds smiling back at him, anticipating what he will say next.

"Really?" he laughs out loud. "Me neither. This could be something to celebrate but it has to stay between you and me for the time being. We can't go public with this yet."

"OK. OK. Now spit it out already so we can get it over with," she pressures him, surprised how well he must have taken the news that he was adopted.

He puts his hand on her arm and stares straight into her eyes with a little smirk. "I got a call yesterday from the owner of a privately-held company in Brazil. He would like to talk to us about medicinal plants they developed over the past five years, which apparently have shown promising results in the cure of certain serious diseases. He would be interested in doing business with us exclusively."

"This is the unbelievable news you wanted to share with me today?" she asks him perplexed.

"Yes, but I am not done yet," Francesco stammers, unsure why Kataryna doesn't seem to be as excited as he is. "The company's assets are also up for sale because the owner has no successors. His children are not interested in the biomedical field and asked him to sell the company so they can open up their own businesses. He agreed to look into it and he wants to offer it to us first. Do you understand what this means? We would be our own raw material supplier, which means no one else will be able to get hold of these plants. This could be huge for us." Francesco grins, expecting her to jump up for excitement.

She just sits there with a blank face trying to hide her disappointment that this conversation is not about their brother/sister relationship. They stare at each other silently for a few moments.

"This is interesting indeed," she finally says.

"Interesting?" Francesco looks at her baffled. "This is the break we have been looking for. I assume that you are on board pursuing this further?"

"Yes, of course," she responds matter-of-factly. "I will discuss it with Stephen when I see him in New York."

"We have to act fast, Kataryna," Francesco implores her. "This is a once in a lifetime break we are getting here. The owner of the company wants us to come over next month to meet with him and tour the area where the plants are grown and harvested. So what should I tell him?"

"Where would we have to go for this due diligence?"

"The shareholders, Mr. and Mrs. Oliveiro, live in the Rio de Janeiro area. They have invited us to stay with them. The manufacturing facility is close to Manaus, Amazonas because the plants are grown on a piece of property located at the border of Brazil and Colombia. We would have to go to all three places to kick the tires, so to speak. I know it would not be an easy trip but I have my eyes on the prize. Nothing ventured nothing gained."

Kataryna sighs. "A challenging trip. How do you know this man?"

"He had been in contact with Roberto and they became good friends over the years. Roberto had been over there several times. He was impressed and said that he could see great potential there for BioMedyca one day. So they agreed that as soon as there was proof that these plants can do what they thought they could do, we would get together to discuss a joint business venture with them. However, at that time there was no talk about selling the company or its assets yet."

"Well, it sounds promising. I just wish Roberto were still on board with us to spearhead this venture. It will be quite a challenge for you, Stephen and me. Was Luca ever involved in any of that?"

"No, not really. Roberto had mentioned it to him at the time but it was premature then. They had just loosely talked about it and tabled it for the future."

"So this would be a case of the blind leading the blind without Roberto, I guess." Kataryna concludes.

"Yes, but I know a little of what is going on there. So let's think positive. I am really excited about this."

Kataryna starts laughing. "I can just imagine Luca's face when I tell him that you and I are going to the Brazilian Amazonas region to check out some plants for BioMedyca."

"Yeah, it probably won't go over easy. I can see him flip out over this. Not to mention that my fiancée won't jump up for joy either."

"In that case we better prepare them well for that conversation," Kataryna says rolling her eyes. "I think I will have to buy some really sexy lingerie and give Luca a night he won't forget before I approach him with our travel plans."

"Yeah, and while you are at it, make sure you have a couple of tranquilizers ready for him to take when you try to coax him into letting you take this kind of a trip."

Kataryna is holding her head. "This day really started out with a bang. Now let's see how the interview with Larissa Dos Santos goes. Between you and me, on paper I am pretty impressed with her. Don't forget, it has to be a person who would also be qualified to take over the CEO role at least on an interim basis in case something happens to you."

"I am fully aware of that," Francesco agrees. "Here's another plus. She speaks Portuguese fluently. Hint. Hint."

"Oh, wow. The universe is aligning again," Kataryna says as they are walking toward the conference room to meet the candidate.

"Good morning Signora Dos Santos," Kataryna welcomes her. "Francesco and I have been looking forward to meeting you. You have an impressive background."

"Thank you, Signora. Taylor. I am pleased to be here. I have been following BioMedyca for many years and I am very excited about this opportunity."

"Great. Please call me Kataryna. I suggest that first we get to know each other a little bit and go from there. So, why don't I start and then Francesco can introduce himself. May we offer you something to drink?"

"No, thank you I am good for now," Larissa responds, delighted with the warm welcome.

Kataryna gives her a reassuring smile. "As you are aware from the press releases, my New York private equity firm just acquired BioMedyca on February 12. My partner Stephen Wagner and I established Adryana Investments LP about five years ago and we are constantly looking for new profitable investments. In order to explore additional European acquisition targets, my partner and I decided to open a satellite office in Europe. Because of our BioMedyca investment, Milan was an excellent place for me to move to but there is also a personal reason for my relocation to Milan. I am engaged to Signor Romano. So all good things came together and brought me here."

Kataryna hands Larissa the BioMedyca organization chart. "This is the current corporate structure. Stephen Wagner and I are Co-Chairmen of BioMedyca. We each hold 45 percent through Adryana Investments LP. The remaining ten percent are still in the hands of the Romano family. Francesco Barone is the Chief Executive Officer of BioMedyca, which became effective February 11 after the previous CEO Roberto Silvestri left the company. Before that, Francesco had held the position of Chief Financial Officer and deputy CEO. We are very pleased that we had such a smooth transition with Francesco on board."

Kataryna signals Francesco to continue with his introduction.

"Thank you, Kataryna," Francesco continues smiling proudly. He turns to Larissa. "I have been with BioMedyca for the last five years. Before that I worked for several years in the Mergers & Acquisitions division of a major investment bank where I was in charge of targets in the medical industry. I had initially intended to become a medical doctor but then changed my mind and left medical school in order to focus on finance and business. But as you can imagine my medical studies come in handy at times, especially here at BioMedyca. As you are aware from following our company, we are focusing on holistic bio-identical solutions rather than the pure chemical approach the pharmaceutical companies are following. My vision for BioMedyca is to expand and find a more natural cure for the worst diseases in this world. With Kataryna's guidance we also want to explore more business opportunities in the United States. Our research team is persistently looking to develop new products in order to come up with more natural solutions. On the personal side, I am also engaged to a Romano family member. My fiancée Patrizia and I are getting married on June 15 this year. And, believe it or not, I am half German on my mother's side. So Kataryna and I have a lot in common. That's it from my side for now. Why don't you tell us a little bit about yourself."

Larissa clears her throat. "Certainly. Let me first say that your vision for BioMedyca sounds great. I can totally identify with your goals. My father is an oncologist. He has been saddened many times by how the treatments he has to administer destroy his patients' quality of life. He is also looking into more natural and holistic cures."

"Good to know," Kataryna says.

"I have been in the CFO position with my present employer for the last ten years, and about five years ago I became the deputy CEO," Larissa continues. "The reason I am seeking this position is, first of all, that I have been waiting for an opportunity to join BioMedyca and, secondly, I don't see a great future ahead for my current employer. The company is owned by two brothers who have different visions, which causes a lot of stress and a high employee turnover. I can't see staying there much longer. I am originally from Brazil and came to Milan when I married a man who was half Italian. I met him in Belo Horizonte where most of my family lives. When my husband died in a car accident a couple of years ago, I almost left to return to Brazil. The only reason I didn't make that move was because of my daughter who grew up in Italy. She did not want to leave Milan and all her friends here. Although my entire family is in Brazil, I couldn't be that selfish and uproot my daughter apart from the fact that I also like it here in Italy."

What a coincidence, Kataryna is thinking. A native Brazilian with these credentials and connections over there.

"Please go on," Kataryna says, anxious to find out more. "What other relatives do you have in Brazil?"

"My brother is an international attorney at a large law firm located in Manaus, Amazonas."

Holy cow, Kataryna scratches her head; you couldn't make this stuff up. She looks at Francesco who is smiling and biting his lip.

Kataryna presses on. "If we were to make you an offer for employment, when would you be able to start?"

"Realistically in about four weeks but I could try to leave earlier. My current deputy would be happy to jump into my position immediately."

"OK," Kataryna responds, "we are going to interview two more candidates today. I will discuss our options with my partner in New York then. We would need to schedule a second interview via video call with him and then make our final decision. Before we adjourn today, do you have any questions for us?"

"Yes, I was wondering why the former CEO left the company fairly abruptly?"

"He left for personal reasons," Francesco answers.

"Yeah, what a shame. He built this company into what it is today but that's life, and we are fortunate to have Francesco in the CEO position now," Kataryna adds.

"Just one more question," Larissa says looking straight at Kataryna. "Why didn't your firm acquire all the shares of BioMedyca?"

"We are still working on how to address the remaining ten percent with the Romano family. That will be settled in the near future," Kataryna advises her. "If there is nothing else that should be it for today. Thank you for coming in. We will be in touch shortly."

Larissa leaves the office satisfied with herself and the interview. Now more than ever she wants this job.

Francesco and Kataryna look at each other grinning.

"Smart woman," Kataryna says. "Just what we need."

"Can you believe this?" he asks. "This is almost too good to be true."

"Yeah," she responds, "I can't wait to see Stephen's face when I get together with him."

Francesco laughs. "What about Luca's face? When are you going to tell him about our little trip to the Brazilian Amazonas rain forest?"

"If I tell Luca you will have to tell Patrizia at the same time otherwise you could be in a lot of trouble for not being forthcoming."

"You are so right. Shall we go for it tonight?"

"Let me see first what the situation is at home. I want him really calm and relaxed for that conversation. It's only just a month since our ordeal in Venice. In addition, I think we need to talk to Roberto to get more information about the Brazilian company and the owner."

"How are you going to pull that one off?" Francesco asks petrified. "Are you saying you want to go and talk to him?"

"Yes, together with you, of course."

"You are really asking for it, Kataryna. Luca is gonna have heart failure when you drop that bombshell."

Kataryna is laughing out loud. "He will have to handle that bombshell, I am afraid. But yes, it will be a tough one. I will send you a text if I decide to tell him tonight. I think I will have to do it, though because we are leaving for New York tomorrow."

After lunch Kataryna and Francesco interview the other two candidates. While they also appear to be qualified, they just can't compete with what Larissa brings to the table. As far as they are concerned the decision is pretty clear but Stephen will also have a say.

Late afternoon Kataryna returns to her office. When she exits the elevator she runs into Luca.

"Hello darling," she greets him cheerfully. "How was your day?"

"It just got so much better," he embraces and kisses her. "I was actually going to call you just now to tell you that I am in the mood for a romantic dinner."

"Are you, my dear?" she flutters her eyelashes at him. "What a coincidence, so am I. I will meet you at home in about an hour."

"I can't wait," he responds. "We have to take this opportunity because after tonight we are going to be in Carlotta's and Enrico's company for the next ten days. I may also have something delicate to discuss with you."

"Another coincidence. So do I." She gives him a sexy smile "This has all the makings of an interesting evening for us."

"Wouldn't it be an even greater coincidence if we both wanted to discuss the same thing?" Luca suggests.

Kataryna smirks. "I very much doubt that."

"OK, Principessa, let me get going to pick up some fabulous food for us from our favorite restaurant. All you have to do is be your sexiest self."

"I will do my best, darling to make this a super exciting evening. By the way, do you like coconut?"

"Yes. Why? Are you picking up dessert?"

"You could call it that," she responds with a trace of mystery.

When Kataryna gets home she takes a quick shower and then applies the organic coconut oil she bought all over her body. She puts the new sexy cobalt blue lingerie on, a slinky piece, which barely covers the naked lower part of her body.

"My darling Luca," she says looking at herself in the mirror, "I want you to enjoy every moment of this because what comes after may not be to your liking."

She sends Francesco a text message: *I am going for it tonight. Wish me luck.*

As she pours the chilled pink Champagne into the glasses on the nightstand, she hears Luca coming through the front door. She walks out of the bedroom to meet him.

"Good evening you dazzling creature, I can't wait to feed you a coconut flavored appetizer." She kisses him sensually on the lips and lets her fingers walk down his spine under his jacket. Sliding the jacket down his arms, she gazes into his eyes and then slowly unbuttons his shirt until it opens completely. She kisses his naked chest. He breathes in the coconut oil on her skin and slowly runs his tongue down her neck to taste it.

"This must be the best appetizer I ever had," he whispers holding her tightly against his body unable to control his impending arousal. "I can't get enough of that. I may even skip dinner."

"I was hoping you would love it and that it would entice you to want more," she purrs as she lays down on the bed positioning her legs into an inviting position.

Luca stares at her half naked body and races to get rid of his remaining clothes. He falls all over her sucking on the soft skin of her thighs to taste more of the sweet oil.

Kataryna moans in pleasure as his tongue assaults her female parts to take in the delicious oil and make her climax deeply while she is moving her body toward him, letting him enter her passionately. When he reaches his orgasm he is exhausted but extremely satisfied. He clutches her tightly.

"Wow," he whispers in her ear. "When I said I was in the mood for a romantic evening earlier, I never imagined how absolutely divine you would make me feel tonight.

I would have settled for a nice dinner and making love later on but this seductive welcome was something much more exciting. You can do that again and again anytime, darling, and that coconut oil on your skin was an extra nice touch. The aroma reminded me a little of our beautiful trip to Hawaii and Princess Kailani."

"I am so glad you liked it, darling," Kataryna says caressing his hair. "I promise to do it again and again," she kisses him softly. "I want you to know that my love for you has no boundaries and making you happy will be my life's mission."

"I truly love you, Principessa. The combination of our raw sexual attraction for each other, the sweetness of the oil and your touch were incredible, for lack of a better word. You once again stunned me in a way I will never forget."

Kataryna is touched that she was able to create such a beautiful moment for them but anxious about what she has to do after dinner.

"Let's have something to eat now and then we will see what pops up next," she says laughing.

"I am pretty sure something is going to pop up later on," Luca alerts her, chuckling. "As a matter of fact I can feel it already."

They sit down at the dining table, which she had nicely set for them.

"How about some wine?" she hands him a glass of Amarone. "Here's to our romantic evening and to our trip to New York," she toasts.

"Here's to all three of you, Principessa, Princess Kailani and Queen of the Nile," Luca makes a toast.

Kataryna laughs. "You get three lovers and I only get one. What's wrong with this picture?"

"Aren't you forgetting that you created these three lovers and that they come in one person, and that this person is the love of my life?"

"Of course not, and you are more than enough for me, darling. I am just teasing you. You are such an easy target."

"You got that right. I am a super easy target when it comes to you. I would do anything for you, my love. I think you know that." He softly kisses her cheek.

"You may get the opportunity to prove that tonight," she challenges him.

"Oh? What do you have in mind? Name it and I'll do it."

"Easy, darling, easy. You may regret that offer," she murmurs, playing with her food.

"Why don't you tell me what you want so I can prove that I mean it. With one caveat, of course."

"Which is?" she asks anxiously.

"No postponement of our wedding."

"Of course not. I am looking forward to becoming Signora Romano." Kataryna smiles sweetly and takes his hand in hers.

"OK. I can breathe easy now." "So what can I do for you, Principessa?" Luca grins, raising his eyebrows.

She bites her lip, trying to find a way to communicate her travel plans to Brazil.

"You had mentioned earlier that you wanted to discuss something with me," she says, "why don't you go first."

"Sure," Luca responds quickly. "I wanted to ask you when would be a good time for us to talk about if we want to have children."

Gee, she didn't expect that subject tonight but it could be helpful to ease him into what she has to tell him. Let's invoke the quid pro quo rule. If I give a little, he will have to give a little, she figures, smiling at him mysteriously.

"That is some smile you are giving me, Principessa. What may I conclude from that?" he chuckles somewhat nervously.

Kataryna breathes in and out deeply. "That is some bombshell you are dropping here the night before our flight to New York."

"I don't think I dropped that bombshell, as you call it, yet. I was just enquiring when would be a good time to activate that bombshell," Luca says jovially.

"How about we do activate that bombshell and another one from my side right now?"

"Now you got me worried. We might have a huge explosion any moment with all these bombshells flying around."

"OK, let's not talk around it any longer. All cards on the table. Here is my thinking. I believe that you would want to have an heir or two."

He nods staring into her eyes. "Two would be good."

"That doesn't surprise me and I am not opposed to that idea."

Luca hugs her tightly. "Gee, thank you. I didn't expect such a quick decision from you tonight. You have no idea how happy I am right now. I wasn't sure how you would react to this subject. I didn't want to spoil our perfect night, but since you asked me point blank what I wanted to discuss with you, I went for it."

"Good, so now that we are both on the same page with that, here comes my explosive newsflash, and I expect you to react as well to that as I did to your bombshell."

"Let me have it," Luca says somewhat concerned now.

Kataryna fills him in about Francesco's phone conversation with the Brazilian company owner and what that kind of acquisition would mean for BioMedyca if the claims they are making were true.

"Sounds exciting," Luca says, "this should definitely be pursued further but where is the bombshell part of that?"

"Francesco and I will have to travel to Brazil to begin with the due diligence, first meeting the owner in Rio de Janeiro, then going to Manaus, Amazonas to look at the manufacturing facility and finally, in order to evaluate the entire process, to the property where the plants are grown and harvested, which is located at the border of Colombia."

Luca's mouth drops open. "Whoa!" He rubs his chin contemplating how to react to this situation.

"Do you have any idea what dangers are lurking in these areas?" he quietly states not letting on that his heart is racing with fear for her safety.

"I wasn't even done yet with the explosives," she responds equally softly, "there is another part to that."

"Now I am really getting scared," he responds. "Are you trying to kill me before we are even married?"

She puts her arms around his shoulders.

"Francesco and I will have to meet with Roberto to learn more about what he has been discussing previously with the Brazilian owner. He has been to the territory several times. Before venturing into this, we really need him to guide us in this potential acquisition in order to fully understand it. Francesco was not part of any of the discussions before. Roberto had only mentioned to him that he met with the owner and that there might be something valuable to follow up on in the future. Apparently, Roberto and the owner also became friends over the last few years and he stayed at his house when he went over there. The owner has invited us to stay at his house on the outskirts of Rio. I am actually looking forward to this journey. Brazil was always on the list of countries I wanted to visit."

"It's a beautiful country. I have been there as a tourist and we had a trustworthy local guide," Luca explains, "but this is different from what you would be doing over there."

"I can appreciate your concern, darling, but in a twist of fate the candidate for the CFO position we interviewed today is Brazilian. Her father, who lives in Belo Horizonte, is an oncologist and he is looking for a more holistic approach to cancer. Her brother is an international attorney who lives in Manaus, Amazonas. I was floored in a good way when she ran down her background. She's just what we need at BioMedyca with this new Brazilian opportunity. So we would have some trustworthy contacts there that could assist us in checking out the company and the claims they are making. Roberto can provide some necessary background information and give us his opinion."

"Well, at least this is a mitigating factor," Luca responds but his face still shows a touch of anxiety.

Kataryna kisses him. "Thank you for understanding that this is something I have to follow through with."

He lets out a deep sigh. "I just hope I won't regret letting you go over there. I would never forgive myself if anything happened to you. On a lighter note, you actually dropped two bombshells on me. The trip and the meeting with Roberto, which I am not at all thrilled about."

"Well darling, you also dropped two bombshells on me," she says smiling.

"How?"

"You indicated you would like to have two kids. Those are two bombshells in my book."

Luca laughs out loud. "You sure are skilled at twisting things in your favor, Principessa. However, we still have to talk about how the meeting with Roberto would go down. What are your thoughts on that?"

"I was thinking that Francesco and I could meet with him at the clinic."

"I ought to have my head examined for agreeing to this," he murmurs holding her close.

Kataryna is relieved. She kisses him on the lips.

"How about returning to the bedroom so I can check out another part of your body while you are examining your head," she jokes hugging him tightly.

He looks at her with a crooked smile. "Aren't you the master of manipulation. You really got me good this time. Don't make me regret this."

"Thank you, darling. I promise to be careful and vigilant. I am a big girl."

Luca gives her a sideways stare. "Isn't that what you told me a few months ago when I tried to warn you about Roberto's behavior after our meeting in Bellagio?"

"Really Luca, that's not fair," she exclaims, "that was a totally different situation."

"OK. OK. One more thing," he requests, "I need to see your travel agenda and who you are meeting with as well as detailed background information on the company and the owner. Preferably try to hook up with the father and brother of the candidate who, I assume, you will be extending an employment offer to. This way you have local contacts in case something adverse happens. Maybe she could also go along with you two. It would make me feel a little better."

"Absolutely," Kataryna responds, satisfied with the outcome. "You will get the itinerary and whatever else you want to see. As far as Larissa Dos Santos, our hopefully new CFO, coming along is concerned, we will have to see how this plays out depending on when she can join BioMedyca."

"By the way," Luca changes the subject, "I put in a call to Vincente but he hasn't called me back yet."

"You are the best, darling. You deserve a reward," she giggles.

While Luca proceeds to the bedroom Kataryna clears the table and sends a text message to Francesco: *I did it. All is well. I just had to agree to have two children. Ha-ha.*

He texts her back: *All done here, too but she is not happy that I am taking such a trip so close to our wedding.*

Kataryna smiles to herself. Two sets of brothers and sisters trying to work with each other, except that one of them doesn't even know that he has a sister. Her thought is interrupted when Luca calls her.

"What are you doing out there? I thought you wanted to examine my body."

"Dr. Taylor is on her way," she yells back laughing, "I expect the patient to be disrobed as well as ready, willing and able to participate in the physical exam."

THREE

"Good morning," Kataryna greets her future sister-in-law Carlotta, her son and his cousin when she and Luca board the Romano jet.

"Buongiorno." Carlotta gets out of her seat to hug the two.

Enrico and Stefano wave at them. "Ciao."

"Ciao. You two must be excited about finally going to New York," Luca says.

"Yeah. We can't wait to explore the city and hang out with Natasha and Sabrina and their friends."

"Make sure you guys behave yourselves, okay? We want to leave again with a favorable impression," Luca requests.

"What do you mean Uncle Luca?" Enrico asks.

"Well, be polite and don't be too forward. I know what can happen. I was 17 once, too." He smiles at the two boys.

"No worries, we will be on our best behavior otherwise we won't be invited there again."

"I am happy to hear that. That's very mature thinking." Luca winks at his sister.

"How are you feeling, Carlotta?" Kataryna asks. "Any more morning sickness or are you over that?"

"I am fine, at least physically," she responds with an eye roll, "but since I just gained a couple of pounds I won't be buying any clothes in New York."

"You can buy me some," Enrico teases his mother with a charming grin.

"While we are the on the subject of spending money, have you made a final decision yet as to which college courses you want to focus on?" Luca asks his nephew.

"What kind of courses should I take if I want to do what you are doing?" Enrico turns to Kataryna.

"Go for an MBA in Finance & Business," Kataryna tells him.

"Can I get a job at your firm when I am finished?"

"Why don't you join as an intern first to see if this is really what you want to do?"

"That's a good idea," Enrico agrees. "But first I need you to help me to get into a good college in the United States next year."

"Your mother and I will discuss it," Kataryna promises him looking at Carlotta for approval.

"I always thought you would join the Romano Holding Company," Luca says, surprised at Enrico's new career choice.

"So did I," Enrico responds, "but I kind of like this private equity business now. I can always come on board the family business later, right?"

"Sure but first you have to get a good education."

"You will be such a good father," Kataryna praises Luca after listening to his conversation with Enrico.

He smiles happily and kisses her. "Thank you. I am looking forward to that."

Carlotta looks at them surprised. "So you have decided to have children?"

Luca sighs. "Yes, but don't ask what I had to agree to in return."

"That's a subject for another day," Kataryna interjects quickly to kill any idea of having to explain that further.

"So what is our agenda while we are in New York?" Carlotta asks.

"I will have to meet with my business partner Stephen on Monday to discuss a few deals and some new hiring options," Kataryna responds. "You guys can do some sightseeing and shopping meanwhile. On Tuesday, I am meeting with the media to give a few interviews. After that I am free for the rest of the week. Next Saturday we have the birthday party for Enrico and the twins. My sister has arranged a private dining room at a popular restaurant with live entertainment for you guys." She looks at Enrico and Stefano.

"Cool," Enrico says, smiling at his cousin, giving him the thumbs up sign.

"Welcome to New York," Aleksandra greets them when they arrive at Kataryna's apartment late afternoon. "I made a nice dinner for you. I figured you all would rather take it easy the first day here."

"That's so sweet," Kataryna hugs her sister. "I am glad we don't have to go out tonight. So what did you make for us?"

"Osso Buco."

"One of my favorite dishes," Luca says.

"Why don't I show you your rooms." Kataryna leads Carlotta, Enrico and Stefano to their guest rooms.

"The twins are really beautiful and there is one for each of us," Stefano says while they are unpacking. "So which one do you want to hang out with, Natasha or Sabrina?"

"I don't know yet. I have to get to know them a little better so I can see their personalities," Enrico responds. "Let's finish unpacking so we can get back out there to talk to them a little more."

After an early dinner Aleksandra and her family leave to let the others get some rest.

"How are our wedding plans coming, Principessa?" Luca asks, kissing Kataryna lightly on her lips when they finally retire to the bedroom.

"Everything is coming along fine. I just didn't have much time lately to attend to that. I will meet with the event planner when we get back. We still have to come up with something for our honeymoon, though."

Luca grins. "I have an idea. Why don't we practice for that right now?"

"I was thinking location, darling." I don't think we have to practice much when it comes to that. We already got that down perfectly, don't you think?"

"We sure do, but you can never practice enough," he whispers in her ear while slowly undressing her.

"God, you are so smart," she breathes heavily, kissing his chest, sliding her hands down his back into his pants.

"Let me just warn you, we can't make too much noise because the walls are really thin here. I don't want the two boys to become witness to our so-called practicing. It might give them some ideas, if you know what I mean."

"I will be as quiet as a church mouse," Luca murmurs as their passion ignites. Kataryna moans under his touch. He softly puts his hand over her mouth. "Shhh, you are going to wake up the boys."

"Why don't you show me how quiet you can be," she giggles moving down to his groin to let her tongue slide all over him slowly but relentlessly. He quickly puts his hands over his mouth when a subdued groan slips out of him as he surrenders to this intense climax.

Kataryna caresses his hair, as they are winding down.

"That was a good practice session, darling, for what we have to do once our kids are sleeping in the room next to us."

"No need, Principessa, our bedroom in the villa has soundproof walls. We won't have to lower the sound effects there."

"Oh really? That was good forward thinking when you had the soundproof walls installed. I can't believe what a clever man I am going to marry," she teases him.

"And I can't believe what a sexy, resourceful and smart woman I am going to marry," he smirks.

"I guess we both hit the wife and husband jackpot." Kataryna kisses his cheek.

"I love you so much," he sighs, "I wouldn't know how to live without you anymore. I hope you understand how worried I am about your trip to Brazil. It really gives me a lot of anxiety. If it wasn't for this important acquisition I have to complete, I would be going with you to watch over you."

"Please don't be worried, darling. I promise to be really careful and Francesco will be there with me. I will check in with you at least twice a day and if anything appears strange I will discuss it with you first before I proceed."

"I am sorry, I just can't help being anxious about it. No matter how well-planned everything appears to be there is always a chance for something to go wrong."

"Yes, darling but that is the case with everything in life. I could cross the street tomorrow here in Manhattan and be hit by a bus or something."

"God forbid!" Luca's palm hits his forehead. "Don't ever put that image in my head again."

"I would be as devastated if something bad happened to you," she responds solemnly. "They might as well put me in a coffin next to you because I would not survive that pain. As a matter of fact when the time comes for us to die, I want to be first so I would never have to go through the pain of being without you."

"I am sorry, Principessa. I just needed to vent because it's constantly on my mind."

"I understand, darling. You have no idea what kind of hell I went through when you were in a coma after Roberto drugged you, not knowing if you would ever wake up. So I have been there. Let me know what I can do to make it more bearable for you. I love you more than anything in this world. I don't want you to be that worried or anxious."

"Thank you for understanding, my love."

◆ ◆ ◆

"Buongiorno." Carlotta joins Kataryna in the kitchen the next morning.

"Good morning, Carlotta. How are you feeling?"

"Very good but hungry. I am eating for two now."

"Yes, you are, my dear," Kataryna caresses Carlotta's belly. "Hello there, little one, you must be hungry, too. We will get something to you right away."

She hands Carlotta a piece of papaya. "You better get that down fast to him or her."

They are both laughing when Luca enters the kitchen.

"We were racing to feed the little troublemaker in Carlotta's belly." Kataryna fills him in.

"Pretty soon, you will also have a little troublemaker in your belly," Luca tells her. "So you might as well get a head start with some pointers from my sister."

Kataryna nods. "Yes, I will. That reminds me, since we are getting married in six months, that I should stop taking the birth control pills soon. I read that you should do that well before intending to get pregnant."

"You should stop very soon because I am shooting for our honeymoon night to get you pregnant."

Kataryna and Carlotta shake their head, giggling at that remark.

"I know that you are really good, darling, but even your consummate skills in that department won't be able to influence Mother Nature that way." Kataryna looks at him provocatively waiting for his comeback.

"Just wait and see, my dear. I may have a direct line to Mother Nature and accomplish that," he counters playfully.

Enrico and Stefano arrive in the kitchen before Kataryna or Carlotta can respond to that statement.

"Time for breakfast," Carlotta announces, trying to hold it together. "My two kids are hungry I suppose."

"I can say with absolute certainty that your 17-year old son is hungry," Enrico throws in casually, heading to the breakfast table.

After breakfast Natasha and Sabrina arrive to pick up the boys. The twins look sharp in their sporty outfits prompting an intense stare from the boys. Carlotta looks at her brother and rolls her eyes.

"Hey guys, remember what we talked about on the plane over, okay?" She hugs Enrico and kisses him on the cheek.

He grimaces somewhat embarrassed. "Of course, not to worry."

Carlotta hands him some money. "Here you go. Why don't you take the girls and Stefano out for lunch later on."

After the kids are gone, Kataryna, Luca and Carlotta get comfortable.

"Are you hoping for a girl?" Kataryna asks Carlotta.

"A girl would be nice. I am sure Roberto is hoping he will have a son. Well, we will find out soon. After Easter I will have the ultrasound exam."

"And then you will go see Roberto and tell him what it is?" Luca asks.

"Yes, that's the plan."

"Francesco and I will also have to meet with Roberto when we get back," Kataryna tells her.

Carlotta glances at Luca and then back at Kataryna.

"Do I dare to ask why?" she says surprised.

"It has to do with a business venture for BioMedyca. He is the only one who knows certain important details of the company we are talking to," Kataryna quickly replies.

"As you can imagine, I am not thrilled about that," Luca admits with a frown.

"Are you ever going to be able to forgive him for what he did to you in Venice?" Carlotta asks her brother.

"I really can't say at this point. This was surreal and I often have to think about it," he responds looking at Kataryna. "Does it ever come back to haunt you?"

"Yes, sometimes but not in a scary way. It just makes me very sad and then there is the business part. I wish he was still in the CEO position, especially now with these new developments."

"Isn't it incredible what we have been through together already considering that we all only met about four months ago?" Carlotta asks. "However, it's not all bad. Look at you two. You found each other and are engaged. I haven't seen a couple more perfect for each other. I am not very lucky in love so count your blessings that you found the love of your life."

Kataryna embraces Luca. "I am grateful for that every day but it's easy to love Luca that much," she responds. "He is everything a woman could want. I wonder if his ex-wife ever regrets betraying him the way she did."

"Probably not," Carlotta sighs. "She was a very selfish person. Everything was always about her."

"Well, for me everything is about Luca," Kataryna declares.

"I don't think I have to tell you that you are the center of my life, Principessa," Luca murmurs. "I still can't believe how lucky I am. As far as my ex-wife is concerned, I am glad that she cheated on me because otherwise you and I would not be together. What appeared pretty painful then was actually a blessing in disguise. You just never know what better situation waits for you around the corner."

"And now consider what Roberto must be going through," Carlotta says. "I bet Kataryna would have been the center of his life too, had they gotten together. In a way I can now understand why he tried to free himself from that emotional pain by taking all these pills. I can tell you from my own experience how unbearable this is. It is a deep pain you can't escape and there is really no cure for it other than hoping that it will pass with time. I am dealing with that every single day. If it wasn't for Enrico, I wouldn't know how to go on."

Kataryna is welling up. She hugs Carlotta whose eyes have also filled with tears. "Not only do I feel your pain but also Roberto's. How will he react when he sees me again? I have never been in a situation where on one side I was deliriously happy and on the other so sad at being the person causing another human being that kind of emotional pain. I never talked about it with anyone but it weighs heavy on me inside and I have nightmares occasionally. But these are my own personal demons I have to go through. I never really wanted to open that up to anyone."

"Well, I am glad you did and no, you don't have to go through this alone. I want to know when something like this is going on inside of you." Luca responds. "Is that why you are tossing and turning at night?"

Kataryna nods. "I feel so guilty."

"What do you have to feel guilty about?" Luca snarls. "This wasn't your fault. Sure, you could have told me earlier that he was still not over you but other than that you have nothing to feel guilty about." Luca turns to Carlotta. "My heart goes out to you. I often wonder what it would have been like for me if Kataryna had ended up with Roberto. Once you are emotionally involved it becomes very difficult to let go, I have to admit. So, yeah, poor Roberto, but I still can't fathom what happened in Venice.

OK, you two, let's bring on some happier thoughts now," he says putting his arms around both of them.

Kataryna smiles through her tears. "Luca to the rescue again. But you know, darling, we have to talk about these things because they won't go away just like that. You also need to work on your feelings toward Roberto and try to forgive him."

"It's not that easy," Luca admits.

The three spend the rest of the day relaxing and planning the next few days' activities.

Monday morning Kataryna heads down to Wall Street to meet with some investment bankers working on one of her U.S. deals. After lunch she makes her rounds of interviews with the financial newspapers going over the BioMedyca acquisition and expansion plans of the company in the U.S. Thereafter she joins her partner Stephen Wagner and Luca for dinner.

"What do you know about this Brazilian company?"

Stephen asks Luca after they filled him in on the proposed acquisition details.

"Unfortunately not much," Luca responds, "Roberto had all the discussions with that company and he kept in close contact with the owner. He was actually planning to go over there next month to see how things are developing and then give me a full report as to whether this was anything we should pursue or not."

"Since he is out of BioMedyca now that's obviously not going to happen," Stephen says, "so now it will be up to Kataryna and Francesco to deal with that."

"Yeah," Luca nods his head, "this could be huge for BioMedyca if it all pans out. Needless to say, though, I am not thrilled about Kataryna and Francesco going over there to explore this claim and in addition having to meet with Roberto first to extract some information from him."

"What exactly are you worried about?" Stephen asks.

"Everything. The trip, the meeting with Roberto, you name it." Luca replies.

Stephen pats him on the shoulder.

"They will be okay, Luca. Don't worry too much. Kataryna is a tough cookie."

"Ha!" Luca shouts out smiling at Kataryna. "Don't I know it. However, the places they are traveling to can be treacherous. We are talking the Amazonas region, and the property where the plants are grown is located at the Colombian border. This is not an easy trip. You know what's going on in these countries not to talk about all the critters and wild animals in the rain forests over there."

"Luca," Kataryna cuts in forcefully, "we will be in the company of the Brazilian owner. He knows this territory very well."

Luca looks at her and shrugs his shoulders. "We better change the subject now."

"Great idea," Stephen says. "By the way Luca, what are we going to do about the ten percent shares of BioMedyca your family still owns? Are you going to sell these to us now that Roberto is out of the picture? You know it was our intention from the get-go to take over 100 percent of BioMedyca."

"Yes, I know but I have another idea, which I hope you will agree to," Luca responds.

Stephen raises his eyebrows. "Oh? Well, don't keep me in the dark. Let's hear it."

"My family was thinking of giving the ten percent of

BioMedyca shares to Francesco and Patrizia as a wedding present."

Kataryna looks at Luca, quite surprised by his proposal. "Wow!" She obviously has no problem with the idea of her brother and future sister in-law becoming a minority shareholder. She gives Luca a reassuring smile.

"Whoa," Stephen exclaims looking at Kataryna for a reaction.

"I wasn't prepared for that one. I thought now that we have eliminated Roberto as a potential shareholder because of his own actions, Kataryna and I would acquire the remaining shares."

"I think Luca's idea is good, though," Kataryna jumps in quickly, prompting a puzzled look from Stephen.

"You do? Really?" Stephen wonders why she doesn't question that plan.

"Yes, I do. I will explain why in due course. Suffice it to say that if Roberto hadn't assaulted us in Venice, he most likely would own these shares now."

Luca addresses Stephen. "Remember at my engagement party last month, I indicated that I had an idea of how to deal with these shares? That's what I had in mind then."

"Is it negotiable?"

"Anything is negotiable," Luca responds, "but I hope that you will agree to my idea. Francesco is a good guy and he will be a great CEO. You really need him at BioMedyca. He deserves this kind of incentive and Patrizia will be his wife come June 15 this year. So it all stays in the family. We will also add a first right of refusal. So before they can sell any of their shares to an outsider they would have to offer them to you first."

Let me sleep on it," Stephen responds. He turns to Kataryna. "I am curious, though, why you are immediately in favor of that idea. Are you afraid that Francesco might leave the company?"

"No. Trust me, Stephen, you will understand when the time comes for me to tell you why I think this is a good idea."

"OK, but before I give up the idea of us acquiring the remaining ten percent, I would like to know what is behind the change in plans," Stephen insists. "In any case, that's a hell of a wedding present."

"The transfer of the shares to Francesco and Patrizia wouldn't take place until June 15 anyway. So, let's just put it on the backburner for now," Kataryna argues to close the subject for now.

"You are speaking in riddles, Kat, but I will wait patiently until you lift the veil," Stephen ends the discussion.

Kataryna and Luca walk home after leaving the restaurant.

"Thank you, darling," she says, kissing Luca as they enter her apartment. "That was a nice surprise announcing that you want to give the shares to our siblings. Your generosity never ceases to amaze me."

"You are welcome, Principessa. And now I hope you have a nice surprise for me," he whispers in her ear.

"You will be very happy with my surprise for you. But remember, the walls are thin here."

FOUR

Saturday evening has come and everyone is getting dressed to the nines for Natasha's, Sabrina's and Enrico's birthday party at a posh Manhattan location. Aleksandra has done a great job arranging the sweet-sixteen birthday party for her twin daughters.

The twin sisters look stunning in their dresses, which they chose carefully to make sure they did not look alike. Natasha decided to wear her hair in a sexy fishtail braided style while Sabrina wears her long blond hair in a high ponytail. She even had the hairstylist give her bangs, just to look even more different than her sister. They have entered an age where they want to be individuals rather than the cute twin girls with the same outfits and hairstyles. That part of their lives is over as far as they are concerned.

When Luca, Kataryna and Carlotta arrive with Enrico and Stefano, Natasha and Sabrina instantly focus on the two Italian guys and introduce them proudly to their friends.

Enrico is wearing a cool black silk Italian suit and Stefano is dressed in dark blue. The twins' girlfriends instantly gather around the Italians bringing on a jealous look from the other young men at the party. Carlotta is watching the spectacle her attractive 17-year-old son is creating among the teenage girls.

Kataryna smiles. "Your son has arrived, Carlotta. Seriously, he is a very attractive and charming young man.

I fully understand what is going on with these girls right now."

Carlotta nods. "So do I. He better know how to handle that. It seems that the girls over here are more aggressive, though. I have seen girls stare at him before in Europe but these girls here are going in for the kill, it appears."

"Well, we will be here for the next couple of hours to watch over that but once we leave and they are alone it will be up to Enrico to master that kind of attention skillfully," Kataryna states.

"I am sure it will be okay," Luca says, "but just in case I will have a little chat with him before we leave them alone here."

After dinner the adults have drinks at the bar while the teenagers start dancing to the live entertainment. The party is in full swing. Enrico and Stefano dance with Sabrina and Natasha when one of the female guests moves in on them. She takes Enrico by the hand in an attempt to lead him away from the group.

"Oh, no you don't," Sabrina scolds her, claiming Enrico back. The girl just shrugs her shoulders and dances away by herself. Natasha gives her a dirty look.

"I told you we shouldn't have invited her," Sabrina says to her sister. "She always creates a situation."

"Well, can you blame her?" Natasha whispers in her sister's ear. "Enrico is just too hot. He brought it out in her. By the way, I think I am totally in love with him. Why don't you dance with Stefano now so I can get closer to Enrico.

"No way. He is mine. So stand back, please," Sabrina responds smiling.

"In that case, we will have to leave it up to him who he wants to be with," Natasha says. "I am not just giving up like that so you can be with him."

"Get ready for a huge disappointment then," her sister responds.

While the twins argue over who will get Enrico, the two Italians have started dancing with other girls unaware of what kind of storm is brewing between the two sisters.

"This is not good," Natasha challenges her sister. "Seriously, what are we going to do about this?"

"As you said, he will have to decide which one of us he wants," Sabrina says walking away from the dance floor. She watches Enrico and Stefano dancing with some of her friends.

"Are you tired?" her mother asks seating herself next to her.

"No, just taking a little break. It's still early," Sabrina answers.

"We are leaving now," Aleksandra tells her daughter. "We will be back around midnight to pick you up. Have a good time. If anything gets out of control, please call me."

"Sure, will do. Thank you."

Sabrina heads back to the dance floor to join Enrico. Her mood is subdued. She doesn't know how to handle the rift her sister has created between them. This has never happened before.

"What's the matter? You look upset," Enrico says.

"I am fine," she responds. "Let's take a break."

Luca approaches them. "Excuse me Sabrina, I need to talk to Enrico for a moment."

They step aside for some privacy.

"You think you can handle all that attention you are getting from these young ladies?"

"No problem, Uncle Luca."

"OK, I just want to make sure that you two guys stay cool. I know this is flattering but if you don't handle this properly, it could easily get out of control."

"Yeah, I know," Enrico responds. "I am not in the least interested in these overly aggressive girls. Stefano and I will hang out with Natasha and Sabrina. See you later."

His phone rings. He picks it up and starts talking to the caller. "Where are you?"

Enrico heads out of the room. "Why did you call me?" he asks Natasha.

"I wanted to make plans with you for tomorrow. It was too loud in the party room. I thought it would be better to talk out here."

"Why don't we talk about what to do tomorrow when my mother and uncle are back. Uncle Luca and Kataryna are going back to Italy Monday night. So they may want to spend the day with us together tomorrow."

Before she can respond Sabrina joins them pulling Enrico away from her.

"Come on, Enrico let's dance." She gives her sister an annoyed look.

"I think it's my turn to dance with Enrico," Natasha hisses at her sister.

"Sabrina and I were interrupted by my uncle earlier, so I really owe her that dance," Enrico responds smirking, heading toward the dance floor with Sabrina. "Why don't you dance with Stefano?"

Natasha waves at him casually and shoots for the ladies room. Once inside she leans against the wall and closes her eyes trying to calm herself down. Her emotions are running high. She is fighting back tears and can't even stomach being close to her twin sister right now.

Sabrina and Enrico stop at the bar to get something to drink and then continue to dance the night away. Around midnight, the adults return to the party.

"Did you have a good time?" Aleksandra asks Sabrina when she enters the party room.

"Yes, this was a great party. Thank you."

"Where is Natasha?" her mother asks.

"I don't know," Sabrina answers. "Come to think of it, I haven't seen her in a while."

"What do you mean?" Aleksandra probes concerned.

"Well, the last time I saw her was about an hour ago when she was going to the ladies room."

Aleksandra is alarmed. "An hour ago?" she raises her voice.

Her husband Brian joins them. "What's the matter?"

"I am looking for Natasha," Aleksandra puffs running in the direction of the ladies room. Kataryna follows her.

The ladies room is empty. No sign of Natasha anywhere. Sabrina looks worried at her mother and aunt when they return without her sister.

"Why don't you call her cellphone, Aleksandra? She must be here somewhere," Luca suggests.

Enrico and Sabrina look at each other speechless. A touch of anxiety develops among the group as Aleksandra dials her daughter's number.

"Natasha," she yells into the phone when her daughter picks up after the third ring, "where in the world are you?"

"What?" Aleksandra shouts. "Why are you at home?"

She continues a brief conversation with her daughter and then hangs up relieved.

Her husband gives her a questioning look. "What's going on?"

"Natasha went home because she didn't feel well."

"Why didn't she call us instead of taking off by herself in the middle of the night?" her husband wonders.

"I don't know. She didn't say. I will have a serious talk with her when we get home."

"This doesn't make any sense," Brian mumbles to himself. "Unless you can shed some light on this?" he asks Sabrina.

She shrugs her shoulders but deep inside she has an idea what prompted her sister to behave so erratically. It never occurred to her that they could be interested in the same guy one day. Unfortunately that day had come.

Kataryna and her sister talk alone for a few moments.

"What do you make of that?" Alexandra asks her. "Did we ever behave like that at that age?"

Kataryna chuckles. "No, and if we had our father would have read us the riot act. Let's just make sure that nothing unusual happened during the party that made her take off like that. This is not like her."

"I will definitely get to the bottom of this," Aleksandra responds.

"Have a good night and thank you for hosting such a great party." Kataryna says, kissing her sister goodbye.

"Have you guys seen anything at the party that could have caused Natasha to take off like that?" Kataryna asks Enrico and Stefano after they get back to her apartment.

Stefano shakes his head. "No, I was wondering where she was all that time but then I got distracted by talking to one of the other girls who actually spoke a little Italian."

Kataryna turns to Enrico. "How about you?"

"Hmm, uh," he stammers.

"If you know anything, Enrico, this would be the time to tell us," Carlotta prompts her son.

"I am not sure," he starts, "but she may have been upset because I didn't dance with her."

"Can you be more specific please," Luca cuts in.

"She had called me and asked me to meet her outside the party room in the lobby after I was talking to you, Uncle Luca. I went outside to meet her. She wanted to make plans with me for later on today alone. I told her that I was sure that we would plan something as a family today because you and Kataryna are leaving tomorrow night. Then Sabrina showed up and asked me to come back inside to dance with her. Natasha gave her a look and insisted it was her turn to dance with me. I told her that I owed Sabrina a dance because Uncle Luca had interrupted us before and I suggested that she dance with Stefano. She then copped an attitude and took off in the direction of the ladies room. That was the last time I saw her."

"Looks like the two sisters are fighting over you. Woo-hoo." Stefano snickers, patting Enrico's shoulder.

"It's not that funny, Stefano," Kataryna cautions him. "Natasha taking off alone in the middle of the night without telling anyone is serious. What if something had happened to her on the way home? Is that all or is there more?" she turns to Enrico again.

"That's all I know," Enrico responds.

"OK, thank you."

After the boys are in their bedroom the three adults discuss the situation.

"Oh my God," Carlotta starts, "I don't know what to say."

"I guess the two sisters are in love with your son," Luca states.

"Let's see how this plays out later on today," Kataryna says. "I will call Aleksandra after breakfast."

"If this is what I think it is, I really feel sorry for Natasha," Kataryna tells Luca after they are in their bedroom. "This could be her first time falling in love and she has to compete with her twin sister. I wish Enrico had a twin brother."

Luca hugs her grinning. "I already sensed at our engagement party last month that these girls were taken with him. Remember how they both said they wouldn't mind spending their summer vacation with us at the Lake Como villa?"

"I sure do."

Luca kisses her softly. "Although I really had some other ideas of how to spend this night with you, I guess we better get to sleep now so we can deal with this situation in a few hours."

Kataryna kisses him passionately and presses her body against him. "Really? You are going to let a couple of teenagers ruin our night?"

"Actually, you just changed my mind," he murmurs taking off his clothes and then hers.

"That's quite obvious now," she smirks running her hand slowly up his thigh. "I think we can take care of this pretty quickly and still get our beauty sleep. So come on down, Signor Romano."

◆◆◆

Enrico and Stefano are up early showing each other the photos they took at the party last night.

"Look at this one, Enrico, isn't she cute?" Stefano asks as he scrolls down the photos he took of the girl he spent most of the time with at the party. "She invited me to her house on Monday."

"Yeah, she is very cute. I hope her parents are on board with that invitation."

"Yes, she asked them when they picked her up last night."

"You will still have to convince my mother to let you go there." Enrico responds. "I don't know if after last night she will be that agreeable."

"What do I have to do with that?" Stefano counters. "That's your problem."

"No, it isn't a problem for me. I like Sabrina. Her sister will just have to deal with that."

"Enrico, the heartthrob. That will be a good story when we get back home."

"Shut up!" Enrico counters heading for the shower.

Kataryna and Carlotta prepare breakfast while Luca and the boys talk. They show Luca some of the photos they put on Instagram.

"I was thinking we could go downtown today and visit the Freedom Tower and 9/11 Memorial, then maybe do a little shopping and have dinner in Tribeca or somewhere around there tonight," Kataryna suggests when she and Carlotta join the guys for breakfast.

"Great idea," Luca and Carlotta agree. "Let's do that."

After their late breakfast Kataryna calls her sister.

"How is everything in your house?"

"I am a little concerned. Natasha won't come out of her room. I wish I knew what's going on with her."

"I think I can solve the puzzle," Kataryna says. She proceeds to tell her sister what Enrico divulged last night.

Aleksandra takes a deep breath. "Natasha won't leave her room and Sabrina is tight-lipped. Sabrina tried to visit her sister earlier but she wouldn't open the door. So this is serious. Now that I know what the problem is, I suggest that we keep the girls and Enrico apart."

"How?" Kataryna asks. "Didn't you invite Carlotta and the boys for dinner on Tuesday?"

"Yes, and they can still come. I will just send the twins to stay overnight with Brian's parents or with some friends that night."

"That's ridiculous," Kataryna responds. "You can't keep them apart until Friday. Carlotta and Enrico will be in New York the whole week."

"If the situation between my daughters doesn't get any better I will keep them from seeing Enrico." Alexandra says determined.

"I was going to ask you if you want to join us for dinner tonight downtown," Kataryna says. "It's Luca's and my last evening in New York."

"Well, Brian and I can join you but we won't bring the girls. Period."

"OK, Aleksandra. It's your call. See you later."

After Kataryna hangs up with her sister she tells Luca and Carlotta what they discussed.

"I guess it's more serious than I thought," she says, "so Aleksandra decided that the girls will not join us for dinner tonight."

"Maybe it's for the best," Carlotta agrees. We don't need any more drama involving my son."

"I am not so happy about that," Kataryna voices her opinion. "I think my sister is jumping the gun here but it's her decision."

Enrico's cellphone rings. A rush of excitement comes over him when he sees Sabrina's name pop up. He excuses himself and heads to the bedroom for privacy.

"Hi, how are you doing?" he greets Sabrina. "I heard Natasha barricaded herself in her room. What's up with her?"

"She hasn't come out and she won't let me in. I don't know but my guess is that she is still upset because you danced with me instead of her."

"What are you doing today?" Enrico enquires.

"I don't have any plans. You want to do something?"

"Yes, if your mother lets you."

"What does that mean?"

"Kataryna talked to her a few moments ago. She said that your mother doesn't want us spending time together because of the incident with Natasha."

"She did? Are you sure?"

"I am positive. Kataryna even made a remark that she doesn't agree with it."

"OK. In that case let's not tell anyone that we are meeting. I will say that I am meeting a girlfriend to see a movie."

"We could be in trouble but let's risk it," Enrico says, smiling to himself.

"Great. Let's meet in an hour. I will pick you up from my aunt's building but I won't come up."

"Stefano will have to come along, though, otherwise it would be too suspicious."

"Fine with me," Sabrina says.

Enrico returns to the living room to talk to Stefano.

"Hey, let's go out for a little while."

"I thought we are all going downtown," Stefano says.

"No, I don't want to do that today," Enrico responds glancing at his mother and Luca.

"OK, then let's cancel that and just go out for dinner later on," Carlotta says. "Enrico, Stefano and I can visit the downtown area sometime this week."

◆ ◆ ◆

Aleksandra enters Natasha's room. "OK, young lady. Let's talk. Why are you hiding in your room?"

Natasha stares silently at her mother.

"Speak, Natasha," Aleksandra demands sternly. "This is getting ridiculous."

"I am sorry. I just need to be alone right now."

"Do you want me to tell you what I think is going on?" Aleksandra asks her.

"I'd rather not talk about it right now."

"OK. Have it your way. Based on your behavior, I have decided that you two are not going to join us for dinner with Aunt Kataryna and her company tonight. Your father and I will go alone. Hopefully this will bring some harmony back to our house."

"Did you reveal that plan to your other daughter already?" Natasha asks her sarcastically.

"First of all, why don't you adjust your attitude and second, no, I haven't spoken to Sabrina about that yet."

Shaking her head, Aleksandra leaves Natasha's room and heads to Sabrina's.

"Hi sweetie, can you shed some light on what is going on between you two?"

"I don't know for sure why Natasha is in such a mood. I tried to talk to her but she won't let me in her room. I haven't done anything to her."

"I see. Could it be about Enrico not dancing with her last night?"

"It's possible, but why don't you ask her?"

"I did. She doesn't want to talk about it. I think both of you are enamored with Enrico. He may favor you, which probably came out last night, and Natasha appears to be quite unhappy about that."

"I can't speak for Natasha. As far as I am concerned, yes, I really like Enrico. I don't think I ever liked a boy as much before. So there, I said it."

Aleksandra hugs her daughter. "I had a feeling that was the case. Obviously your sister has the same feelings for him. Look, he lives in Italy. I don't think that you can develop a normal relationship with anyone under these circumstances."

Sabrina gasps. "Mom, I don't think this is up to you to decide who I can have feelings for and develop a relationship with. These feelings are there, whether you like it or not. And by the way, Aunt Kataryna also had a long distance relationship with Luca who lives in Italy and now she also lives over there and they are getting married."

Aleksandra laughs lightly. "You can't compare these two situations. Your aunt is an adult woman who can come and go as she pleases and live wherever she wants to. You are a minor. I am not letting you go to live in Italy."

"I wasn't planning to move to Italy. Enrico will come over here next year to attend an American college."

Aleksandra is stunned. This seems to be more serious than she thought.

"Well, then let's see what happens next year if he does come over here to go to college, but for now I don't want you to get any closer to him. Since he will be at the dinner tonight, you girls will not join us."

Sabrina's first reaction is to protest. She quickly changes her mind knowing that she will see Enrico in a few minutes anyway. She has never lied to her mother before, however, the omission of this fact seems to be justified in light of this situation, she decides.

She shrugs her shoulders. "OK, let's see how things will develop. I have to go now. I am meeting a friend of mine in a few minutes."

She grabs her bag and kisses her mother. "See you later. Should I pick up dinner for myself and Natasha then?"

"No, I am going to make a pasta dish for you two for tonight. Have a good time."

"Thank you, mother. I will." She rushes out the door.

When she arrives at her aunt's building, Enrico and Stefano are already waiting for her outside.

"So what do you want to do?" Enrico asks her.

"Let's just get away from here first so no one sees us."

They start walking toward Central Park.

"This is a first for me," Sabrina says. "I have never hidden anything from my mother before, but it's her own fault for being so unreasonable."

"I don't understand why we are not supposed to get together," Enrico states.

"Because my sister seems to have a problem with us hanging out together," Sabrina asserts. "She won't even talk to me. I haven't seen her at all this morning."

"Wow!" Stefano exclaims. "She must have it bad for you, Enrico."

Enrico is slightly embarrassed and turns it around. "Or she is upset because you spent the rest of the night with this other girl."

Sabrina giggles. "I am afraid it's you Enrico. I wish we could clone you."

He smiles at her mischievously. "And I wish there was only one of you so we wouldn't have this drama."

"How about a photo of you two together?" Stefano suggests. "Why don't you move a little closer to Sabrina."

Enrico puts his arms around her. Sabrina gives him a cute look. They take a series of photos with their phones and Instagram them.

"You two make a cute couple," Stefano cajoles. "Now should I send these photos to your mothers?" He laughs out loud.

"You are flirting with disaster," Enrico counters, amused, making a fist.

"What are you doing tomorrow?" Sabrina asks Enrico.

"My mother and I will go to a Broadway show in the evening. I wish you could come along."

"So do I," Sabrina responds with a frown but then lightens up. "I have an idea. How about you text me where you are going to be during the day and I arrange to run into you accidentally?"

"That could work. I am sure my mother wouldn't mind if we were to 'run into' each other."

Stefano rolls his eyes. "I am not sure how she will react to that but I wish you luck. It would have been much simpler if your sister and I had hit it off, but she seems to have the hots for Enrico."

The two guys escort Sabrina home after the movie. Enrico kisses her softly and she embraces him before she heads around the corner to enter the building she lives in. Her heart is beating faster than usual. She is pretty sure she is in love and it feels good, but it would be so much better if this dark cloud weren't hanging over it.

When she opens the door to her family's apartment her sister is standing in the foyer. The two stare at each other for a moment and then start crying. Sabrina runs into her room to let her tears run freely. Natasha is in the kitchen heating up the pasta dish their mother made for them when Sabrina comes out of her room. They sit down at the kitchen table. After a long uncomfortable silence Sabrina makes an attempt at a conversation with her sister.

"We have to talk this out, Natasha," she starts. "I know this is totally awkward and painful but there is no way around it."

Natasha nods. "Now that Enrico is out of our lives, we have to try to get back to normal."

"What do you mean, he is out of our lives? He is an important person in Aunt Kataryna's new family. How do you figure he's out of our lives?"

"Well, we don't have to see him. After all he lives in Italy and we are thousands of miles apart." Natasha shrugs her shoulders casually.

"Are you serious? Do you really think that Aunt Kataryna is going to play the hiding game every time we all get together for holidays and vacations?" Sabrina shakes her head in disbelief.

"Well, I guess we all won't get together anymore like this. Aunt Kataryna will have to decide whom she wants to spend her holidays with, either Luca's family or her own."

Sabrina grunts. "Good luck with that approach. I am sure she will tell us how this is going to work on her terms. I can guarantee you that she wants Enrico and his mother around for these events. They have become very close."

"If our mother has anything to say about it, Aunt Kataryna won't be able to have it her way if she wants to see us." Natasha states.

Sabrina decides to end this conversation. After dinner she retires to her room and starts texting with Enrico.

Enrico and Stefano are getting dressed for their evening out with the family. When they are done, Enrico goes to see his mother in the other bedroom.

"Ciao, Enrico. You look very nice." She kisses him on the cheek. "What did you two guys do today?"

"Mamma, please sit down. I have to talk to you about something," he says nervously.

"We are leaving in a few minutes. Can't this wait?"

"No, it has to be now before we meet the others. When Stefano and I went out earlier we met Sabrina and we spent the whole afternoon with her."

"You ran into her on the street?"

"No, we met intentionally. After Kataryna told us that the twins were not allowed to join us for dinner tonight, I spoke with Sabrina. We then arranged to meet during the day but not tell anyone."

"Why Enrico?" Carlotta asks concerned. "Just out of spite? Or what were you thinking?"

"I really like her. I wanted to spend some time with her. Well, actually the word like doesn't quite describe what I feel. I don't think I ever had feelings like this for a girl before. I have enjoyed hanging out with certain girls in Milano but I never thought of them later on or was this excited about them. It's different with Sabrina, though. I have been thinking about her since Uncle Luca's engagement party when I met her for the first time and we spent some time together in Milano."

Tears are welling up in Carlotta's eyes as she realizes that her son may be in love for the first time and may face an uphill battle here not unlike her own with Roberto. She hugs him tightly and lets the tears run down her face. Before she can say anything, Kataryna walks into the room to remind her it's time to leave.

"Carlotta," Kataryna cries out. "What happened?"

She closes the door and runs to hug both of them.

"Please sit down, Carlotta. Can I get you some water or anything?"

Carlotta shakes her head. "No, thank you. I am sorry I just got a little emotional. I will be okay." She attempts a smile.

Kataryna senses something is wrong but decides to let it go for now. The three join Luca and Stefano who are waiting for them by the door to leave for the dinner.

After finishing the appetizers Kataryna and Aleksandra visit the ladies room together.

"How are the girls?" Kataryna asks her sister.

"Natasha was still in her room when we left and Sabrina was out with one of her friends. Before she left I had a talk with her and she opened up about her feelings for Enrico. So that is one more reason I don't want them to see each other anymore. The girls are both at home and had dinner together. Looks like things are getting back to normal again. I don't know what would have happened if I had let them join us tonight."

Kataryna gives her sister a surprised look. "Do you really think this is the way to handle this? You should have let them come to dinner with us tonight. What do you have against Enrico and Sabrina seeing each other? He is a very responsible young man."

"It's for the best if they don't see him and fight over him."

"Fight over him? It's not that he played both ends here. He chose to hang out with Sabrina last night and Natasha will have to learn how to step back when a young man chooses her sister over her. We are talking about human feelings and not about a piece of merchandise that someone can acquire with the highest bid. Didn't you prepare them for something like this?" Kataryna admonishes her sister.

"I don't think we need to discuss this any further. I am hoping that the out-of–sight-out-of mind rule will be successful here," Aleksandra returns.

"Well, if the girls come to stay with us during their summer vacation, I am not restricting Enrico from being at the villa. He is used to spending time there in the summer months and this is not going to change. So they will meet again in the future. It's just a matter of time. Why don't we sit down with them and hammer it out tomorrow?"

"No worries, Kataryna. I am making other plans for them for their summer vacation."

"I hope you know what you are doing. It looks like Sabrina and Enrico like each other. You may alienate your daughter taking that stance."

"I know what I am doing."

Kataryna turns around to leave the ladies room. She has had enough of that conversation.

During the main course, Kataryna mostly chats with Carlotta and the boys while Luca is entertaining Aleksandra and her husband.

Aleksandra turns to Enrico and Stefano. "I am sorry guys but the girls will not join us when you come to our house for dinner on Tuesday."

Enrico is disappointed to hear that Sabrina will not be at the dinner. He looks at his mother, lost for words.

"Oh, that's too bad," Stefano says casually. "We were hoping to spend some time with them. I guess we can catch up with them on Wednesday or Thursday then since we are going back to Italy on Friday." He lightly kicks Enrico under the table. Enrico smiles, anticipating Aleksandra's response.

"They haven't seen their grandparents for a while so I suppose they will stay there for a few days," Aleksandra quickly kills that idea.

Kataryna feels her blood pressure rising. Big mistake, she thinks. She sees Enrico's disappointment in his face and becomes even more irritated. Luca senses his fiancée's uneasiness. It is apparent that she is totally out of character. He takes her hand and looks at her sweetly, hoping to bring her back to her usual self.

She kisses his cheek. "Let's call it a night, darling. I am a bit tired and I have to get up early tomorrow. I am going to introduce Enrico to a few people at my firm, so when he takes the internship we are offering him, he will already know some of the staff."

Aleksandra's face drops when she hears that Enrico will come to New York as an intern in her sister's firm. Knowing that her sister is already upset with her over the entire issue, she chooses not to react to that disturbing piece of news.

Back at the apartment, the two guys proceed to their bedroom while Kataryna, Carlotta and Luca sit around the fireplace after changing into more comfortable clothes.

"How are you doing, Carlotta?" Kataryna takes the bull by the horns attempting to get Carlotta to explain her tears before they left for dinner.

"I have seen better days," Carlotta sighs.

"Would you like to talk about it?" Kataryna probes.

Luca looks at the two. "This has been a really weird evening. First the tension between you and your sister," he addresses Kataryna, "and now this back and forth between you two. Can someone please clue me in as to what is going on or have you two already forgotten the pact we made after the Venice fiasco? NO MORE SECRETS!"

Carlotta buries her face in her hands and exhales audibly.

"What now?" Luca asks anxiously. "Is it the Roberto quandary again?"

She shakes her head. "While that is still lingering, my immediate concern right now is with Enrico."

"What are you worried about? He looks fine to me." Luca questions his sister.

"Before we left for dinner tonight, he came to my room to talk to me." She lowers her voice making sure he can't hear her in the other room. "He told me that he and Stefano met up with Sabrina today and that he really likes her a lot. Actually it sounded more like he is in love."

"Wow! So Sabrina met Enrico against her mother's will?"

"Yes, she told her she was meeting a girlfriend."

"Ha-ha," Kataryna starts laughing. "I am not surprised but obviously my sister doesn't understand that people will find a way to be together when they start having feelings for each other."

"I don't like what I am hearing. This could turn into a war between our families, Principessa," Luca leans back running his hands through his meticulous hair.

FIVE

Kataryna and Enrico arrive at her private equity firm's office the next morning. She gives him a tour of the facilities after introducing him to Human Resources, the business development and the due diligence teams.

"I suggest that we let you work in each department for about three months," Kataryna advises him. "That will give you a good oversight of what these teams are doing. And for the rest of your term you can decide which area you want to focus on a little more."

"Sounds great," Enrico responds. "I am really excited about that, although it is still some time before I can start this internship."

"Yes, of course, but now you know what to expect when the time comes. You can prepare yourself already. I will give you some material to read and then we can go over any questions you may have. That will make it easier for you and my firm's staff once you start the internship."

"Thank you. Great plan."

"Maybe you can already assist me a little in Milano soon. Francesco and I are expecting to work on an exciting deal in the near future. We will need all the help we can get when that ball starts rolling."

"Awesome," Enrico exclaims. "I would love to assist you with that."

"How about a little lunch now?" Kataryna suggests.

"I could eat something," he agrees.

"Your mother told us last night that you met and spent the day with Sabrina," Kataryna opens up their conversation after they are seated in the restaurant.

"Sabrina decided that we should get together after I told her that your sister said she wanted to keep us apart. She told her mother she would be meeting a girlfriend. I didn't tell her to do that and Stefano was with us, too."

I wasn't suggesting that, Enrico." Kataryna pats his arm reassuringly.

"Why doesn't your sister like me? I haven't done anything wrong," he says kind of sad looking.

"It's not that she doesn't like you, Enrico. She just wants to protect her daughters. I don't agree with how she is handling this, but it's her call. She is their mother."

"Protect them from what?"

"Apparently both of the girls like you. So if one gets to be with you, the other may be quite hurt. I think Aleksandra believes that if you don't get to see either one, then everything will go back to normal and the girls won't have anything to be upset about."

"But I really like Sabrina and I believe she likes me."

"Yes, I get that. This is where my sister may go wrong. She assumes everything will be okay once you are gone. What she doesn't seem to realize is that she may have a problem with Sabrina if she tries to keep you two from spending time together while you are here in New York."

"Can you talk to her and explain that?" Enrico looks at her hopeful. "Sabrina wants to come to Italy during her summer vacation and I was very much looking forward to that."

"I will give it a shot," Kataryna promises, "but let me ask you this. Do you think you would be able to sustain a long distance relationship with her?"

"I haven't thought about it seriously yet. If she comes over in July and we spend some quality time together I may be in a better position to answer that question."

"And what happens after she leaves?" Kataryna asks.

"If everything goes well, I was thinking that I could come to New York in the fall again for a few days. Maybe if you have to come back here for business, I can join you?"

"Have you forgotten that your uncle and I are getting married at the end of September? We will be on our honeymoon in the first two weeks of October. I will have a lot of work waiting for me once we return. I have no idea how the deal, Francesco and I are exploring, will go and where I will have to be in the fall. So, I can't make that kind of commitment now. In addition, your mother will have the baby sometime in September, so she won't be able to go with you either."

"What about Christmas?" Enrico enquires.

"We will spend Christmas at your grandparents' house in Bellagio this year."

"Sabrina could join us there," he suggests.

"Possibly but let's not get ahead of ourselves. I will have a talk with my sister to see if she would be open to anything like that."

Enrico's phone rings. He looks at Kataryna, grinning.

"It's Sabrina. She wanted me to let her know where I will be today."

"Go ahead, answer it."

"Hi Sabrina. I am at lunch with your aunt." He hands Kataryna the phone. "Sabrina would like to speak with you."

"Hi, Aunt Kataryna," she greets her. "I need you to talk to my mother about letting me see Enrico."

"Hello, Sabrina. How are things between you and your sister?"

"It's a long story. She thinks that neither one of us will get to spend time with Enrico but she is wrong. I am not prepared to let this go regardless of what my mother says."

"OK, sweetie, I will be right over to deal with this."

She hands the phone back to Enrico who chats with Sabrina for a while.

"Why don't you go home now, Enrico," Kataryna suggests. "I am going to meet with my sister and the twins. Please tell your uncle that I will be back at the apartment at 5p.m. the latest so we can leave for the airport then."

Sabrina opens the door when Kataryna arrives at her sister's apartment. She hugs her aunt and whispers in her ear. "Are you going to help us?"

"I will do my best." She kisses her niece.

Aleksandra appears from the kitchen. "Oh, what a surprise. Aren't you leaving in a couple of hours?"

"I have to clear the air before I go back to Italy," Kataryna says. "Why don't you get Natasha, so we can talk."

Aleksandra looks at her sister nervously not knowing what to expect next. "It would be best if you let this go, Kataryna."

Kataryna shakes her head. "Sorry, I can't. We have to settle this before I leave."

Sabrina calls her sister. "Natasha, come to the living room please. Aunt Kataryna wants to talk to us before she goes back to Italy."

Natasha appears. "Hi, Aunt Kataryna. I thought you were already on the way to the airport."

"Yeah, I don't have that much time but we need to talk."

They all gather in the living room.

"OK, here is what I have to say. As you know, I am getting married to Luca in September. With that I will have another extended family including two sisters-in-law and their children. Enrico will be an important member of my family. In addition, he will most likely join my firm once he is finished with college and before that as an intern. So you can see where this is going. I will not jump through any hoops so you can avoid that the girls come into contact with him. He is a responsible young man and I love him dearly. Therefore, Aleksandra, you will have to choose to either be reasonable when it comes to him having any contact with your daughters or we will have pretty limited visitation in the future. Your daughters are always welcome in my house if they want to come over but not at the expense of Enrico. He will be spending a lot of time at the Lake Como villa during the summer months. Period. End of story."

Aleksandra takes a deep breath. "I don't' know what to say."

"I recommend that you do some soul searching before you decide anything. And you two," Kataryna points at the twins, "you have to grow up and let it sink in that this can happen any day again with some guy over here. Unless you two find a set of male identical twins, where each of you can have one like the other, you may have a big problem if you don't get this under control."

The two girls stare at their aunt silently. Kataryna focuses on Natasha.

"Why don't we let the cat out of the bag, Natasha. Enrico likes your sister and wants to spend time with her. As far as I can tell the feeling is mutual. You guys are still young and this might be a short-lived attraction and blow over soon. Or it could get serious. Then what? You cannot forbid someone from having feelings for another just to not upset the other sister/daughter. Life doesn't work that way. The sooner you understand and accept that the better off we will all be. I have a lot on my plate the next few months and I won't have time for this kind of nonsense. If you want to spend any quality time with me in the future, you will have to accept Enrico as a part of my new family. If you don't, we will not be able to spend holidays together and you guys won't be able to attend my wedding either because he will be there for all of it."

Natasha starts crying. "What about my feelings? If I see these two together I will be very upset."

"And if Sabrina can't be with him because it upsets you, she will not take it well either, I assume. So, one of you has to bite the bullet. Since Enrico likes Sabrina back, I am afraid, Natasha, that you will have to live with that."

Aleksandra sits next to Natasha and embraces her, wiping the tears of her face.

"Remember this, sweetie. When one door closes another one opens. I am sure your dream boyfriend will appear soon and then we will all laugh about this moment right here."

Kataryna gets up to leave. She kisses her sister and the girls goodbye.

"Enrico will be expecting your call Sabrina. Hopefully you can spend the rest of the week with him. Carlotta wants to invite you to go to dinner and a Broadway show with her and Enrico tonight."

Sabrina smiles happily. "Thank you, Aunt Kataryna."

"So, what's the verdict?" Enrico asks when Kataryna arrives back at her place.

"Sabrina will join you and your mother tonight."

Enrico gives her a huge smile and a hug. "Thank you. You are the best."

"You are welcome. I am glad I was able to turn this around but please don't make me regret sticking out my neck for you, OK?"

"Nicely done, Principessa." Luca embraces her.

"It was a bit of a tear jerker, though, seeing Natasha that emotionally upset over this. I am glad we are leaving today, darling, but not just for that reason." She grins at him seductively.

◆ ◆ ◆

After a long but comfortable night flight, Luca and Kataryna arrive back at the Lake Como villa.

"Home sweet home," Kataryna says. "I really missed this place. New York was so loud and hectic." She looks out to the lake. "I will never get tired of this view."

Luca smirks. "As much as I will never get tired of the view of you here."

She turns around to face him. "You always know how to say the right things to fit the occasion."

"Thank you, Principessa. I don't even have to think about it. You inspire me, so these words flow easily."

"Wow, darling, that was very poetic. Might you have an ulterior motive, like trying to arouse me?" Kataryna gives him a tempting smile.

He hugs her tighter. "Is it working?"

"Would you take my word for it if I said it isn't?"

"Ah, no way," he moans in her ear. "I trust you but I think I will make sure for myself."

He unzips her pants and slides them down her legs with one hand while the other takes down her underwear at the same time. She slowly steps out of them and then undresses him.

"Shall we take a shower together," she whispers.

"Too late for me," he breathes heavily, "and by the state of your highly obvious arousal it's also too late for you. I don't want you to cool off. We are just seconds away from the grand finale here."

"That was just the right medicine after our stressful trip to New York," Luca murmurs.

"You can say that again," Kataryna agrees. "That was the trip from hell. First, all the business appointments and interviews, then not being able to sound off while making love and if that wasn't enough already, the situation with Natasha, Sabrina and Enrico. We surely deserved this divine moment."

"I am so glad we are on the same page with that." Luca responds sweetly, kissing her. "How about a little nap, a shower afterwards and then a late Italian lunch?"

"Absolutely," Kataryna responds, closing her eyes and putting her head onto Luca's shoulder.

A couple of hours later, the two sit happily and freshly showered at the dining table awaiting one of Mariya's delicious dishes.

"Shall we call Carlotta and Enrico to see how their evening went?" Luca asks.

"Good idea, but the real test actually comes tonight when they will be at my sister's for dinner."

Luca checks his watch. It's 9:30 a.m. in New York. He dials Carlotta's number.

"Buongiorno Carlotta. How is everything?"

They go off in Italian. Kataryna listens carefully to pick up some new Italian words and phrases. She believes she pretty much understands what Luca is saying. That's progress.

"Everything is okay over there," Luca explains after he hangs up with Carlotta. "They had a really nice evening with Sabrina. My sister believes those two are really into each other."

"Yay!" Kataryna lets out a joyful scream. "I think they make a cute couple. My sister is probably having a cow over that. I can't wait to hear about the dinner tonight."

"I think you and I also make a cute couple," Luca says.

Kataryna nods. "We are a perfect couple."

"I am a little concerned, though, about the long distance aspect between these two." Luca contends. "They are so young and may not have our maturity to work through this. They are also just beginning to have these feelings for the other sex. Today it is Sabrina and tomorrow Enrico may like a girl over here who is geographically closer to him."

"Yes, you got a point there but it will be a good experience. They'll either go their separate ways or surprise us and work it out somehow."

"I just hope no one's heart will be broken. I don't think Carlotta could handle any more drama involving her immediate family, especially when it comes to Enrico."

"Speaking about immediate family, we need to talk to Vincente about my brother. Another week has passed but I doubt that he told Francesco the truth by now."

"I will call him after we are done with lunch. Right now I just want to savor this tranquility and have a nice relaxing meal with my beautiful future wife."

Kataryna sneers. "You really know how to appease me, darling. What can I possibly say when you make such a charming statement?"

"Actions speak louder than words, my dear. You can show me your appreciation at the appropriate time." He kisses her hand.

"Yikes, you got me," Kataryna laughs. "I am in your debt again."

"That's right. You know what would really make my day?"

"I could think about a few things." Kataryna teases him smiling mischievously.

"How about...," he pauses for a moment, keeping her in suspense, and then continues, "you giving up the Brazil trip."

"Wow, that was the last thing I would have expected," she says almost disappointed, staring straight into his eyes. "No can do, Signor Romano. You better make peace with that idea. We have been through this already and had a deal. Two kids for one Brazil trip." She kisses him softly. "But I love you for being so concerned about me," she adds, hugging him tightly.

"It was worth a try, though," he responds.

Kataryna's cellphone rings. "Ciao Francesco. I was going to call you too in a while. So how does our agenda look for this week? Oh, good. Let's go over everything tomorrow. I will come to your office around 9 a.m. Good job."

She turns to Luca. "Francesco has prepared the employment offer letter for Larissa Dos Santos. So that will go out tomorrow. Hopefully she can start soon. I am so glad that Stephen immediately liked her when we had that video call with her and that he agreed to offer her the CFO position."

"Excellent," Luca states, "you two are really on the same page with everything as far as I can tell."

"Yes, we better be, otherwise our 50/50 partnership would never work."

"Has he made any more comments about my intentions to give the remaining ten percent shares of BioMedyca to Francesco and Patrizia for their wedding?" Luca asks.

"No, we didn't discuss it any further while we were in New York. I will bring it up next time I speak to him, though, because I want this out of the way."

"Yeah, we are approaching the end of March and they are getting married on June 15. I would really like to get the ball rolling and prepare the paperwork to transfer the shares to them as of June 15," Luca replies.

"Sure darling, so do I. Oh, by the way, Francesco just mentioned that he set up a meeting with Roberto at the clinic for us on Wednesday. We need to find out what he has to say about the Brazilian company we were offered before we continue with any further talks or negotiations. They want us to come over there mid April."

Luca rolls his eyes and shakes his head.

"Here goes our relaxing lunch. I am already agitated hearing the name Roberto."

◆◆◆

"Buongiorno Signora," Francesco greets Kataryna with a big smile when they meet the next morning. "How was New York?"

"Good, except for a few little snags," she responds. "So let me see the information you got from Brazil meanwhile."

He hands her a folder. "I went through it already. It looks promising but let's see what Roberto has to say. We will meet him at 10 a.m. tomorrow."

"Great. How is your mother?" Kataryna asks anxiously.

"Not so good. She hardly gets out of bed these days. We are very concerned. I am going over for dinner to my parents' house tonight and I'll stay overnight. My father needs the support, if you know what I mean."

"Yes, I do," Kataryna says empathetically. "Make sure you spend as much time as you can with your mother. I never got a chance to say goodbye to mine before she died unexpectedly and it still haunts me."

"I will," Francesco replies gently. "She is the best mother in the world. Since I am the only child she was able to have, she poured all her love into me."

Kataryna is fighting tears, painfully aware that his world will come crashing down soon. Could this be any more difficult for both of them? She swiftly changes the subject.

"Why don't we sign the employment letter for Larissa so you can messenger it over to her this morning?"

"Yes, let's do that. I spoke to her yesterday and alerted her to expect it. She is so thrilled to join us. She said once she receives the offer letter, she would try to get out of her current position immediately."

"Would be great if she could start here right away," Kataryna says.

When Kataryna arrives back at her office she first calls Luca to fill him in about Francesco's mother's condition asking him not to call Vincente Barone for now. She then starts focusing on the company information received from Brazil. The company's financial condition looks good on paper but will have to undergo further stress tests to be done by the international accountants, including a SWOT analysis to determine the company's strengths, weaknesses, opportunities and threats. This is the kind of area she knows expertly. However, the medical aspects and the claims of what the plants can do when properly converted into bio-identical products have yet to be proven. According to the information memorandum they supposedly can cure or at least ward off some nasty diseases. The Food and Drug Administration in the U.S. and similar agencies in the European Union countries and the rest of the world would have to be involved and do their analysis and subsequently approve the end products. Another thought hits her. Can bio-identical products be patented? Knowing how bureaucratic these agencies are, this could be in trials for a long time. She wonders if the Brazilian owner is aware that they would not close the deal before all these facts are proven. Maybe Roberto has a better understanding if these claims are realistic and can decipher that for her.

The thought of seeing Roberto tomorrow makes her somewhat uneasy. This is the first time that she will face him since Luca and she visited him in the clinic by his request. That was after he drugged Luca and almost raped her in Venice due to his abuse of anti-anxiety drugs and whatever else he took then. However, this time the psychiatrist will not be in the room with them. Francesco hasn't seen Roberto at all since that time. How will he handle this up close meeting with his former boss?

Her life has become so crazy since she met Luca, Roberto and Francesco. Luca, the love of her life and soon-to-be husband. Roberto, a former BioMedyca key executive she lost because of his inability to let go of his infatuation with her, and Francesco who turned out to be the brother she didn't know she had until a few months ago. These three men are dominating her life right now and they are all entwined in one way or another. Yeah, tomorrow will be a tough day for all of them.

◆ ◆ ◆

After Larissa Dos Santos and her lawyer have carefully reviewed the employment offer for the Chief Financial Officer position at BioMedyca, she resigns her current position. She puts in a call to Francesco Barone to tell him the good news.

"That is fantastic," Francesco tells her. "Kataryna will be extremely happy. So when would you like to start?"

"How about the day after tomorrow?" she asks.

"Fine with me," he responds elated. "The sooner the better. We got something interesting brewing here, which we need your assistance with."

After he hangs up with Larissa, he calls Kataryna.

"Our new CFO will start the day after tomorrow," he informs her.

"Wonderful," she exclaims. "I will come over after she is settled in so us three can have lunch together and go over the Brazilian deal. By then we will also have the information from Roberto."

"Exactly," Francesco responds. "Everything seems to be falling into place. So, I will see you tomorrow at 10 a.m. at the clinic."

"Yes, let's meet inside at the reception area. By the way, how do you feel about seeing Roberto tomorrow?"

"I am a bit apprehensive but I am sure it is more uncomfortable for you after what happened in Venice."

"I am trying not to think about it that way. Between you and me, I feel sorry for him," Kataryna reveals.

"Honestly, me, too. I miss him around here. Not that I am complaining that I am in the CEO position now, but he was a huge asset to this company and as you can see we have to consult him now on this proposed acquisition. I think you and I are somewhat out of our comfort zone with this deal. Let's just hope that he can educate us quickly tomorrow. We are supposed to meet with the Brazilian owner in about three weeks. By then, I want to know what I am talking about."

"Me, too," Kataryna says. "See you tomorrow."

SIX

Kataryna arrives at the clinic a little before 10 a.m. She checks in with the receptionist who prepares the entry badges for her and Francesco, which have to be worn in the restricted area of the clinic. A staff member approaches her shortly thereafter.

"Everything is set up for you to meet with Signor Silvestri in one of the therapy suites. I can take you in there now," she offers.

"I am still waiting for Signor Barone, who is also joining this meeting," Kataryna advises her.

"Sure. I will be back shortly then to let you in."

Kataryna's cellphone rings displaying Francesco's number.

"Kataryna, I am so sorry but my mother just had a seizure. We are waiting for the ambulance to take her to the hospital. I can't leave here now."

"Oh my God, Francesco," Kataryna shouts out. "I am sorry to hear that. Please take care of your mother. I will call you later."

The idea of meeting Roberto by herself brings up some anxiety at first but she manages to dismiss it.

"Thank you for understanding, Kataryna," he responds. "If you don't want to do this alone, we can postpone it."

"No, Francesco. We don't know how things will develop with your mother. Let me do this so we can move forward."

She heads toward the locked entrance of the clinic's psychiatric wing. The staff member meets her half way.

"Signor Barone has a medical emergency at home. He is unable to join me," Kataryna explains, thinking what am I doing? Luca is going to have a fit when he finds out.

"Would it be possible to see Dr. Giordano for a few minutes before I meet with Signor Silvestri?" Kataryna asks.

The employee unlocks the door to let her enter the restricted area.

"Let me check if he is available." She disappears in one of the rooms.

"Signora Taylor," Dr. Giordano greets her. "Good to see you again. How have you been?" He motions her to join him in his office.

"To be perfectly honest, I am struggling a bit with this situation. I have to think about it all the time."

"That's normal. Your mind needs to process this traumatic experience before you can move on." Dr. Giordano explains.

"I mean I feel guilty about what Roberto is going through because of me. I would like to know if he has resolved his feelings for me yet, but you probably can't talk about that with me."

"I can talk about certain things. He signed a release form," the doctor explains. "While he is making good progress in general, his feelings for you will most likely always be there. He loves you deeply and said he will probably go to his grave with these feelings for you. I can't wave a magic wand and make that go away. My goal is for him to just acknowledge these feelings but then move on. In order to restructure his life, we have discussed an early release with therapy on an outpatient basis so he can get professionally engaged again rather than brooding over what could have been and so on."

"As Signor Barone has explained to you, we need his input professionally right now," Kataryna says. "So this visit has nothing to do with his therapy or his unresolved feelings for me."

"Yes, I am aware of that. Engaging him professionally is good for him. Roberto needs to get the feeling that he is doing something valuable to redeem himself. So this meeting might be helpful on various levels."

"Thank you for taking the time to speak with me, Dr. Giordano. I feel a little better now."

"Anytime Signora Taylor. While you may have been the cause for his meltdown you can also be part of the solution. I don't suppose Signor Romano has forgiven Roberto yet?"

Kataryna shakes her head "No, I am trying to get him there also for his sake."

"Let me know if I can help," Dr. Giordano offers.

She leaves the doctor's office. A touch of nervousness appears as she sets one foot in front of the other to walk the short distance to the room she and Roberto will be meeting in. An orderly greets her and opens the door for her.

"Please knock on the door when you are finished and I will let you out," he advises her, locking the door behind her.

Roberto and Kataryna face each other, both unable to speak at first. She finally manages to catch herself but these few intense moments felt like an eternity.

"Ciao Roberto," she starts. "Francesco's mother had a serious medical situation this morning. He is unable to attend this meeting."

"I am sorry to hear that," he says, his voice shaky. "I know how much he loves his mother."

Kataryna feels her head pounding. This is more difficult than I imagined, she thinks. She tries hard to bring her emotions under control hoping he won't realize that she feels unstable around him. She opens a folder to review the questions Francesco and she prepared for this meeting.

"How have you been?" he asks, glancing at her engagement ring as her hand scrolls down the questions.

Kataryna feels the blood draining from her head. How do I answer this question, she ponders? When she looks up and their eyes meet again, she tears up.

"Every single day I wish the incident in Venice had never happened," she responds. "Then again, the Venice episode was only the inevitable waiting to happen. The real problem actually began way before that. Unfortunately I was not perceptive enough to realize that these emotions could lead to tragedy. I am as much to blame as you are for the ill-fated outcome. I should have known better. By trying to play the heroine, who could save the day, meaning saving yours and Luca's friendship, I ruined your life. I don't know how I can ever live with that. I could have averted this disaster by putting an immediate stop to it if I had told Luca about your continued infatuation with me. This way, there might have been one big bang among us three but we could have worked it out somehow. No secrets, no overmedication and none of the pain all of us are going through right now. And when I say all of us, I am also including Carlotta as well as Luca because I think deep down he is also suffering. He just won't admit it yet."

"Please don't do that to yourself. There is nothing you could have done. My feelings for you were so strong already when I returned from our dinner in Berlin. I would have fought Luca tooth and nail for you if it had come to that. My anxiety attacks started right after that. It's safe to assume that I would have taken the medication anyhow, and who knows what I would have done under these circumstances to get what I wanted so badly."

"It still makes me the culprit, though. If I hadn't shown up in your lives, you two would still be close friends and you wouldn't be in here."

"That's life, Kataryna. I don't blame you for anything. We don't have a choice who does or doesn't show up in our lives. I guess we all had to learn something. I learned that I am capable of having these deep feelings for a woman, which would be liberating if it had worked out. At least I now understand the meaning of the saying 'It's better to have loved and lost than never to have loved at all'."

Kataryna is wiping the tears from her face. "I will have to do some soul searching to determine what I had to learn from this. We better talk about what I came here for now."

"You will be alright, Kataryna. You have Luca in your life. I know he will take good care of you. He is a great human being and has a lot of love to give. Unfortunately he will probably never be in my life again in a meaningful way, except for the fact that I am the father of his future niece or nephew. I will miss that close relationship with him, but let's not rehash that. I am trying to move on to get out of here and rebuild my life somehow."

"How much longer do you have to stay in here?" she asks.

"My therapist will let me go home to celebrate Easter with my parents and my daughter. We will see what happens afterwards. We discussed to continue the therapy on an outpatient basis. He just wants to make sure that I am not a threat to myself or you and Luca for that matter."

"That's good news. I am happy for you. What are your plans when you get out of here?"

"For starters, I need a change of scenery. My friend Sergio, another friend and I will be taking a fairly strenuous trip into the wilderness together. There will be no luxury hotels or anything like that. We will sleep in tents and try to catch and hunt our own food and make sure we are not eaten by wild animals. You feel like a new human being after surviving a venture like that and this is exactly what I need right now."

"Wow, this sounds dangerous," Kataryna exclaims.

"For people who have never done that, you bet it would be dangerous, but all of us are former Special Forces military. It definitely gets the adrenaline going. Needless to say, we will be well equipped for our protection."

"I wish you well." Kataryna directs her attention back to the questions she has for him.

"What exactly do you know about this Brazilian company and these plants?"

He takes a deep breath. "I started talking to Ernesto Oliveiro about the plant fields he owns five years ago. He took me to the area where the plants are grown. He kept me pretty up to date on all developments over the years. It already looked good then but he didn't have the proof yet for the claims he was making. We had discussed an exclusive distribution contract once he could provide the proof that these plants can indeed be used to produce bio-identical medication.. It appears they are a couple of steps further now and can prove the claims. That he wants to sell the entire company is new to me. We never had any discussions about that."

"He explained to Francesco that his children are not interested in running the company once he steps down or dies. They would rather have the money and expand their own businesses. So there would be no successor in the family."

"Makes sense to sell then," Roberto agrees. "I would advise you to take a closer look at this. These plants could be a huge asset and advantage."

"I think I don't have to tell you that Francesco and I are not as experienced in this area as you are. Would you be willing to be our consultant and advisor in this proposed acquisition? You could deal with the regulatory agencies and work with Francesco on the due diligence."

"Generally yes, but do you think Luca would approve of you and I working together on that basis?"

"I will discuss it with him once you agree. You would mostly work with Francesco anyhow."

Roberto smirks. "Good luck with getting Luca to agree to that. I am already more than surprised that he let you meet with me today."

"At the moment he is more concerned with me taking this trip to Brazil. You know the areas Francesco and I will have to travel to well."

"Oh, I don't blame him there. You are going deep into the rain forest areas up the Amazon. Let me tell you, this is not an easy trip to take under the best of circumstances. When I went over there everything was well arranged by Ernesto Oliveiro and his staff, though, and it was easier than I had initially thought. However, I have to advise you there are certain dangers in that area regardless of how well organized the trip is. First of all, it is not a very populated area. There are some native tribes around there and you never know how the natives react to outside visitors trespassing in their territory. They are not fond of intruders of their space. In addition, the area where the company's plants are grown is bordering on Colombia. Another hotspot to be careful about. We are talking unchartered territory here."

"So what are you saying?" Kataryna is somewhat irked by Roberto's warning.

"Honestly? You and Francesco should not go there alone. On second thought, I don't think you should go there at all. At least not to the remote area where the plants are grown. You can meet with Ernesto in Rio and maybe go to Manaus, the capital of Amazonas, where the manufacturing facility is located but not to the other place."

Kataryna gives him a disconcerted look. She would prefer to dismiss his warning but she has a gut feeling he knows what he is talking about.

"Look," he continues, "I am quite experienced in wilderness trips. I just told you that my friends and I are planning one of these trips soon. When I went over there, I knew what to expect and I took appropriate precautions. In my opinion you two are not cut out for that kind of trip. I can maybe see Francesco going with another man, preferably one who knows this kind of territory, but I would strongly advise against you venturing out there."

"I guess I will have to take that under consideration," Kataryna responds.

"I can offer to go there with Francesco and show him around if Luca agrees that I can join you as a consultant. You can either stay in Manaus while we go there or you can fly home."

"I might as well fly back home then unless there are any more important meetings planned after you visit the plant fields."

"I think you can arrange that all the important meetings take place before we go there."

"Sure. That should be possible." Kataryna is kind of pleased with this new plan. "However, someone has to go there and make sure that these plants really exist and continue to be there after we complete the acquisition. The plants are the only reason we are even entertaining this acquisition."

"OK. I am in, but good luck fighting the battle with Luca over the consultant position for me," Roberto says grinning.

Kataryna smiles mischievously. "I believe in this case you might be the lesser evil because he is so concerned about me taking this trip."

"And rightfully so. If he knew what I know, he would never let you go there. I wouldn't if I was in his position."

"I am going to have our lawyer prepare a consultancy agreement and have it messengered over here tomorrow with a review copy to your lawyer."

"I am looking forward to it," he responds, "but please clear it with Luca first."

Kataryna nods. "Of course. We wouldn't want to start World War III."

She leaves the clinic happy with the outcome. This was not only a productive business meeting but she was also able to express her feelings to Roberto and his therapist about the Venice incident. A heavy burden has been lifted from her chest. Now if she could only tell Francesco that she is his biological sister, everything would really be wonderful. But that has to wait. She calls him to see how he is doing.

"Francesco, I am done with the meeting. How are you and how is your mother?"

"My mother is in a coma."

"I am sorry to hear that. Is there anything I can do for you?"

"No, thank you. Patrizia is here with me."

"OK, good. I just didn't want you to go through this alone. Why don't you call me later so I can fill you in about my meeting with Roberto?"

"I will. Thanks for everything, Kataryna."

It's almost 1 p.m. when Kataryna gets into her car. She calls Luca. "Hello darling. Would you like to have lunch with me?"

"Absolutely," Luca responds, "then you can tell me all about how you met alone with Roberto."

Kataryna rolls her eyes. Oh gee, he found out before she could tell him.

"I will tell you every minute detail, darling," Kataryna says laughing.

"I fail to see the humor in this." His tone is serious.

Oh, oh, he is upset, she thinks. This is not starting out well. How will he react when he hears the rest?

"Let's meet at our usual restaurant in a few minutes," she says in a more somber tone. "Please don't be upset. It's all good."

They meet in the restaurant a half hour later.

"So how did your visit go?" Luca asks her with a stern face after they are seated.

"Really well," Kataryna replies. "You will never guess what happened."

"Roberto proposed marriage again?" Luca hisses sarcastically.

She looks at him with pursed lips. "Come on, Luca, let's not go there. You know we need his advice in this acquisition. This was a really productive meeting. I am prepared to have him come on board as a consultant for the Brazilian deal."

"WHAT? Hello! Come again. You can't be serious."

"I am deadly serious and I am sure you will agree. Here is why. Roberto has been over to Brazil to visit the company and the area where the plants are grown. He advised me against going to this remote area and he explained why in detail. After hearing what he had to say, I tend to agree with him. So he will take the trip to the remote plant fields at the border of Colombia with Francesco and I will come back home to you while they are fighting snakes, tarantulas and the native tribes people out there."

She gives him a huge smile expecting him to do a victory dance. Luca stares at her shaking his head.

"Do you seriously expect that I'll let you go to Brazil with Roberto? I'd rather trust the snakes and tarantulas with your company than him. No way! He had his walk on the wild side with you!"

"Luca, my darling, you are overreacting here. Please take a step back."

"You want me to take a step back so that he can step in?" Luca presses his lips together. "Did I not discuss with you how dangerous this trip might be? And you ignored me. However, Roberto convinced you that it would be too dangerous for you. Why does he have more credibility than I do?" He raises his voice.

"Oh my God," Kataryna shouts out, "this is totally going in the wrong direction. I think the Venice incident has affected you deeper than you are willing to admit. There appears to be so much pent up hurt and anger here, Luca. Maybe you should have a chat with Dr. Giordano about what this is doing to you."

"I strongly recommend that we end this conversation right now. This is going downhill fast, I am afraid." Luca is still steaming.

Kataryna is at a loss for words. Wow, this didn't go at all how she had imagined. She was sure he would be so pleased that she would not have to travel to the dangerous areas they had been talking about.

"OK, let's shut this down. I will take the trip then, period," she states determined, upset with his reaction.

They finish their lunch and head back to work. Kataryna stares at the wall in her office. She is still stunned at the direction her conversation with Luca took. Be smart, Kataryna, she tells herself. This could be the blow-up of the century. Luca needs to talk to someone about his feelings toward Roberto otherwise he is going to flip out completely. She calls her partner Stephen in New York to discuss the recent developments.

"We need Roberto on board with us," he determines. "Francesco, you and I don't have a clue what we are up against here. In addition, Francesco is preoccupied now with his mother's medical condition. I am going to call Luca and tell him that business is business. He will have to suck it up and live with it."

Kataryna lets out a deep sigh. "But not today, Stephen. Please wait a day or so to let him cool down. As a matter of fact, I would prefer if you do it next week after Easter. I don't want a family drama playing out at our holiday gathering in Bellagio."

"Yeah, okay but meanwhile you have the lawyer prepare the consultancy agreement for Roberto so we can get that signed next week."

"You bet. Have a nice Easter, Stephen."

A few minutes later Francesco calls her.

"Ciao Kataryna, I am sorry but I won't be in the office tomorrow," he informs her, "my mother's condition is touch and go. I just remembered that Larissa Dos Santos is starting her position with us tomorrow. Could you possibly meet her and welcome her to the company in the morning?"

"Yes, I will. How is your father holding up?"

"He is in bad shape emotionally. I am trying to support him as much as I can."

"I am so sorry, Francesco."

"Was the meeting with Roberto helpful?" he asks.

"Yes, it was but please don't worry about that for now. All the best. We'll talk soon."

What a day, Kataryna thinks. Judging by Luca's earlier mood, the evening could also be challenging.

"Hello Universe, can I get some assistance, please?" she says out loud looking up to the sky.

◆ ◆ ◆

When Larissa Dos Santos arrives at her new employer the next morning, she is surprised to find Kataryna Taylor in Francesco's office.

"Buongiorno and welcome, Larissa," Kataryna greets her. "Unfortunately Francesco has a family emergency and won't be in the office today. So I came over to get you settled in and show you around a bit."

"Thank you, Kataryna. How nice of you."

"My pleasure. I suggest that you meet with our head of Human Resources first to get all the paperwork out of the way and then I would like to invite you for lunch, let's say around 1 p.m."

"I am looking forward to that," Larissa replies.

Kataryna and her lawyer discuss the terms of Roberto's consultancy agreement while Larissa is getting settled. They agree to finalize the paperwork after Easter. She feels a bit uneasy knowing that Luca is not aware of what is about to happen. She dismisses it, hoping to soften him up over the Easter holiday before Stephen talks to him next week.

"We are really happy to have you on board, Larissa," Kataryna says when the two meet for lunch. "Now that you have officially become an employee, I can fill you in on the latest confidential developments at the company." Kataryna explains the proposed Brazilian acquisition deal.

"This is exciting news," Larissa exclaims. "I think I can add some value here. What's the next step?"

"Francesco and I will be going to Brazil in about three weeks to meet with the current owner and do our preliminary due diligence. I hope you can give me some pointers for the trip to Brazil."

"Yes, sure, which area are you going to?"

"Rio first, then Manaus, Amazonas and at the end there is a trip planned to the area where the plant field is located, which is at the border of Colombia. We have to make sure that these plants really exist."

"Wow. You have to cover a lot of territory. I think I mentioned before that my brother lives in Manaus."

"Yes, I recall you did. I was wondering if you could put us in contact with him so we will have a reliable person to turn to if something unusual happens over there. In addition, we do need a Brazilian legal counsel and an accountant for various due diligence matters."

"I would be delighted to introduce you to my brother. His law firm has an accounting arm, too. He could set up a meeting with the partners there."

"Outstanding," Kataryna responds enthusiastically. "Maybe you can even accompany us to Brazil? This way we have a native Portuguese speaker with us."

"I am sorry but that won't be possible. I have a friend from out of town visiting me during that period. We had planned that for a long time and I am really looking forward to spending time with her. I have been cooped up at my home for too long."

"I understand. Too bad," Kataryna says. "So what are you doing for Easter?"

"We, that is my daughter Eliana and I, don't have any plans. I suppose we will have a nice Sunday Easter dinner together and just relax at home."

"I guess you don't have any family over here?"

"No, I don't. My family lives in Brazil, as I mentioned, and my husband passed away a couple of years ago. I have some close friends but they are all out of town for Easter this year. My daughter and I had initially planned to go away but then this job offer came in and I decided to stay home."

"How old is your daughter?" Kataryna enquires.

"She just turned 17." Larissa gets out her phone and shows Kataryna a photo of her daughter.

"She is very beautiful. She looks like one of these exotic Miss Universe contestants who always win and they are usually from a Latin American country."

"Thank you. She takes a lot after my late husband, though," Larissa explains proudly.

After lunch Kataryna goes to see Luca at his office.

"How did everything go this morning?" he asks her, looking up from his desk.

"Good. I just came back from lunch with Larissa Dos Santos. I was wondering if your parents would mind if we invite her and her daughter up to Bellagio for Easter Sunday? They are all alone here."

"Should be okay," Luca says. "Let me call my mother to make sure."

"Ciao, mamma," he greets her continuing in Italian. They talk for a while. He gives Kataryna a sign that it is okay to invite Larissa.

"How lovely. We would be delighted to come to Bellagio for Easter Sunday," Larissa responds when Kataryna calls her to extend the invitation.

"Good, we will see you and Eliana on Sunday around noon then. I will email you the address in a moment."

◆ ◆ ◆

Luca and Kataryna get home to the Lake Como villa late Thursday night. They both made a dent in their heavy workloads before the holiday and then had a quick dinner before driving up to the villa.

Kataryna gets ready for bed. Exhausted from work and the events of the past days, she is asleep the minute her head hits the pillow.

Luca is awake mulling over Kataryna's trip to Brazil. He wanders around the house to relieve the nervous tension he is feeling. He stares out to the lake, which usually helps him to relax. Not tonight, though. Imagining Kataryna traveling into the wilderness gets him more and more agitated. No, he can't put her in that kind of danger. An idea hits him. Yeah, that could be the solution. Finally at ease, he goes to sleep.

Kataryna wakes up around 9 a.m. Luca is not in bed. He is probably in his office downstairs, she thinks when she hears his and Mariya's voices outside the bedroom. The double doors to the master bedroom suite open and Mariya, followed by Luca, delivers a serving cart with breakfast.

"Buongiorno," Luca greets her smiling. "How about breakfast in bed?"

"That's an excellent idea. I was just going to call Mariya and ask her to bring me a cup of tea."

"All you have to do is wish for something and I make it happen," he says charmingly.

"Good to know," she responds smiling, "let me wish for something else now to see if you can make that happen, too."

He hands her a cup of tea and sits next to her. "What else did you wish for? Or should I rather not ask?"

"I am not saying, otherwise it won't come true." She takes a sip of the hot tea. "I was out like a light last night. When did you finally come to bed?"

"After I came up with the solution for your Brazil trip."

"I am afraid to ask what you came up with," she murmurs putting the cup on the nightstand.

"I think you will like it." He puts his arms around her. "Ready?"

She nods not knowing what to expect.

"Here is how this trip is going to go down," he starts. "You and Francesco will go to Rio and Manaus to have the meetings with the owner of the company and inspect the production facility. Once you are done you will fly back home. The day you leave, Roberto can arrive in Manaus to meet Francesco there and then go up to wherever these plants are to do the due diligence."

Kataryna gives him a broad smile. "Nice plan, my dear. You can be quite creative when it comes to keeping Roberto and me apart. Well, if it works out flight schedule-wise we shouldn't have a problem doing it that way."

"It will work out because our corporate jet will bring you home so we don't have to worry about flight schedules."

"Oh great," Kataryna smirks. "Now I know what I have to do when I want to travel on your company jet for business. I just have to invoke a Roberto situation."

"Don't get cute now," Luca says kissing her passionately.

"I hope you are not too hungry because we are going to seal that solution now with an act of love," she whispers.

"Great minds think alike," Luca responds softly, kissing her neck and moving on to her cleavage when his phone rings.

Kataryna grabs his phone to answer the call. She wants Luca to continue what he is doing right now.

"Pronto. Ciao Carlotta," she laughs into the phone while Luca is moving down her body.

"What are we doing?" she repeats Carlotta's question. "Aah," a slight moan escapes her as Luca is hitting a certain spot.

"Are you not feeling well?" Carlotta asks, hearing her moan.

"Oh no, I am feeling really good," Kataryna responds attempting to get Luca's lips off her for a moment.

Luca tears the phone out of her hand, says something briefly to Carlotta in Italian and then drops the phone quickly to continue on his sexy mission to first climax her and then himself.

"Wow, darling. That's what I call multitasking at its best," she praises him. "What did you say to Carlotta before you hung up on her so abruptly?"

He laughs out loud. "I told her she has lousy timing."

Kataryna cracks up. "Oh, my goodness, I am sure with that and my sound effects she figured out what was going on here. We better call her back now. I guess she and the boys just arrived home from New York."

"Let's have our relaxing breakfast in bed first and then call her." Luca feeds her some of the fruit. "By the way, that was very nice of you to invite your new CFO and her daughter for Easter," Luca praises her.

"Thank you," she replies, "no one should be alone on a major holiday like that. She is part of our corporate family now. So what is the general agenda for the next few days?"

"We'll go up to Bellagio tomorrow evening and stay with my parents until Monday. Sunday morning we'll all go to Easter mass and then have lunch at my parents house."

"That sounds so nice. I am looking forward to getting together with everyone again. Hopefully Francesco's mother will get better soon. Let me call him to see what's going on there."

"Ciao Francesco. How is everything?" They talk for a while.

"Apparently his mother is stabilized," she explains to Luca after she ends the call. "They are cautiously optimistic about her condition."

Luca sighs. "That must be so tough to go through. Not really knowing what causes her condition and what can be done about it. That also means you will have to be more patient about Francesco being told that you are his sister."

Kataryna's face turns sad. Luca hugs her. "When the time comes and the news is out, we will have a huge celebration."

Luca's kind idea makes her smile. He always knows how to make her feel better. Yeah, that's the kind of person you want to be married to, she confirms to herself.

"I guess it's time to call Carlotta back. Where is my phone?" Luca is searching the bed.

Kataryna laughs. "You threw it somewhere earlier in the heat of passion."

"The situation called for it," he says playfully continuing the search. "Ah, here it is under the covers."

Kataryna is amused watching Luca roll his eyes and pressing the speed call button with his sister's number. He talks to her in Italian. She loves to hear him speak Italian. It always sounds as if something exciting is going on. After a while he hands her the phone grinning.

"Carlotta, how are you and the boys? Was there any more drama in New York?"

"We are fine. Enrico got to spend some time with Sabrina. They are so cute together. Tuesday night we had dinner at Aleksandra's house but Natasha wasn't there. She spent the night at one of her girlfriend's house. I figured she didn't want to see Enrico and Sabrina together."

"I can sympathize with that. So we will see you and Enrico tomorrow night at your parents' house. By the way, your parents were so kind to allow me to invite the new BioMedyca CFO and her daughter for Easter lunch. You will like her."

"I am looking forward to meeting her," Carlotta says. "Has Patrizia met her yet?"

"No. She just started yesterday."

Carlotta giggles. "What does she look like? Does Patrizia have anything to worry about?"

"I can't believe you asked that," Kataryna says laughing. "No, of course not. She is a nice looking 38-year-old woman. Very smart, professional and devoted to her daughter. Nothing overly sexy or so."

"I was just kidding," Carlotta says. "Well, obviously she is single."

"She is a widow, believe it or not. Her husband died in a car crash a couple of years ago. She hasn't mentioned anyone else in her life. We will all get to know her better on Sunday. So, welcome home, Carlotta. I better get out of bed now."

◆◆◆

Luca and Kataryna take the boat up to Bellagio Saturday late afternoon. They sit tightly embraced enjoying the beautiful scenery around Lake Como, this time as a couple.

"Remember the first time we were on this boat together going up to Bellagio for our business meeting?" Luca asks her with an enigmatic smile.

"How can I forget?" Kataryna grins back at him provocatively. "That was one thrilling ride. I tried to keep my sexual attraction for you at bay and you were constantly fueling the fire."

"I was?" Luca teases her.

"Don't act innocent," she teases back. "You knew what you were doing. I thought I would get a break once the business meeting started but then Roberto started flirting with me. I just couldn't catch a break that day."

"I hope you weren't sexually attracted to him," Luca states in a more serious tone.

"Let's not even go there," Kataryna responds equally serious. "Just so you know, he will be up in the area at his parents' house for the weekend. Dr. Giordano agreed to let him spend Easter with his family. If all goes well, he will also let him continue his therapy on an outpatient basis starting the end of next week."

"Thanks for the warning," Luca replies sarcastically, "I will have the villa locked down so he can't break in."

"You do that, darling." Kataryna glances at him with a crooked smile as the boat docks in Bellagio where Carlotta is already waiting for them to take them to their parents' villa.

The family has a quiet dinner together. Carlotta tells them all about her and Enrico's stay in New York.

"So, Enrico, you have girlfriend in New York now?" his grandfather comments.

"I guess I do." Enrico tries to play it cool glancing at his phone screen.

"You and Sabrina are so cute together," Carlotta says.

"Cute? Mamma, please," Enrico counters making a face.

"OK, I am sorry," Carlotta says, "let's say you make a nice couple."

"Do we really have to talk about me?" Enrico becomes impatient with his mother.

Kataryna jumps in to change the subject. "What's the latest with your mother, Francesco?"

"She appears to be stable but who knows what to expect. My father will spend the holiday with her in the hospital. I am going to visit her on Monday again."

"By the way," Luca cuts in, "you and Kataryna should make sure that you get vaccinated for your trip to Brazil. You should do that next week."

"Yeah, we will make an appointment with Dr. de Angelis so he can advise us on what is required for such a trip."

Kataryna looks at her fiancé. "Gee, Luca, you are really micro managing our trip."

"I just want you to take all precautions, Principessa", he responds. "Better safe than sorry."

He turns to Francesco. "As far as the agenda is concerned, Kataryna and I have agreed that you two do the due diligence meetings with the owner and the production facility staff in Rio and Manaus. Kataryna will come back home then and you and Roberto will go to the Amazonas region where the plants are grown to check out everything there."

Francesco nods. "Sounds like a good plan."

"Not to me," Patrizia, his fiancée sounds concerned.

"Roberto, is going to Brazil? How is that possible?" Carlotta is totally surprised.

Luca gives her a sign that they will explain everything later.

"Why don't we have an early evening," Riccardo Romano suggests. "Tomorrow will be a busy day here and we will also attend Easter mass in the morning. So no sleeping late."

On the way to their bedrooms Kataryna explains Roberto's new situation to Carlotta. She is stunned to hear that her brother agreed to that but also pleased to learn that Roberto will get to go home and start a normal life.

"Are you really comfortable working that closely with him?" Carlotta asks Kataryna.

"First of all, he will work closer with Francesco and only interact occasionally with me, and second, yes, I am confident that he will not step out of line."

"Good. I am pleased to hear that. I will meet him after I have had the ultrasound next week," Carlotta explains.

"Oh, that's right. Would you like me to go with you?" Kataryna offers.

"I wouldn't mind the company if you are not too busy with your new deal."

"Don't worry. I will make time for that," Kataryna promises.

"Thank you, that is really sweet. Have a good night."

After the Sunday Easter mass the family returns to the villa. The priest joins them for lunch. Larissa and her daughter Eliana arrive at noon and are introduced to everyone by Kataryna. Enrico is pleased that another person his age is part of the holiday gathering. It also doesn't hurt that she is a stunning looking girl in an exotic kind of way. He is recalling a snippet from the earlier sermon at Easter mass when the priest said that God is working in mysterious ways. He got that right, Enrico thinks, checking out Eliana. She seems to be equally pleased to have someone her age to talk to and walks right up to him.

After lunch Luca and Kataryna briefly discuss their wedding plans with the priest. Kataryna leaves them to join Carlotta and Larissa for a chat.

"You have a beautiful family," Larissa says facing Carlotta. "I miss my family. They are so far away. I am planning on going to Brazil for Christmas." She turns to Kataryna. "Do you think I can take a short vacation at the end of the year?"

"I don't see why not. We should have wrapped up the Brazilian acquisition by then. Even if not for whatever reason, no one works over the Christmas holiday anyway."

"Are you in a relationship?" Carlotta asks Larissa.

"No, I am not. After my husband died I needed time to get over it. We had a great marriage. I miss him a lot and I haven't met anyone who could take his place in my heart. How about you?"

"I am currently single but I am also pregnant. The relationship with the father of my child didn't work out and I am divorced from Enrico's father."

"I was single for a long time before I met Luca," Kataryna explains. "I wouldn't rush into a relationship either. You are better off single than with the wrong person."

"Yes, that's how I see it too but there are moments now when I wish I would meet the right person." Larissa says.

"Well, who knows, Mr. Right could be just around the corner," Kataryna pronounces looking at both of them.

"Thank you, for instilling hope in us," Carlotta says somewhat cynical. "Hey Larissa, how about you and I go out together one evening? I know in my present state I won't be attracting any men but we can have a nice dinner somewhere."

"I would love that, Carlotta. Let's plan something real soon."

Luca is still in a conversation with the priest, Kataryna notices. Wondering what they are discussing so intensely, she walks over to join them. Their conversation ends as she approaches. After a few words the priest excuses himself.

"So, darling, what did you and Father Antonio talk about so seriously? Did you confess how naughty you have been?" she jokes.

"Oh sure, Principessa, I described everything I do to you in detail," he whispers in her ear.

"That is pretty one-sided, darling. Why didn't you also tell him what I do to you?" She has fun with this flirtatious conversation, which surely is stirring them both up.

"I wanted to leave something for his imagination." Luca grins at her playfully.

"He is a Catholic priest. He has no experience in that department. How could he possibly imagine that?" She smiles impishly.

"Unbelievable. You always have to have the final word." He kisses her on the lips as Carlotta walks up to them.

She sighs seeing them kiss. "At least someone is happy here."

Kataryna gives her an 'I am so sorry look'. "Well, at least you made a nice new friend today and I am always here for you."

"Where is Enrico? I haven't seen him for a while." Luca asks his sister.

"He and Eliana are in papà's study watching a movie," Carlotta replies. "What a beautiful girl."

"Hey, aren't you forgetting that Enrico is supposedly in love with Sabrina?" Kataryna reminds her.

Carlotta shrugs her shoulders. Let's see how this works out with the geographic distance."

SEVEN

Tuesday morning Kataryna and Francesco meet with Dr. de Angelis at the clinic to discuss their vaccines for the Brazil trip.

"How are you Francesco? We are still working on your mother's test results. Hopefully we will know soon what's causing her condition."

"Thank you, Dr. de Angelis. I am sure you are doing your best here."

Nice to see you again, Signora Taylor. I trust Signor Romano is well?" Dr. de Angelis enquires.

"Yes, he is fine. Thank you for asking."

"I understand you two have to travel to various regions in Brazil."

"Yes," Francesco responds, "Kataryna will only go to Rio and Manaus, which is in the State of Amazonas but Roberto and I will have to go all the way up the river close to the Colombian border. So what kind of vaccinations do you suggest for us?"

"Other than the typical, like tetanus, we recommend all hepatitis shots as well as yellow fever, typhoid and a malaria prevention drug. I will also give you antibiotics to take with you in case you get an infection."

"That's a lot of vaccinations. Is that really necessary?" Kataryna asks.

"I am afraid so. We have learned that a couple of people who went up the Amazonas contracted yellow fever and died. Malaria medication is a must, and you have to protect yourself from mosquitos in the Amazonas region because we know that there were outbreaks of dengue fever for which there is no vaccination or preventative drug available. Is either one of you allergic to eggs?"

"Not that I know of," Francesco says, "I have eggs all the time."

"Me neither," Kataryna says, "why are you asking?"

"Because the yellow fever vaccine is egg white based. Why don't we do a total physical with all blood work, urinalysis, etc. just to be on the safe side? In case you come back with any unusual symptoms we know what you didn't have before you went there."

"Sounds like a good idea," Kataryna says. "I didn't have a full physical for some time. You may as well do some genetic tests for me, too because I am planning to get pregnant after my wedding in September."

"I am getting married in June, so why don't you do all these tests for me also?" Francesco adds. "Good thinking, Kataryna."

"Sure. Especially in your case, Francesco, we want to be sure that you are in good shape because of your mother's yet undetermined illness and her weak immune system, in case you inherited any of that," Dr. de Angelis says.

No chance of that, Kataryna is thinking.

The doctor calls the lab. "I am sending two patients down for a complete blood count and a few other tests."

He hands Francesco and Kataryna each an instruction sheet to take to the lab.

"OK, you're all set. You can make an appointment to come back for the results and the inoculations in about three days."

They head down to the lab to have their blood drawn.

When she returns to her office, Kataryna finds the draft for Roberto's consultancy agreement on her desk. After reviewing it she instructs the lawyer to have it sent to Roberto with a copy to Francesco.

A calendar alert comes up reminding her of Carlotta's ultrasound appointment next week. She activates the snooze feature to set a reminder for the night before and another one for her vaccination appointment Friday afternoon.

♦ ♦ ♦

Friday morning Dr. de Angelis reviews Kataryna's and Francesco's blood test results. He stumbles upon something unusual and examines it closer by pulling up another patient's chart. Distraught by the findings he shakes his head and calls the medical director of the clinic's lab up to his office.

"Ciao Salvatore." The lab's medical director enters his office. "What's so urgent that I had to rush up here?"

Dr. de Angelis lets out a deep sigh. "I think we have a huge problem in the lab."

He hands the printed lab tests to his colleague. "Take a look at these results. This is scientifically impossible. The lab technician who performed these tests must have used the wrong blood samples. I have no idea how this could have happened but if this gets out we will have the press all over the clinic. God knows, how many other mistakes like that happened in your lab. I want you to immediately start an investigation but do it quietly and remove the technician from this kind of work for the time being without telling him or her why. Give that employee a special assignment not involving lab tests and report back to me ASAP."

"What happened?" the lab director asks stunned, reviewing the results.

"Look at the test for Francesco Barone and Kataryna Taylor. They are not related to each other but show a high DNA combined relationship index. Then when I look at

Sylvia Barone's DNA, hers and her son's don't match at all."

"What? How in the world is that possible?" the lab director yells out. "Let me investigate this immediately. I cannot imagine how this could have happened."

"You tell me," Dr. de Angelis groans, throwing his arms up in the air. "I am terrified to find out what may have happened. We will have to terminate the responsible technician without giving the real reason. This cannot get out to the public."

"I will do the new tests personally," the lab director states still in shock, "but we need new blood samples."

Dr. Angelis calls Kataryna. "Ciao Signora Taylor. Unfortunately, we had a little accident in the lab. Yours as well as Francesco's blood samples were dropped and are compromised now. We need to take a fresh sample from both of you today."

"Oh no! Let me get in touch with Francesco. We will be at your office shortly."

Kataryna is not happy. Neither is Francesco when she calls him with this news.

"I was hoping to get these vaccinations over with well ahead of our trip in case either one of us has a reaction to them," he says irritated.

"Me, too, Francesco but accidents happen. So let's just go there and give them our blood again."

After three days the lab director appears with the new test results in Dr. de Angelis' office.

"You are not going to believe this, Salvatore. The tests came out the same and I did them myself with no other blood samples close to me."

The two doctors stare at each other too stunned by the results to speak.

"This is a nightmare," Dr. de Angelis finally declares. "Signora Taylor and Francesco are due here any moment."

"You can give them the vaccinations. It has nothing to do with the DNA test," the lab director says. "Let me know what other steps you want to take."

Dr. de Angelis' assistant followed by Kataryna enters his office as his colleague exits. "Signora Taylor has arrived."

"Ciao Dr. de Angelis. Francesco will be delayed due to a longer than expected business meeting," Kataryna explains. "Why don't we take care of my vaccinations so I can get back to work. He will be in a little later."

"Sure, but first I need to discuss something with you," he says in a serious tone.

Kataryna gives him a concerned look expecting bad news about her health.

"You are scaring me. Do I have some kind of dreadful disease?"

"No, you are in good health," Dr. de Angelis starts. "However, something highly unusual has shown up and we are unable to explain it at this time. We will have to investigate this further."

"What is it?" Kataryna asks anxiously.

"We ran the tests twice. Each time with the same result. Yours and Francesco's DNA are a close match as indicated by the combined relationship index. We are puzzled because we have never seen two biologically unrelated persons having such a close match."

Kataryna feels a touch of anxiety coming on. She takes a deep breath and then slowly exhales.

"I think I can solve this mystery," she says quietly.

The doctor looks at her bewildered. "How?"

She hesitates then takes another deep breath.

"This has to stay between us for now."

"It's covered under the doctor-patient confidentiality."

"I recently learned that Francesco is my biological brother."

"WHAT?" He looks at her as if she had two heads.

"Let me explain," she continues. "My father told me in November last year that my parents had a child, a boy, which they gave up for adoption right after he was born. I vowed to find my brother and hired an attorney to locate the adoption papers. He did and informed me mid February, right after the Venice incident with Roberto, that Francesco is my brother. My fiancé already discussed it with Francesco's adoptive father, who requested that we don't make this public yet because of his wife's medical condition. He said she would be devastated if she found out that I am Francesco's sister and that they had to tell him and their other family members that they are not his biological parents."

Dr. de Angelis is stunned but relieved at the same time. His lab's integrity is intact but what a story.

"So you are saying that Francesco doesn't know that he was adopted and they haven't told him yet?"

"He has no idea. Dr. Barone wants to wait telling him until his wife is in stable condition."

"I suppose you would not have revealed this if he had been here with you right now," he says.

"No. I promised that I would wait until Sylvia's condition has improved. So you can't divulge this when Francesco comes in later on."

"He won't hear it from me," the doctor assures her, "but it would be best if he would be told soon. He is worried that he might get Sylvia's illness one day. However, we now know that he doesn't have anything to worry about."

Kataryna sighs. "Believe me, I'd rather tell him today than tomorrow but I can't."

"At this point, we don't even know what exactly causes Sylvia's condition. This could be a long drawn out process," he advises her.

"That's what I am afraid of." Kataryna gets up to leave as the doctor's assistant ushers Francesco into his office.

"Sorry about the delay," he apologizes. "This was a never-ending meeting. OK, doc, what's the verdict? Am I gonna live?" he jokes.

The doctor nods. "You are in excellent health. Let me give you the shots."

"I'll see you later, Francesco."

Kataryna heads to her car with mixed emotions after they leave the clinic. She goes straight to see Luca.

"You never guess what just happened." Her face is serious.

"Does it have anything to do with Roberto?" Luca asks with an even more serious face.

"No, it has to do with my brother."

"What about him?"

"I had asked to include genetic tests while taking the physical for the Brazil trip because of our plans to get pregnant after the wedding. So did Francesco. The test results showed a close DNA match for Francesco and me. Dr. de Angelis figured something was wrong in his lab and said they would need to investigate this further. So, I had to tell him that Francesco is my brother. He won't say anything but this is getting hairy now."

Luca sighs. "Yes, it is. "After you two are back from Brazil, Vincente has to talk to him regardless of his wife's condition. If she is still in bad shape, they should just not tell her."

"I will hold you to it, Luca." She leaves his office calmer than before. At least they have agreed on a time frame now.

Her assistant hands her the messages when she returns to her office. A message from Roberto is right on top with a phone number he can be reached at. She returns his call.

"Ciao Kataryna. My lawyer reviewed the consultant agreement. I am prepared to sign and messenger it over to you."

"Good. Are you still in the clinic?"

"No, I am at home."

"OK. I would like to set up a meeting with Francesco, you and Larissa Dos Santos, BioMedyca's new CFO."

"Sure. When would you like me to come in?"

"How about Monday at 8 a.m.?"

"See you on Monday. Have a nice weekend."

"Thank you. Same to you."

She instructs her assistant to send out the meeting invitation to all parties.

◆ ◆ ◆

As soon as Roberto hangs up with Kataryna he calls Carlotta. The sound of his voice sends electrical currents through her body.

"Did I catch you at a bad time?" he asks, sensing she was startled.

"No, I just wasn't expecting to get a call from you."

"I wanted to let you know that I was released from the clinic. I am back home. If I recall correctly, you are going to have the ultrasound exam next week. I would like to go with you."

"Actually Kataryna is going with me," she advises him.

"Well, that doesn't preclude me from going, too. After all I am the father of this child."

Carlotta clears her throat nervously. "Let me get back to you. I will think about it and discuss it with Kataryna."

"Do you need Kataryna's permission for who may come to your ultrasound exam?" he asks somewhat miffed.

"Not her permission but I would think that she would want to know that you are coming along."

"I am going to start to work for BioMedyca as a consultant on Monday. So I will see her then anyway. I don't think she would have a problem with me joining you."

"Yeah, but Luca might have a problem with that. I will let you know. Have a good weekend. Ciao."

Carlotta is all torn up inside. Just his voice brings back the memories of the time they spent together before his 'Kataryna melt-down' in Venice. She was so in love with him then and it appeared that he was, too. Was? Who am I kidding, she thinks? I am not over this man. Tears are streaming down her face. The deep emotional pain is back with a vengeance. Could there still be a chance for them, flashes through her mind? "NO! Cancel that thought," she says to herself. However, there will always be a part of him in her life because of the child she is carrying. She touches her baby bump.

At 5 p.m. Kataryna arrives to pick her up to spend the weekend with her and Luca at the Lake Como villa.

"You are very quiet," Kataryna remarks as the three have dinner together Saturday night. "Are you feeling okay?"

"Yeah, just a little tired. It's been a long week for me."

Luca looks at his sister. Something is off, he decides.

Carlotta senses her brother is not convinced. "Must be the hormones," she tries to make him believe.

"I am kind of under the weather, too," Kataryna says. "I think it's from all the vaccinations. I am ready to go to sleep."

Sunday after breakfast Carlotta and Kataryna take a walk by the lake while Luca attends to some business matters in his home office.

"I got a call from Roberto Friday afternoon. He wants to join us for the ultrasound exam. What do you think?"

"That's entirely up to you, Carlotta. If you are okay with that, I don't really have to go. I offered to go with you because I didn't want you to be alone."

"I really don't know what to do," she responds. "One side of me wants him there but I am not sure how I would react."

"I can see why. I guess there are still some lingering feelings for him inside you. As a matter of fact, I am going to see him tomorrow morning. He signed the consultant agreement. We will have an introductory meeting regarding the Brazilian company I intend to acquire."

"It goes a little deeper than lingering feelings, I am afraid." Carlotta admits. "I'll let you know by Tuesday what I decide."

◆ ◆ ◆

"Buongiorno Roberto," Kataryna greets him when she enters Francesco's office Monday morning. "This is Larissa Dos Santos, our new CFO." She introduces the two.

"It's a pleasure to meet you, Roberto," Larissa says appearing somewhat nervous. "I have read a lot about you."

He gives her an uncertain look and then smiles.

"Only good things, I hope."

"Yes, of course. You have done an amazing job here."

"Why don't we start." Kataryna hands Roberto a presentation folder. "This is the material we received from Ernesto Oliveiro. How about we go over the details and you can give us your opinion how realistic their facts and assumptions are."

"Sure," Roberto nods.

"By the way, Roberto, Larissa is Brazilian," Kataryna informs him. "It just so happens that her brother is a partner at an international law firm in Manaus. We need to have a reliable attorney over there. I would like you three to have a conference call with him tomorrow. He should send us his firm's information package and a retainer agreement for review."

Roberto describes the company's operations and his prior discussions with Ernesto Oliveiro in detail. He then reviews the presentation material Kataryna gave him.

"I will make a couple of calls to some other contacts in Brazil tomorrow to check on a few things," he explains.

"Perfect," Kataryna responds. "We should also go over our travel plans tomorrow. Francesco and I will go over first to meet with Ernesto at his house in Rio de Janeiro. He invited us to be his guests. He's going to have a welcome party for us so we can meet all the important players over there. Then we will go to Manaus to inspect the production facility. Thereafter you can fly over, Roberto, and do the rest of the trip with Francesco."

"I take it that you got the necessary vaccinations for that trip?" Roberto asks Francesco.

"Yes, both Kataryna and I did," he confirms.

"OK then. Get ready for snakes, exotic spiders and a few other obstacles," Roberto smirks, patting Francesco on the shoulder.

Francesco sighs. "Sounds adventurous."

"Yeah, we have to be really careful. Seriously, the spiders I am talking about are quite poisonous and their bite could be fatal."

Francesco scratches his head. "I feel an illness coming on. Maybe I should stay home."

Kataryna gets up. "I've got to get back to my office. Please keep me updated on all new developments."

Francesco, Larissa and Roberto break for lunch after Kataryna left.

Larissa gets home around 7 p.m. She sits down to have dinner with her daughter.

"How was your day, mamma?" Eliana asks.

"Exciting," Larissa responds with a certain grin.

Eliana looks at her mother, intrigued to find out more.

"Can you talk about it or is it confidential?"

"Yeah, I have to talk to someone about it before I burst."

"That exciting, huh? In that case, please don't keep me in suspense any longer."

Larissa takes a deep breath. "We had our first meeting today with the former CEO of BioMedyca. He is coming on as a consultant for an acquisition I can't talk about yet."

She grabs her daughter's arm. "He is sooo good-looking and he has this mysterious aura about him. I don't really know how to explain it. In a way I wish he were still the CEO. Don't get me wrong, I really like my boss Francesco but when Roberto came into the meeting it just took an entirely different direction. He is so good at what he does, so in control. I was totally mesmerized. I think I am in love."

"That's great, mamma," Eliana says surprised. "I am so happy for you. Well, guess what. I have a huge crush on Enrico. So it looks like we both have something to be excited about."

"Ooh, Enrico is a cute guy," Larissa admits. "I can see you with him. I noticed you two hit it off right away at the Easter get-together."

"I am going to hang out with him tomorrow," Eliana adds with a broad smile.

"Good for you. Now I have to find a way for Roberto to ask me out." Larissa giggles.

"I am sure you will come up with something." Eliana encourages her.

Larissa shrugs her shoulders. "I believe he is divorced but I don't know if he is seeing anyone. Besides, I haven't been in the dating scene for a long time."

"Why don't you ask Kataryna or Carlotta if he is available? They seem to know him well."

"No, sweetie, I don't want to open this up to them. That would be so unprofessional. I can't help wondering why he left the company and is coming back as a consultant now. Apparently he left for personal reasons. I am really curious what could have caused this drastic step."

Larissa's phone rings. "Pronto. Ciao Carlotta. How are you?"

"Pretty good. I am calling to see when we can meet for dinner."

"How about tomorrow or Wednesday?" Larissa suggests.

"Wednesday is good. Shall we say around 8 p.m.?"

"Yes. I am really looking forward to it. Ciao Carlotta."

Eliana smiles at her mother. "I am so glad that you are starting to go out more."

"Me, too but please, not a word about my interest in Roberto to anyone, okay?"

"I won't say anything, mamma," Eliana promises.

After hanging up with Larissa, Carlotta calls Roberto.

"If you still want to go to the ultrasound exam, meet me at the doctor's office on Wednesday at 3.p.m."

"I wouldn't miss it for anything. Should I pick you up from the office?"

"No, thank you. I don't want Luca to see you pick me up. I don't feel like having any lengthy discussions about you with him."

"Of course. I don't want to upset Luca either. He's already not happy that I joined BioMedyca as a consultant. What about Kataryna? She will know because she was supposed to go with you."

"She won't say anything to him. She is trying to keep him calm about her trip to Brazil already."

"OK. See you Wednesday, Carlotta. Ciao."

◆◆◆

Francesco, Roberto and Larissa meet the next day to tackle the proposed acquisition details. Roberto updates them with information he received from Brazil overnight. Larissa is mesmerized again by the way Roberto is taking charge. She has a tough time focusing on business matters and promptly misses a question he just asked her.

"Larissa, do you have an answer for me?" he addresses her more directly.

She struggles. It went right over her head. She has no idea what he just asked her. A heat wave runs through her as the adrenaline takes control.

"Can you repeat the question, please?" she quickly asks trying not to show her embarrassment.

"What kind of free cash flow does BioMedyca have to complete this acquisition or do we need to go for financing?"

Francesco jumps in. "We should discuss that with Kataryna."

"Yeah, sooner rather than later," Roberto murmurs. "When we get a positive response from Anvisa, we should immediately submit our letter of intent to Ernesto Oliveiro before some other company nabs the deal."

"Anvisa?" Francesco repeats, glancing at Roberto.

"That's the Brazilian equivalent of the FDA."

"OK, let me call her," Francesco reaches for the phone.

"What's up, Francesco?" she answers his call.

"Have you and Stephen decided how to pay for the Brazilian acquisition if it goes forward?"

"We are thinking of using free cash flow. Please have Larissa send over updated financial statements."

"You'll have it within the hour," he ends the call and turns to Larissa.

"Kataryna needs the latest financial statements. Can you have that ready for me in the next half hour?"

"Sure," she responds gathering her things to head to her office. She calls up the reports on her computer, reviews them and then emails them with some footnotes to Francesco.

Still uneasy about the earlier incident at the office, Larissa pours herself a glass of wine when she gets home and calls her girlfriend Claudia.

"Ciao Larissa. How is the new job?" Claudia asks.

"So far, I really like it but I am also in a somewhat touchy situation."

"Why? What's going on?" Claudia is curious.

"Remember the former CEO, Roberto Silvestri who you and I used to fantasize about when we saw his photo in the papers?"

"How could I not remember him?" Claudia answers. "That's the kind of man who shows up in your dreams."

"Well, he just came on as a consultant in connection with an acquisition we are looking at, and I have to work closely with him on this project."

"Wow. Lucky you. What is he like? Is he a flirt?"

"He is amazing. The project we are working on is not easy but he seems to manage it with such ease. I really would like to know why he left the CEO position."

"So what is the touchy situation you mentioned?"

Larissa takes a moment to respond. "Hmm. I am totally in love with him."

"Good for you. I am happy you are finally starting to date. I was getting pretty worried about you."

"We are not at the dating stage yet. I don't even know how he feels about me," Larissa sighs, "but I am head over heels in love with him. I have never felt like this before."

"I see. So what's your plan?"

"I was hoping to get some advice from you," Larissa says anxiously. "How do I go about this? I am so out of touch when it comes to dating and all of a sudden it hit me so hard. I even had trouble concentrating today and totally missed a question he asked me."

"Oh, oh. You got it bad," Claudia giggles. "I love it. Do you know if he is available?"

"No, I don't know much about his personal life."

"Why don't you ask him to go out for a drink after work?" Claudia suggests. "That'll give you an opportunity to find out what's going on in his life."

"I don't know if I have the nerve to do that. What if he says no? Don't forget I have to work with him until we close this deal."

"Just say you would like to get his input on something in connection with the deal. He may be flattered that you are seeking his advice. Or play 'the damsel in distress'. That usually works well. Then you slowly ease into his personal life to find out if he is seeing anyone."

"That's not a bad idea," Larissa admits. "I am just afraid this may come across as unprofessional. Maybe I should wait until the deal has closed."

"I wouldn't wait that long with a man like him. If you want this bad enough, you will come up with something. Why don't you practice your approach for a couple of days and then just do it."

"Easy for you to say," Larissa chuckles.

"Come on. You can do it." Claudia eggs her on. "If I weren't married, I would go after him in a heartbeat."

Larissa laughs out loud. "Oh dear, this is so difficult. I can't stop thinking about him."

"Then do something about it," Claudia responds. "Next time you call me, you better have some juicy details to report."

"Oh my God, Claudia. Now I am even more scared just thinking about it. Let me go. I have to get my beauty rest. Ciao."

"Ciao Larissa. Call me soon."

Larissa hangs up the phone with a grin. After finishing her wine, she feels a bit more relaxed about the whole thing.

◆ ◆ ◆

Wednesday afternoon Roberto meets Carlotta at her obstetrician's office.

"Here is your baby," the doctor explains to Carlotta and Roberto pointing to a spot on the monitor as she performs the ultrasound exam. Excited they both stare at the screen.

"Everything looks good. Do you want to know the gender?" the doctor asks.

Carlotta looks at Roberto. "Do you?"

"I would like to know if you are up for it," he says softly.

"Go ahead," Carlotta instructs the doctor. "Tell us."

"It's a boy." The doctor smiles at the two and then leaves the exam room.

"I guess that's what you hoped it would be," Carlotta says.

"Yeah, I have to admit that makes me very happy," Roberto responds. "Are you disappointed that it's not a girl?"

"It would have been nice to have a daughter but a healthy child is more important than gender."

"I agree," Roberto says. "Can I tell Verena?"

"Sure, you can tell your daughter. I will also tell Enrico but let's limit it to close family for now."

Roberto nods. "OK. Would you like to go out to have a bite to eat and talk about the arrangements for our son?"

"I already have dinner plans for tonight," Carlotta replies. "Let's get together another night."

"I'll give you a call next week to set something up. By the way, I will be going to Brazil soon on a business trip."

Carlotta glances at him. "I know, with Kataryna and Francesco."

"I will travel with Francesco. Your brother made sure that Kataryna will be nowhere close to me in Brazil."

Carlotta chuckles. "Can you blame him?"

"I guess not," he says somewhat sad.

"I am sorry," Carlotta touches his arm, "I didn't mean to open old wounds."

"I can't change what has happened in the past. I can only do better in the future. We better stick to talking about our child and moving forward when we get together."

"I wish I could move forward as easily as you seem to be able to."

"You don't know what I am going through, Carlotta. Please don't assume anything. Can I give you a ride home?"

"No, thank you. I have to run a couple of errands in the area. Have a nice evening." She turns around and walks away.

"Buonasera," Carlotta greets Larissa when they meet for dinner at the restaurant. "I have really been looking forward to our evening out."

"So have I," Larissa responds. "I don't go out that much."

"Other than family gatherings, I don't get to go out that much either," Carlotta admits. "It's really refreshing to have dinner with someone new. I can't wait to hear more about your life."

Larissa smiles. "My life is pretty boring. Well, it was at least up to now."

"So what is going on now that may have turned it around?" Carlotta asks.

"Well, for starters, I love my new job at BioMedyca, and I already met some very nice people because of it, including you."

"Thank you. The feeling is mutual."

Larissa grins mysteriously. "I think I may have finally fallen in love again."

"Oh, wow," Carlotta exclaims, "good for you. Being fresh in love is the greatest feeling in the world."

"Yes, I am totally excited but I don't want to talk about it yet. It's way too early and I don't want to jinx it."

"I understand. I am not going to pry. I just hope you are luckier in love than I am."

"Why? What's going on with you in that department?"

"I don't want to go into too many details but I also was very much in love recently. Turned out that my dream man was in love with another woman. I was pretty shocked when I found out and I am still not entirely over him."

"I am sorry to hear that, Carlotta. This doesn't sound like it could have a happy ending."

"Believe me, I am trying to move on but it is really tough because he is also the father of the baby I am carrying. The pregnancy was an accident, though."

"How did you find out that he was in love with another woman? Did he tell you or did you catch them together?"

Carlotta hesitates. "It came out in a dramatic way. Today was especially difficult because he joined me for the ultrasound exam and we found out that we will have a son. He was so accommodating and even wanted to take me out for dinner afterwards. Thank God, I had plans with you otherwise I might have accepted his invitation." Carlotta looks sad.

"What a scoundrel," Larissa tries to comfort her. "I can see that this is pretty painful for you."

Carlotta nods fighting back tears. "We better change the subject."

"So I understand that Enrico and my daughter have become quite close," Larissa tries to distract her.

Carlotta lightens up again. "Yes, Enrico mentioned that he has been hanging out with her a couple of times."

"Eliana really likes him and so do I," Larissa adds. "I wouldn't mind if they started dating. How about you?"

"Well, I think your daughter is a very beautiful girl but he just started a closer relationship with my future sister-in-law's niece. She lives in New York but Enrico wants to study over there anyway. So Kataryna and I will arrange to get him into a college in the New York area next year."

"Oh," Larissa sounds disappointed. "I had no idea."

"Yeah, the whole thing started with a bit of drama because Kataryna's niece has a twin sister and they both kind of fell for Enrico. Their mother was not happy about that but we managed to work it out in the end."

"But isn't this pretty difficult with the long distance between them?" Larissa asks.

"Time will tell. Sabrina will come to Italy during her summer vacation. They have been on video calls almost daily since we came back from New York."

"OK. I will prepare Eliana before she gets too interested in him."

"Yes, you better do that, Larissa." Carlotta signals the waiter to bring the check. "I had a really good time tonight. It felt good to talk a bit about my personal predicament. Let's do it again soon."

"I would love to get together again. How about next time you come to my house and I'll make dinner for us?"

"Excellent. Maybe by that time you have more to tell about your new love interest."

Larissa rolls her eyes and crosses her fingers. "I really hope so. I can't wait to get closer to that man."

When Larissa arrives home, Eliana is waiting for her in the living room. "Ciao, mamma. How was your dinner?"

"Very nice. Carlotta is such a lovely woman. I really enjoy her company."

"Did you two talk about Enrico and me at all?" Eliana giggles.

"We did. I hate to tell you but Enrico has a girlfriend. It's Kataryna Taylor's niece Sabrina. Did he ever mention her?"

"He mentioned that he celebrated his birthday together with her and her twin sister's birthday in New York but he didn't say she was his girlfriend."

"Carlotta told me that they are in a relationship. She will come to Italy for her entire summer vacation and next year Enrico will to go to college in the New York area."

Eliana is visibly disappointed. "Really? I wonder why he wouldn't tell me that."

"What did you two talk about when you met up?"

"Music, movies and school stuff. We also talked a lot about New York and what else he did over there."

"Was it just you two or were you in a group?"

"Him and his cousin and another girl."

"I see. So nothing romantic."

"No, but we only got together twice since we met at Easter. I was hoping the next time he would ask me out on a date. Just me and him, you know."

"Unfortunately that's not gonna happen."

"We'll see. If he asks me out, I am not going to say no," Eliana says determined. "Sabrina is far away and maybe it's not as serious as you think."

"According to Carlotta, they are seeing each other every day via FaceTime. That looks pretty serious to me. Please don't interfere. After all we are talking about my big boss's niece. I don't need any complications like this in my new job and neither does Carlotta who is already going through a lot of personal stuff."

"I am really not happy right now, mamma." Eliana frowns.

"I know, sweetie but you have to learn how to deal with disappointments in life. Not everything will go your way all the time. Just look at the hand I was dealt. I never imagined to be a widow at this young age."

Eliana starts crying. "It's not fair that I have to suppress my feelings for Enrico."

"I will help you through this." Larissa embraces her daughter.

EIGHT

"Good morning, Larissa. Would you please finalize the five-year projections for BioMedyca," Kataryna requests when she calls her. "I need these by tonight so I can review them with my partner in New York. Roberto will deliver the assumptions for the proposed Brazilian acquisition to you later on."

"Sure, Kataryna. I will do my absolute best to put this together for you by 8 p.m."

"Thank you, Larissa. That would be great. How is everything going for you so far?"

"Very well. I couldn't be happier here, Kataryna."

"We are really glad to have you on board, Larissa."

Francesco enters Kataryna's office.

"Good morning. Are you ready to go over the retainer letter for the Brazilian law firm and a few other things?" He hands her a folder.

"Absolutely. So you spoke with Larissa's brother in Manaus?" she asks.

"Yeah, we did. He made a good impression. Have a look at the folder with his firm's presentation and the retainer letter."

"Good. Everything seems to come together nicely," Kataryna says looking at the law firm's profile. "Why don't you send the retainer letter to our lawyer for review?"

"Consider it done," Francesco replies.

"How is everything working out with Roberto?" she asks.

"So far so good. If I didn't know what I know, I would never think that he would be capable of what he did. Anyway he is as brilliant as ever and we are all getting along just fine. Between you and me, I am glad that he is on board for this transaction. As much as it might irk Luca for personal reasons, it was the right business decision."

"I know. You and I couldn't pull this off alone, Francesco. I highly respect you but Roberto is the one with the experience and knowledge when it comes to this acquisition."

"Say no more. I fully understand and agree, Kataryna."

"I am happy to hear that. How is your mother?"

"Still shaky but I know she is in good hands with Dr. de Angelis."

"I hope she recovers soon."

"So do I, especially since we are leaving for Brazil soon."

"I'll keep my fingers crossed," she says.

◆ ◆ ◆

"Here are the assumptions for the acquisition, Larissa," Roberto says handing her some handwritten notes. "How are the financial projections coming?"

"I should have something to go over around 6 p.m.," she responds.

"OK, so let's get together in an hour and finalize everything." He turns around to leave her office.

Larissa closes her eyes after he is gone, trying to calm down from the excitement of having him that close to her. She can't recall ever having been that head over heels for any man including her deceased husband. Take a deep breath and relax, Larissa, she tells herself. You've got an important job to do here. No room for errors. She takes a sip of water attempting to simmer down her thoughts about Roberto when Francesco walks in.

"Is everything okay, Larissa? You look a little flushed. Hopefully you are not coming down with anything," he says concerned.

"Oh no, I am fine," she tries to convince him quickly. "Roberto just gave me the assumptions. What time would you like to get together to go over the projections?"

"I have to leave soon. It's my father's birthday today and we are having a little get-together. Please review the numbers with Roberto and then email everything to me and Kataryna."

"OK. Expect an email between 7 p.m. and 8 p.m."

"Perfect. Thank you, Larissa. See you tomorrow."

Larissa starts working on including the acquisition assumptions in the projection model. She has trouble concentrating. "Get it together before you make a huge mistake," she commands herself. She manages to focus on the figures and carefully prepares the Excel sheet with the numbers she received from Roberto.

"How is it going? Any problems?" Roberto stands over her, appearing out of nowhere.

"Uh. You scared me," she shrieks, grasping her chest. "What time is it?"

"I am sorry. I didn't mean to startle you." He checks his watch. "It's 6:15 p.m. You said you might have this finished around 6 p.m."

"I had no idea it was that late already. Here you go." She hands him a printout with the projections.

He reviews it intensely giving her the opportunity to study every inch of him.

"I think we have to do some tweaking in the gross profit position in year three," he recommends still looking at the numbers.

"These numbers are based on the assumptions you gave me," she counters softly.

"Yeah, I need to revise that." He takes a look at his prior notes and starts correcting some numbers. "Sorry Larissa, my mistake. I transposed some numbers."

She smiles at him coquettishly. "That's gonna cost you."

"I accept the responsibility. Since it is my fault that you have to stay this late, how about I take you out for dinner after we are done? I am sure you don't want to go home and cook this late."

"I gladly accept," she responds happily. "I am starving. I didn't have a proper lunch. Just nibbled on something."

"Me neither. I will make a reservation for us while you are updating the projections."

She nods and quickly hits the keyboard. Dinner with Roberto. That came totally unexpected. Her heart is beating faster.

"Buona notte," the hostess greets them when they enter the restaurant around 8:30p.m. She seats them at the reserved table.

"How do you like your new job?" Roberto asks her.

"I absolutely love it. I have been following the company for many years and always hoped to get a position at BioMedyca one day."

"Yes, it is a great company with an excellent outlook, especially now with the upcoming Brazilian acquisition."

She looks at him somewhat apprehensive. "Can I ask you why you left the CEO position?"

"Aw, it's a personal thing. I'd rather not get into it."

"I am sorry," she quickly responds embarrassed, "I didn't mean to pry."

"No problem, Larissa. I can understand why you might be wondering about my fairly abrupt resignation. I can assure sure you it has nothing to do with the company. You are in good hands there."

"Thank you for saying that. What are your plans after the acquisition has closed?"

"First of all, I have to stay on and integrate the target into BioMedyca. After that's completed I am planning on a somewhat adventurous vacation with a couple of friends of mine. Nothing fancy. Just us guys in the wilderness for a week or so to get the adrenaline pumping. We might even try some wing suit flying."

"Wing suit flying? That sounds dangerous."

He shrugs his shoulders. "I am aware of the dangers. I am trained in parachute jumping."

"And professionally?" she probes still in awe about his wing suit flying plan.

"I have no concrete plans at the moment. It's all wide open."

"Do you have a family?" she is waiting for his answer with bated breath.

"Yeah, I have a daughter. She is 21. She is studying business and finance. I might do something together with her in the future, business wise."

"Oh, that sounds nice. What about your wife, does she work?"

"We are divorced." His cellphone rings. He picks up the call. "Ciao Kataryna."

Larissa watches him talking to Kataryna. She recalls his words. He is divorced, going on vacation with some guys, no mention of any significant other in his life. So far so good.

"Kataryna says hello and great job on the projections," he tells her after he ends the call.

"Thank you. When are you three going to Brazil?" she continues.

"Kataryna and Francesco are leaving next week. I will join a few days later."

"So it's going to be a shorter trip for you?"

"Yes, just a few days. I will fly directly to Manaus. Francesco and I will take the trip up the Amazonas River to the area where the plant fields are located."

"Kataryna is not going with you?"

"No, I advised her against it. It's a rough territory for various reasons but I know my way around there."

"Actually she had asked me to join them on this trip but I have a girlfriend visiting from out of town during that time. They will be meeting with my brother in Manaus, though."

"Yes, I know."

Larissa is trying to get back to a more personal subject. She is dying to find out a little more about his private life and communicate somehow that she is available without being too obvious.

"By the way, I have a daughter, too," she cleverly turns the conversation around. "Eliana is 17. My husband died two years ago in a car accident."

"Oh, I am sorry to hear that," he states empathically. "Would you like anything else? If not, I am going to ask for the check."

"No, thank you," she responds, disappointed that he seems to be in a rush to end their dinner. Well, it's late and they had a long day, she rationalizes, but if it were up to her they would get to know each other some more.

She gets home still stirred up from the excitement of her dinner with Roberto. She wants to take about it with her girlfriend.

"Ciao Claudia. I hope I didn't wake you but I really need to get something off my chest."

"Wake me? It's not that late. You know I am a night owl. Anything exciting going on with the sexy Roberto?"

"We had dinner tonight."

"Whoa!" Claudia shouts out. "I underestimated you. I didn't think you would dare to do something that fast."

"I didn't. He asked me but don't get too excited. It was more in the context of a business dinner. Actually, come to think of it, he didn't even ask me one personal question. I don't think he is interested in me."

"Of course he would behave business like," Claudia tries to convince her. "First of all you two are colleagues and second you can't expect him to fall all over you the first time you are out together. He behaved like a gentleman."

"I didn't expect him to fall all over me. I just don't get the feeling he likes me in that way. I didn't detect any spark of interest from his side."

Claudia sighs. "You haven't been dating in a while, Larissa. Things have changed in the dating world. He is probably playing it cool to test the waters unless he is in a committed relationship."

"No, I don't think so based on what he told me."

"So, he did volunteer personal information? That's a good sign."

"Not really. I asked him about his wife and he said they are divorced but then Kataryna Taylor called him and we got off subject. And here's another thing I noticed. His voice and demeanor totally changed when he talked to her."

"Can you be more specific?"

"When he talked to me it was straight laced in a more serious polite professional tone. When he was on the phone with her his voice became mellow and soothing and there was an underlying smile on his face, although they talked business."

"Aha. What are trying to say?"

"Believe it or not, I was actually a little jealous in that moment. They seem to be closely connected."

"My goodness, Larissa. Are you serious? That reaction almost sounds a little crazy. They have known each other for a while. Of course they are comfortable with each other. You can't expect that he is like that with you this early on. Give him a chance to get to know you."

Larissa exhales relieved. "You are right. I think I lost my mind. I have never felt this way before. He is all I can think of."

"You have to be calm and confident around him otherwise it's game over before it has started."

"I don't think I am appealing enough for him. I am sure he would want someone like Kataryna or Carlotta Romano. However, Kataryna is engaged to Luca Romano and Carlotta is pregnant with another man's child, who she is in love with, but who seems to be in love with another woman. Can you believe all this?"

"There you go, my dear. Both of these ladies are not available so he is free for you."

Larissa is laughing out loud. "I can always rely on you to make me feel better. Let me get some sleep so I look good for him tomorrow. Good night, talk soon."

Before she goes to bed she inspects her wardrobe looking for a figure-flattering dress to wear at work the next day. I have to turn up the heat, she thinks. Time for a makeover. She looks at herself in the mirror. A new hairstyle wouldn't hurt either and maybe some highlights. This boring look has to go. She inspects her body, imagining Roberto touching her. Oh, yes, she wants him badly. She can feel his lips on her neck going down her chest. "Oh God," she moans, feeling an arousal coming on like never before.

◆ ◆ ◆

"Hi Enrico," Kataryna greets him when he arrives at her office the next day. "How is everything?"

"Pretty good. Looking forward to learning some new things. What can I help you with?"

"OK, then let's get started." She gives him some instructions.

"How is everything going with Sabrina?" she asks casually.

"Good. We speak via FaceTime almost every day," he responds, "but it's not the same as if she were here."

"Yes, I know what long distance romance fells like," she chuckles patting him on the shoulder. "Believe it or not, this is a good test for your relationship."

"I guess so."

"If I may give you a word of advice, please be honest with yourself and her. If this long distance thing doesn't work for you just say so."

He nods. "Sure, thanks."

"By the way, we'll have dinner together later this evening with your mother and uncle as well as Patrizia and Francesco."

"How are your wedding plans coming? Is everything set?" Kataryna asks her future sister-in-law Patrizia when they meet in the restaurant.

"Yes, pretty much," Patrizia responds. "I am just not too happy about that Brazil trip you and Francesco are embarking on soon."

"Neither am I," Luca grabs the opportunity to express his concern again.

Kataryna rolls her eyes. "Look, you two, you better quit while you are ahead. I can't hear this anymore."

Luca tilts his head to the side smiling playfully at Francesco and Patrizia. "Let's talk about something more pleasant. Your wedding."

"That's an excellent subject," Kataryna agrees.

"More precisely your wedding present from our family." Luca continues.

"We are all ears," Francesco responds jovially.

"After discussing it with Kataryna and her business partner Stephen, who graciously agreed to it, our family will gift you the ten percent shares in BioMedyca we still own. Five percent for each of you."

Francesco and Patrizia gaze at each other.

"Are you sure?" They look straight at Kataryna.

"Yes. I thought it was a great idea when Luca ran that by me in New York."

"That's very generous," Francesco states. "Thank you for agreeing to that, Kataryna. I recall that you and Stephen were striving for a 100 percent ownership."

"My pleasure. I figured as a shareholder you will work even harder." She laughs wickedly.

"I knew there had to be an ulterior motive," Francesco kids her.

"We'll start the paperwork with the lawyers in the next few days so everything will be done by June 15, your wedding day," Luca adds.

"Congratulations, Patrizia. Now at the ripe old age of 27 you will be a shareholder in two major companies, the Romano Holding Co. and BioMedyca," her sister Carlotta says. "Not too bad."

◆ ◆ ◆

Larissa arrives at the office the next morning wearing one of her more figure emphasizing dresses. She feels a little more confident but there is room for improvement. An appointment with her hair stylist is next on her list. Shortly before noon she decides to visit Roberto in his office.

"Any further news from Brazil?" she sticks her head in his office. Just looking at him turns up the heat in her.

He looks up startled. "Um, I am not expecting any news from over there. What are you referring to?"

"Oh, I thought there were some loose ends?"

"Not really. I am putting everything together right now for our meetings in Brazil."

"Good. I am heading out for lunch. Would you like to join me?" she asks him sweetly when Kataryna suddenly walks into Roberto's office.

"Ciao Larissa," Kataryna greets her. "I spoke to your brother yesterday at length. Looks like we are going to hire him as our Brazilian counsel."

"Great. I am happy to hear that," she responds, irked that Kataryna is interrupting her attempt to have lunch with Roberto.

"Hi Kataryna. What brings you here?" Roberto gets out of his seat to meet her half way.

"Didn't Francesco tell you that I wanted to have a lunch meeting with you two to go over the travel agenda and a few other things?"

"No, he didn't. I for sure would have remembered that." He gives her a broad smile.

Larissa awkwardly watches the two interact, joking about Francesco forgetting to mention the lunch meeting. She is in a kind of daze. He never smiles at me like this, she thinks. She feels a couple of stabs in her chest.

Francesco strolls by and spots Kataryna in Roberto's office. He hits his forehead. "Uh, oh, I forgot about our lunch. I guess the exciting news last night totally put that in the shadow."

"Yeah, we were just talking about that," Kataryna tells him smiling.

"That must have been some news," Roberto concludes looking at them curiously.

"Let's go eat," Kataryna says cheerfully, "we will tell you all about it."

"Have a nice lunch," Larissa manages to get out.

Another failed attempt to get closer to her dream man. Ready to go back to her office she sees Roberto's cellphone on his desk. She grabs the phone and runs after him trying to catch him before he leaves the building. Too late, they are gone. She returns to her office staring at the phone in her hand. She presses some of the keys. Let's see what I can find out, she thinks. She immediately feels guilty about invading his privacy but proceeds. Her curiosity is stronger than her guilt. The name Verena Silvestri pops up. Who is Verena? The daughter or the ex-wife, she wonders? She comes across some other female names, shrugging her shoulders. God knows who these women are and what roles they play in his life. Frustrated she opens the photo gallery, scrolling up and down.

"NO!" she shouts out in shock when a photo of Roberto embracing Kataryna appears. Right behind that one another one of them equally disturbing. Her heart is racing like crazy as she swipes through the intimate photos. They are having an affair, she concludes. I knew it. She is sick to her stomach, holding her head staring at the photos, fighting tears.

Francesco's assistant approaches her. "Larissa? Are you okay? What's going on?"

"I, ahem," she stammers quickly sliding the phone under a piece of paper. "I don't feel well," she completes the sentence.

"Let me get you some water." The assistant hurries out of Larissa's office and returns with the water.

"Here you go." She hands her the glass, noticing Larissa's hands trembling. "Should I call a doctor?"

"No! I will be good in a moment." She takes a large swig of the water almost spitting it out again.

"What is it, Larissa? Are you ill?" The assistant looks at her scared.

"I think it's low blood sugar," she lies. "I haven't eaten anything today."

"In that case, let me get you some orange juice. That will perk you up in no time."

After drinking a bit of the juice, she heads to the ladies room managing to sneak Roberto's phone back on his desk on the way over there. Returning to her office, she calls Francesco on his cellphone to excuse herself and leaves for the day.

Her emotions are all over the place when she arrives at her home. Her disappointment turns into sadness and then into rage. She starts talking to herself.

"Poor Luca. He doesn't deserve that kind of betrayal. Who wouldn't be happy with a man like him?"

Highly agitated she gets the vial with Valium from her medicine cabinet and takes one. It's been some time since she needed these but this situation calls for it. As the tranquilizing effect kicks in, she starts thinking about how to handle this situation. Should she tell Carlotta that her brother is being deceived by his fiancée and Roberto? Bad idea, she would jeopardize her job. Pursuing a relationship with Roberto seems to be out of the question now, or is it? Kataryna can't keep it up with two men forever. Who will she end up with? The wedding in September is still on as far as she knows. Oh, but wait, Kataryna and Roberto are going to Brazil soon.

"Nicely done, Ms. Taylor. Going on a 'business trip' with your lover far away from your fiancé," she snarls. "That woman has some nerve. I can't get even one of them to take a closer look at me and she is hot and heavy with both. Maybe that's why he left the company so abruptly?"

A visit to the mirror confirms her disgust with her appearance. Time to do something about it. She picks up the phone.

"Bom dia, Marcos. How is everything?"

"Uh, Larissa. I haven't heard from you in a long time. I was just asking about you the other day. Your father said you have a fantastic new job."

"Yeah, I do. It's a biomedical company. We may have some exciting news soon."

"Great. When are you coming over to Brazil for a visit again? I would like to catch up with you."

"Well, maybe soon."

"That would be great. Any time frame yet?"

"Not yet but I need to discuss something delicate with you. Please keep this confidential."

"Of course."

"I would like to discuss a plastic surgery procedure with you."

"For you?"

"Yes. I don't like the way I look. The grieving for my late husband has left its traces in my face. I am just not myself anymore."

"What kind of procedure are you thinking about? Some injections, like fillers or Botox?"

"Oh no. I want a more radical change. A full face lift of some sort."

"Really? Why? You are not even 40 yet."

"Well, I don't like the way I look. As a matter of fact, let me send you a photo so I can show you the look I am going for."

"OK, but I don't like the way this sounds, Larissa. Are you in some kind of crisis?"

"Yeah, I am when I look in the mirror. The crisis is my face."

"You have a beautiful face. Did something happen to it?"

"Let me send you the photo and you will understand."

"OK. Send me a recent photo of you so we can discuss some options."

She uploads two photos and hits send. "Did you get them?"

"They are coming through now." He pauses waiting for the photos to appear. "OK. Got it. Who is this stunning woman in the photo? An actress?"

"Oh yeah, she is an actress, all right," slips out of her mouth sarcastically. "Can you make me look like her?"

Marcos starts laughing. "I am a plastic surgeon not God. This lady has a chiseled face with high cheekbones and you have a more flat and square face. It would take major reconstruction to sculpt a face like this from yours. I would never attempt that on you. This is way too risky. You could end up looking like Frankenstein's bride. On top of that this lady has blonde hair and blue eyes. I know you can dye your hair but you can't dye your eyes. Larissa, be reasonable. I can't turn a Brazilian into what looks like a northern European woman. Who is she and why do you want to look like her? This is not like you at all. You were never vain."

Larissa sighs. "She is a woman who has two very attractive men and I want one of them."

"Oh. So this is about a man," Marcos states. "I knew something unusual was up. This is not the way to go about it, though. You never know why a man may be attracted to a woman. It's not always just the looks, Larissa. A lot has to do with personality, too. Even the most beautiful woman may be totally boring or completely unattractive if she has an ugly personality. I can tell you from my own experience that looks alone are not enough. It's the certain something in a woman which makes her desirable, and every man has different trigger points there."

"Well, I still don't like my face," she responds softly, getting a little sleepy now from the tranquilizer.

"I can offer you a couple of little nips and tucks to rejuvenate your face but nothing major. The rest you have to do with hair and make-up to reinvent yourself. A word of caution, though. You should only do that for yourself but not because you think it will help you get a certain man."

"I'll think about it, Marcos. Please don't tell anyone what we discussed."

"Of course not. Be well, Larissa. Looking forward to seeing you soon."

Larissa hangs up the phone, lies down on the couch and closes her eyes. She soon drifts off into dreamland.

NINE

Kataryna calls Stephen in New York to set up a video conference in preparation for her trip to Brazil.

"We need to hire a Director of Clinical Research after the deal has closed," Kataryna suggests after they finished discussing the payment details for the Brazilian acquisition.

"You can do that after you return from Brazil."

"Yeah, but we should put our feelers out soon. I will call the headhunter tomorrow so he can start searching for suitable candidates and present some CVs after I am back here," Kataryna says.

"By the way, Kat, you never told me why you agreed so readily to have the remaining ten percent BioMedyca shares transferred to Francesco and Patrizia. I recall when Roberto was still on board, you and I had discussed to only give the senior management equity shares if they met certain performance covenants after a year. What changed your mind? Did Luca pressure you into this transfer?"

Kataryna is uncomfortable with the subject. "No, Stephen. He didn't pressure me into it. He suggested it and I agreed for a reason I can't get into this minute. I promise I will tell you after I am back from Brazil. It's something personal."

"Personal? I am really at a loss here," Stephen sounds disappointed with her answer. "Why can't you tell me now? We have always been totally upfront with each other. Honestly, this just doesn't sit well with me."

"Please give me this time, Stephen. Trust me, you will understand when I tell you."

"OK. Have a safe trip and good luck with everything. I hope we don't run into any snags with this deal. Pretty soon our competitors will get wind of what kind of a treasure may be growing over there."

"Yeah, I know. I can't wait to get this behind me. As soon as this deal is done, Luca and I are taking a nice romantic vacation. The poor guy had to put up with a lot of long working hours, his and mine. So we need some time just for ourselves."

"Where will you be going?"

"We are thinking Capri."

"Ooh, nice. You deserve a break, Kat. Two major acquisitions in a row. Hell, you should probably relax for the rest of the year."

"Well, I basically will. By the time we come back from our trip, we will be looking forward to Francesco's wedding in Portofino in June. Thereafter I'll be busy with the final touches of my wedding in September, and Luca is determined to get me pregnant during the honeymoon. So that'll be the rest of my year."

Stephen laughs. "On that note, see you in September."

Luca sticks his head through the door. "Ciao bella, are you ready to leave?"

"Ready whenever you are." She grabs her bag and coat.

"I am going to work from home tomorrow so we can spend the day together before you leave for Brazil the day after tomorrow," Luca mentions when they take off to Lake Como.

"That's very sweet of you, darling. We'll have a fun day."

"Anything special in mind?" he asks.

"Let's just be spontaneous."

Luca grins approvingly. "Feel free to interrupt me from work anytime."

"I may not let you work at all tomorrow."

"OK, you are on. I won't if you keep me entertained."

"Really?" Kataryna challenges him. "What if you get an important business call about your hot acquisition deal?"

"I will count on your amazing talent to prevent me from taking the call," he responds as they are arriving at the Lake Como villa.

Mariya meets them in the foyer. "What time would you like me to serve dinner?"

"We'll eat right away," Kataryna responds.

"By the way, darling," Kataryna says when they are sitting down at the dining table, "I have a surprise for you."

"I love surprises, especially when they are coming from you," Luca responds seductively.

"I am glad you are in such a good mood, even though I am leaving for Brazil the day after tomorrow," Kataryna observes.

"Well, Principessa, I made peace with that idea because there is nothing I can do about it anyway. I just wish I could go with you."

Kataryna takes his hand. "We will go to Rio together next year. Ernesto Oliveiro sent me a message today. He will get us tickets for the 2014 Soccer World Cup games. Isn't that exciting?"

"Wow! That is a great surprise. I wonder if we could get another ticket for Enrico."

"You must be the greatest uncle," Kataryna praises him. "Enrico is one lucky guy to have you in his life. Are you going to be the same with Carlotta's second son, knowing that Roberto is his father?"

Luca gives her a long stare.

"Are you?" Kataryna pushes him further.

"As much as I wish that this wasn't the case, he will not be treated any different," Luca assures her. "I still can't fathom though how Carlotta let it come to that."

"I think it's time that you let that go, Luca. Accidents do happen. It is what it is. However, with our travel plans to the World Cup next year, we better plan my pregnancy so I can make it over to Brazil in June or July for the games. I don't think our honeymoon will work to plant that seed, if you know what I mean. Otherwise I may deliver the baby right in the stadium when the German soccer team wins over Italy." She cracks up laughing watching Luca's face who is trying to digest what she just said.

Luca takes a deep breath. "You are in rare form, my dear," he starts out, chuckling. "However, your wild imagination about Germany beating Italy won't happen anyway. Here's an idea. How about we start right now getting you pregnant so you are done with the delivery by February 2014, the latest."

"Well, Luca Romano, what do you think Father Antonio would say if I told him what you just suggested? No way! Have you forgotten the ancient rule that first comes love then comes marriage and then comes Kataryna with a baby carriage?"

Luca shakes his head laughing. "Thanks for the reminder."

Kataryna gets up and sits on his lap. "Get used to it, darling, you know I will always be a step ahead of you. Having said that, I can offer you a practice run now for that big event."

"Practice makes perfect," he says leading her to the bedroom.

"I was just thinking how absolutely perfect it would be if I, like my sister, would get pregnant with twins. Then I would be done the first time around."

"I'll do my best to make it happen," Luca winks.

The two have an extended breakfast in bed the next morning. Kataryna's cellphone rings just when they are becoming amorous.

"Ciao Roberto. Did you finish the presentation yet?"

Luca throws his arms up in the air and rolls his eyes. She shakes her head at him, mouthing "stop it," and then continues her conversation with Roberto. "OK, could you email the draft to me, please? I will get back to you in the afternoon, in case we need to make any changes. Grazie. Ciao."

She turns to Luca. "What was that all about again?"

"This guy has an uncanny talent to disturb us."

"Luca, you are being unreasonable. You know that he is a huge asset to the deal I am trying to close. I can't do it without him. I have done many deals but none like this one. I am on unchartered territory and he knows his way around. He has not made any advances toward me since he left the clinic, has shown remorse for what he did to us and respect for our relationship."

"I am doing the best I can to deal with this," he contends.

"Good, and while we are on the subject already, I would like you to know that it would really be helpful if he would join us sooner rather than later on this trip. I would feel more confident having him by our side during the early meetings with Ernesto Oliveiro."

"No, no, no! Don't go there, Principessa," he states, kissing her neck passionately. "It took a lot for me to swallow the idea that you need him as a consultant, and the only reason I agreed to that was that he would not be with you in Brazil at the same time. Case closed."

Realizing that this conversation is going nowhere fast, Kataryna retreats and continues where they left off before their sensual moments were interrupted, maneuvering her hands and lips into Luca's pleasure zones, making him forget all about Roberto for now.

"That was an amazing recovery from the earlier disruption," Luca whispers in her ear. "Don't forget, you promised to entertain me the whole day."

"I will. How about taking a walk along the lake now and then have a nice lunch with some excellent wine?"

"Sounds like a super charming plan. What kind of entertainment do you have planned for later on?"

"A sexy lottery game," Kataryna proposes ardently.

"Uh, that sounds extremely intriguing. How does it work and what can I win?"

"Well, darling, I will let you write all the things you would want me to do to you on little pieces of paper which we then fold and put in a bowl. I will draw one of the entries and whatever is on there, I will do."

"Whoa," Luca yells out laughing, "you sure have some exciting ideas. I can't lose."

"Not so fast," Kataryna interjects grinning. "You get to put three wishes into the lottery pool and then we will add one entry which is blank inside."

Luca frowns. "So what if you draw the blank piece of paper? I get nothing?"

Kataryna can hardly contain herself. "Not only will you get nothing done to you but you have to do to me what I then choose."

"Gee, Principessa, that is cruel."

"That's why it's called a lottery, darling. You either win or lose. There has to be a downside in a lottery."

"You are unbelievable," he protests, "but I am getting all excited already thinking about it."

"You better restrain your enthusiasm," she cautions him. "I may end up drawing the piece that is blank."

After their walk along Lake Como, they stop by their favorite restaurant.

"It's so nice to have a leisurely lunch like this on a day we would normally work. I am glad I took the day off," Luca remarks. "It's going to be tough without you here."

"It'll go so fast," she says. "You will be busy with your acquisition and before you know it, I will be back. Maybe while I am gone you can have a word with Vincente about finally telling Francesco that he was adopted."

"Consider it done."

The lottery of love game later on that evening turns in Luca's favor.

"Thank you for the beautiful day and evening," he says kissing her good night.

"It was my pleasure," she grins, snuggling into his arms. "Sweet dreams."

Kataryna can't fall asleep. She is apprehensive but tries to stay still. She doesn't want to alarm Luca. He is restless, tossing and turning, unaware that she is not sleeping either. Eventually they succeed to doze off. When the alarm comes on in the morning, they are still tired wishing they didn't have to get up.

"I didn't sleep well at all," Luca reveals trying to keep his eyes open.

"Me neither," Kataryna admits.

"Do you have second thoughts about this trip?"

"No, I never sleep well before I travel," she quickly responds stretching the truth a bit.

"At least you can sleep on the plane," Luca says, "but I have to go to the office and deal with all the stuff I didn't

get to do yesterday, however, it was well worth it." He smiles at her happily.

◆ ◆ ◆

The jet is ready for takeoff. Kataryna and Francesco get comfortable in their seats.

"You are very quiet," Francesco says. "Did Luca have a tough time letting you go?"

"He was okay with it but when I tried to talk him into letting Roberto go with us today, he did not want to hear it."

"I don't blame him. He is very protective of you, Kataryna. You are his life."

"I know and he is my life. After we are back and have closed the deal, I will not be involved that much in the day-to-day business anymore. I hope with Larissa on board you will be able to take over."

"Sure. How long do you think Roberto will stay on as a consultant?"

"At least until the entire integration of the Brazilian company has taken place. So that'll give you plenty of support."

"That's great. I have to admit that I don't have his skills and experience yet but don't worry, I will get there."

"I am not worried, Francesco. I know you will be very successful in this position. There is no one else I would trust as much with this company."

"Aww, thanks for saying that. I also want to thank you again for agreeing to give the remaining ten percent shares of BioMedyca to Patrizia and me. I never expected this kind of wedding gift. This is beyond amazing."

"You deserve it, Francesco. Pretty soon you will understand why it was a no-brainer for me to let you have these shares."

He gives her a puzzled look. "So there is a reason?"

She nods and grins, patting his hand. "Let's just say it was meant to be."

"I don't know what that means but I gladly accept this precious gift. I told my father the other day how floored I was when Luca announced it and how great a gesture I thought it was from you to agree to that just like that. He gave me this strange almost sad look. I asked him if he wasn't happy for me. He said he was. However, something didn't match up. Patrizia thinks he might be a little jealous that we are getting such a highly valuable wedding gift from the Romano family side."

"He will get over it," Kataryna sighs. "He has a lot to deal with already these days."

"On another note, my assistant told me that when you, Roberto and I had our strategy lunch the other day, she found Larissa totally out of it in her office. She said she was white like a wall and shaking. When she asked her what was wrong, Larissa apparently tried to pull it together and said she hadn't eaten that day and assumed it was low blood sugar. She then left for the day."

"Really? I hope she isn't sick with something. That's the last thing we need right now. Did you tell Roberto?"

"Yeah, I mentioned it to him yesterday. He said he also noticed some kind of odd behavior lately. He will keep an eye on it and let us know if anything else comes up."

"Good. If you don't mind, I need to get some sleep now. I am really tired."

After the jet touches down in Rio de Janeiro, Kataryna calls Luca. "Hi darling, I hope I didn't wake you. Just reporting in to tell you that we have arrived in Rio. Ernesto came personally to pick us up with his driver. What a service."

"You know I wouldn't go to sleep before talking to you," Luca says. "The pilot texted me already that you arrived safely. I was just waiting for your call."

"So all is well and I got some much-needed sleep on the flight. I am in great shape now. I will call you again tomorrow but don't panic if it isn't exactly at the time we agreed. I don't know what Ernesto has planned for us but tonight he is giving a welcome party for us at his house."

"Just text me if you can't call so I know you are okay."

"Yes, Sir!" She giggles. "What would we do without this technology?"

"Well, we don't have to worry about that, my dear, Luca responds. "Check in with me tomorrow, please."

"Kataryna! Francesco!" Ernesto Oliveiro greets them, opening his arms to embrace her after she exits the plane.

"I am so excited to finally meet you in person. I promise you will have a great time here this week. Besides work, I have some nice activities planned so you also get to see our beautiful country a bit."

Kataryna smiles at him. "I am so happy to be here. I always wanted to come to Brazil but so far it never worked out. This just goes to show that you have to trust the universe to put it all together for you. I get to acquire a fabulous company and see Brazil at the same time."

"That's true, Kataryna. You always have to trust that things will come to you at the appropriate time. So let's get going. My family can't wait to meet you two. What a shame that Roberto wasn't able to join us this week. He is like a son to me. That's why I had talked to him some time ago about taking over my company if my children would decide not to succeed me, which they just did."

"Well, lucky for us then, their loss is our gain," Kataryna replies happily, glancing at Francesco.

"So, Roberto has been ill for some time? Is that why he stepped down as CEO?" Ernesto asks.

Kataryna nods. "We will let him talk about his situation when he gets here next week. He is on board as a consultant for now and will be working with Francesco on the due diligence, the closing and the integration of this company into BioMedyca."

"Good to know," Ernesto responds. "He is brilliant and fully understands this business. It's kind of tough for me to let go of this company, however, knowing that Roberto is involved to integrate it into your company makes it so much easier."

"We are extremely grateful for this opportunity and respect that Roberto was the reason you offered it to us," Kataryna assures him, "and we are all looking forward to moving ahead together."

"We will drink to that in a moment," Ernesto cheers, as the car enters through a private gate opening up to a spectacular driveway.

"Wow, Ernesto, this is a gorgeous home you have here," Kataryna marvels looking at the estate in front of them. "I wish Luca was here to see this."

Ernesto smiles proudly helping her out of the car.

"Yes, this is my pride and joy. My paradise on earth, and I am honored to have you here as my guests."

When they enter the foyer, Amanda Oliveiro rushes toward them. "Bem-vindo a Rio de Janeiro. I hope you had a nice flight?"

She ushers them into a room with floor to ceiling windows leading to a terrace overlooking a majestic swimming pool with a waterfall streaming into it surrounded by tropical trees and plants.

"Here's to new friends and a successful transaction," Ernesto hands them a glass of Champagne.

"Here's to life, new friends and family," Francesco toasts as they clink their glasses.

"Here's to family," Kataryna says as hers and Francesco's glasses meet.

"Kataryna and I are going to be in-laws soon," Francesco exclaims smiling. "I am going to marry Patrizia Romano in June and Kataryna will get married to Luca Romano who is Patrizia's older brother."

"Well, we have more beautiful events to celebrate then this year," Ernesto cajoles. "As I mentioned in one of our phone calls already, Kataryna, I will make arrangements to get tickets for the 2014 FIFA World Cup for you, your future husband, Francesco and his soon-to-be wife. Needless to say, you will be our guests here again."

"Thank you, Ernesto," Kataryna gives him a sweet smile. "We are so looking forward to it. Do you think it would be possible to get another ticket for Luca's nephew? We will of course pay for it."

"Absolutely, please bring him along but I will not accept any payment from you. And by the way, I also invited Roberto to join us."

Kataryna nods silently. Francesco raises his eyebrows at her. He turns to Ernesto. "I would like to invite you and your wife to my wedding in June in Portofino."

"Thank you. We would be honored to attend your wedding," Ernesto accepts the invite.

"Hopefully you will also come to my wedding," Kataryna chimes in.

"We wouldn't miss it for the world," the Oliveiros respond. "Why don't we let you get some rest now so you are in good shape for tonight's festivities. You will be meeting the high society of Rio and our most important business partners."

A staff member appears with the luggage.

"Please follow me." Amanda Oliveiro escorts them to their guest rooms. "The reception will start at 8:30 p.m."

Once in her room, Kataryna takes some photos of the tropical gardens from her balcony and sends them to Luca in an email.

Greetings from Rio, she writes, wish you were here. I just managed to get another World Cup ticket for Enrico. We sure will have fun here next year. All is well. Love you.

Luca's phone pings alerting him that an email has arrived. He smiles looking at the photos Kataryna sent him and then calls his sister. "Ciao, Patrizia. In case you haven't heard from Francesco yet, they are fine. I just got an email from Kataryna."

"Thank you, Luca. I am still waiting for an email from my fiancé."

"Be patient, this is Francesco's first huge action as CEO. I am sure he wants to show Kataryna that he is well prepared for the upcoming meetings there. Relax and have a good night."

◆ ◆ ◆

Larissa is in a good mood the next morning. Kataryna is in Brazil and out of the way.

"Time to make my move," she says to herself, getting dressed in a more daring outfit, which shows off her legs and some cleavage. When she arrives at work, she heads straight to Roberto's office, which she finds empty.

"When do you expect Roberto to come in?" she asks the assistant who had just returned to her seat with a cup of coffee.

"I don't think he is planning to come in today."

"Are you sure?" Larissa enquires.

"He told me yesterday, he would work from home. Can I help you with something?"

"No, thank you."

Disappointed, Larissa heads to her office and dials Roberto's cellphone number.

"Ciao Roberto. I wasn't aware that you wouldn't be in today."

"There is no need for me to be in the office. Kataryna and Francesco are gone, and I have nothing urgent to do there. I am making some calls from home and will be speaking with them later on after their first meeting in Rio."

"I see. So you won't be in the whole week?"

"No, I won't and as you know, I'll leave for Brazil in a few days to do the Amazonas trip with Francesco. Give me a call if you need anything but as far as I can see everything is under control."

When they hang up, she is close to tears. Her plan failed again. Nothing seems to be going her way. She calls her girlfriend who arrived from out of town to visit her.

"Ciao Manuela. I will be home earlier than I thought. I made a reservation for us at one of the top restaurants in Milan for 8 p.m."

"I am looking forward to a nice dinner tonight," Manuela responds, "as well as the continuation of the story about the man you are in love with."

"I haven't gotten very far with that," Larissa frowns, "but I need to talk about it. Maybe I am doing something wrong."

Larissa tries to get some work done but can't really focus on anything. At noon she leaves for the day.

"Wow!" her girlfriend exclaims when she comes through the front door later that afternoon. "Look at you. A new hairstyle and blondish highlights. You look amazing. I almost didn't recognize you."

Larissa smiles sheepishly. "I couldn't look at my old self anymore. Is it too radical of a change?"

"No, it suits you well. I just didn't expect you to come home looking like this."

"Yeah, it was a spur of the moment thing. I had to cheer myself up."

"Oh, oh, what happened?" Manuela asks.

"Roberto didn't come to the office today and when I called him he told me he won't be in until they all return from Brazil."

"Aww, you poor lovesick puppy. I guess you'll have to wait a while to catch him."

"Or I find a way to see him before he leaves," Larissa responds.

"That'll be tough to pull off without raising some kind of red flag. I would wait."

"Yeah, as usual you are the voice of reason."

"Hey, listen. You are just starting with this whole dating thing. You haven't been interested in anyone for the last two years. So you'll have to ease into this."

"It's difficult to be patient now that I have gotten a taste of falling in love again."

"Trust me, Larissa. Men don't like overly aggressive women. Show some interest but don't go overboard. Enjoy the being-in-love feeling and look forward to what's to come."

"I get it, Manuela, but do you have any idea how difficult this is? Just thinking about him gets me so excited. It is a high I have never been on. Something has to happen soon before I go insane. Well, I better freshen up now and change into something uplifting to go along with my new hair."

When they arrive at the upscale restaurant, they are seated right away. A couple of men give Larissa a second look as the two women pass by their table. Manuela notices and smiles.

"Well, my dear, you sure are attracting some attention tonight with your new hair and that figure-hugging emerald green dress."

"I wish Roberto could see me now. He might not be able to resist me anymore." Larissa says coquettishly.

"I wish you all the happiness in the world," Manuela responds raising her glass to make a toast. "Here's to you and Roberto."

"Thanks," Larissa grins broadly, "I am more confident about him tonight. Must be my new appearance and the attention I got when we walked in here."

"I am telling you when you feel good about yourself everything is so much brighter."

"Thank you. You are good for my ego. You should…," Larissa stops in the middle of the sentence. Her mouth wide open.

"What is it?" Manuela asks.

"You are not going to believe this but Roberto just walked in. Don't turn around now. He is being seated at the bar. I am going over to say hello and ask him if he wants to join us, if you don't mind." She almost knocks her glass over jumping out of her chair.

"Whoa," Manuela giggles, "take it easy. You don't want to mess up your dress right now."

Larissa darts off to the bar.

"What a small world," she laughs nervously when she reaches Roberto. "Fancy meeting you here." She touches his arm.

Roberto looks at her perplexed. "Ah, gee, Larissa."

He is trying to recover from the surprise of her altered appearance. "How is everything?" he asks in a monotone voice.

"Great but now even better with you here," she flirts.

He takes a sip of his drink trying to figure out how to handle this unwelcome situation. Is she coming on to me, he thinks? Awkward! He gives her a weak smile.

"I am here with a girlfriend who is visiting from out of town. Would you like to join us for dinner?" she excitedly asks him, anticipating a resounding yes.

"I am afraid Roberto is already taken for the evening," a woman walking up behind her answers that question.

Carlotta hugs her hello and then kisses Roberto on the cheek. "Sorry I am late."

A feeling like ten thousand volts of electricity runs through Larissa's entire body.

"Carlotta?" she stares at her with wide eyes. "What a surprise."

"Speaking about surprise. I didn't even recognize you at first. You changed your hair. Looks great, and that dress, very nice, Larissa. Are you out for some excitement?"

Roberto is relieved that Carlotta arrived just when it got more uncomfortable. He watches the two women chat. Something is off with Larissa, he notices. She is struggling to speak coherently. Well, Francesco had alerted him already about some unusual behavior the other day.

"Signor Silvestri, I have your table ready," the host of the restaurant approaches them.

Roberto gestures Carlotta to follow the host. "Have a nice evening, Larissa," he wishes her politely before taking off to his table.

Larissa stands there staring after them. What the hell does that mean, she wonders? Her heart is beating out of her chest. Is he going after Carlotta now, too?

"Is everything alright, Signora?" the host startles her as he returns to the bar area.

She doesn't respond, her eyes still glued on Carlotta and Roberto who have been seated at their table.

"Signora?" the host tries to get her attention again.

Manuela watches the spectacle from afar. She notices Larissa's dazed look.

"What happened?" she asks gingerly when Larissa returns to the table. "Are you okay?"

"No, I am not," she hisses. "I have no idea what this means." She chases down the wine in her glass. "This is not happening. Why is everything turning against me? I think I'm about to lose it."

"So, obviously Roberto is dating someone?" Manuela reckons. "Do you know her?"

"This is Carlotta Romano. Luca Romano's sister. Luca is engaged to my top boss Kataryna Taylor."

"Yeah, so?" Manuela purses her lips and raises her eyebrows.

"For starters, Carlotta is pregnant with some man's child whom she told me she doesn't have a relationship with because he fell in love with another woman. As far as Roberto is concerned, I have reason to believe that he has been having an affair with Kataryna Taylor. So what is he doing here on a date with Carlotta now? This whole thing doesn't make any sense." Her voice is cracking. She struggles to suppress tears.

"Calm down, Larissa. I realize that you are in love with this man but you don't know the whole story here. Don't jump to conclusions. And why do you think he has been having an affair with Luca Romano's fiancée?"

"Keep this to yourself, please. I saw photos on his cellphone showing him and Kataryna intimately embracing. It made me throw up."

"Gee, I don't know what to say, Larissa." Manuela is flabbergasted.

"I want to go over there and yell it in his face before Carlotta gets more involved with him," Larissa voices angrily.

"I am not going to let you do that, Larissa. You will look ridiculous and bitter. After all, his private life is none of your business."

"It is if I know something that could prevent Carlotta from getting hurt."

"You are speculating based on some photos you have seen. Who knows in what context these were taken. In addition, I have to wonder why you would want to date him, if this is really true."

"Well, I was hoping that I could make him forget Kataryna once he is involved with me," Larissa asserts. "I was willing to give him some time to change course."

Manuela shrugs her shoulders. "Come on. If he really is in love with her an entire stable of horses couldn't make him forget her. Besides, don't you think Carlotta could make him forget about Kataryna? Look at her. She is a knockout. Why were you snooping around on his phone, anyway?"

"Stop, stop, stop!" Larissa yells, attracting the attention of other restaurant guests. "I don't want to talk about it."

"I am getting very concerned about you," Manuela says quietly. "Let's finish our dinner and go home or have a drink somewhere else so you don't have to look at these two together."

Larissa asks for the check. She wants to go home, take a tranquilizer and forget what just happened.

"Honestly, Larissa, I think you should drop the idea of a relationship with Roberto. This just doesn't look good. It brings out a side of you I have never seen, and that's not a compliment."

"Thank you for your concern, Manuela. I would like to go to sleep now. It's been a long and difficult day for me."

"Good night. See you at breakfast." Manuela hugs her friend tightly. "If you need to talk don't hesitate to wake me. I am here for you."

Still haunted by last night's event, Larissa gets to the office a little later than usual the next morning. She dials Kataryna's number and gets her voice mail. She tries Francesco next. Voice mail again. Her phone rings. She quickly answers.

"Pronto."

"Ciao, Larissa, it's Carlotta. How are you?"

"Fine, I guess. Although, I was astounded last night seeing you out for dinner with Roberto."

"Yeah, you looked kind of frazzled. That's why I am calling to fill you in on some news. So here it goes. Roberto is the father of my child. Other than our close family no one has been told yet. So we discussed it last night and decided it's time to make it public."

Larissa is trying hard to breathe normally.

"Hello, Larissa, can you hear me?" Carlotta asks when she doesn't get a reaction from her.

"Yes, I heard you. I don't know what to say, Carlotta."

"I am sorry to drop this on you like that but when we saw you last night we figured we better announce it publicly now."

"So he is the man you were in a relationship with who fell in love with another woman?"

"Yes, but that has been resolved meanwhile. The other woman is no longer an issue. As a matter of fact they never had a relationship."

"You are not making any sense," Larissa responds with a bit of an attitude.

"Yeah, I am not prepared to get into this any further. Let's just leave it at that."

Larissa takes a deep breath. "How do you know that they didn't have a relationship and that he is not still into her?"

"Rest assured, we have moved on, Larissa."

"OK. So I suppose you two are back together then?"

"Time will tell where we are headed as far as a committed relationship is concerned but as the father of my child he will always be in my life, one way or another."

"Do you still love him?" Larissa dares to ask, although she doesn't really want to hear the answer.

"If I am honest with myself, yes, I do."

Larissa smirks. "Well, Carlotta my intuition tells me you should keep your guard up."

Carlotta laughs. "Are you saying you are psychic?"

"Just be careful. I don't want you to get hurt by him again."

"Thank you for watching out for me, Larissa but I have known Roberto since childhood. We have a history. He just got a little lost for a while. Anyway, I have to get back to work now. Hope to see you soon."

Tears are streaming down Larissa's face as she hangs up the phone still stunned about Carlotta's disclosure. Just when you thought you were safe, here comes another roadblock, goes through her mind.

"Well, Roberto," she says out loud, "I am not giving up on you yet."

She dials Kataryna's number. "You have reached the voicemail of Kataryna..," is coming on again. She hangs up in the middle of the message and then dials another number to make a call.

Luca's assistant enters his office. "I am sorry to interrupt you, Luca but I have Larissa Dos Santos on the phone for you. Will you take the call?"

Luca looks at her surprised. "Did she say why she wants to speak with me?"

"No, I didn't really ask her and she didn't volunteer anything. I figured it might have to do with Kataryna in Brazil or so."

"According to the agenda, Kataryna and Francesco should be in Manaus today meeting with Larissa's brother and visiting the manufacturing plant. So I better take the call."

"Ciao, Larissa," Luca greets her. "Is everything okay in Brazil?"

"Yeah, as far as I know but I haven't been able to get Kataryna on the phone yet."

"Well, it's still early over there and she has back-to-back meetings from what I can see on her itinerary. What can I do for you?"

"I was wondering if you have a couple of minutes to meet with me today?"

"Unfortunately, no. I have a meeting in about 30 minutes and that will go on for the rest of the day and into the evening."

"How about tomorrow?"

"I have to admit, I am kind of curious what this is all about. I am only a minority shareholder of BioMedyca. You better get hold of Kataryna when she is available again."

"It's not about BioMedyca, and I would prefer to have this conversation with you face-to-face."

"I will let you know tomorrow." Luca hangs up shaking his head.

He calls Kataryna and gets her voice mail. "Please call me when you get this. It's urgent, and I also would like to hear your voice."

His assistant buzzes him. "Luca, your guests have arrived. I have seated them in the conference room."

"Thank you. I am heading over there now. If Kataryna calls, you have my permission to interrupt me. I really need to talk to her."

"Will do, Luca. Anything else?"

"Please call my father and ask him to meet us in the conference room."

"Ciao, Patrizia," Luca's assistant greets her when she approaches the office. "They are still in a meeting."

"Oh." She looks upset.

"Yeah, I expect this to go for another hour or so and then they have a reservation for dinner. Shall I tell Luca that you came by?"

"Yes, please. I need to talk to him before he leaves for the business dinner." Patrizia heads back to her office.

Luca's meeting concludes. He excuses himself for a moment heading straight to his assistant's desk.

"So Kataryna didn't call?" he asks her glancing at some other messages she handed him.

"No, I was at my desk the entire time."

Luca checks his cellphone. No message or email from Kataryna. He dials her number and is directed to her voice mail again. "Kataryna, I had left an urgent message earlier for you to call me. I know you have a busy day but I need to speak with you. Something is up with Larissa. She called me earlier to make an appointment to see me but said it had nothing to do with BioMedyca. Can you please call me back ASAP or call her first and then let me know why she wants to see me? I really don't have the time nor do I want to get involved with whatever problem she is having. Thank you, darling. Love you. Call me."

Heading back to join his business partners for dinner, he runs into his sister Patrizia.

"I came by earlier, Luca. Have you spoken to Kataryna yet today?"

"No, they are having a crazy meeting schedule today and who knows what kind of situation they are dealing with but I just left her another message to call me urgently. Why?"

"I haven't been able to reach Francesco either. Not even a text from him."

"Yeah, as I said they are having a busy day and don't forget about the time difference between Italy and Brazil." Luca tries to reassure her but he isn't too pleased either that Kataryna hasn't contacted him at all today. He takes a deep breath and rejoins his business partners.

The business dinner is dragging on. Luca is fidgety and has a problem focusing on the conversation. His father gives him a concerned look. He suspects something is bothering his son. Luca's cellphone rings. The caller id shows Roberto is calling him. "What does he want from me?" Luca is mumbling to himself. "Damn, the whole world is calling me except the person I really want to speak to." He considers letting the call go to voice mail but then changes his mind.

"Ciao, Luca," he hears Roberto's voice say. "Have you spoken to Kataryna yet?"

"You are the third person who asked me that today," Luca responds impatiently. "No, but I am expecting her to call me any minute."

There is a moment of silence between them.

"Hmm. I just received a call from Ernesto Oliveiro saying that Kataryna and Francesco were supposed to be at the company's manufacturing facility over an hour ago but they have not arrived there and he has not been able to reach them on their cellphones either," Roberto explains.

"WHAT?" Luca jumps out of his seat knocking over his glass in the process. Everyone at the table is staring at him. He leaves to go to a quiet area. "What are you saying, Roberto? They are missing?"

"Well, I don't know, Luca. I just found out myself. I was standing by for a video conference call with them. So I don't know any more than you do."

Luca closes his eyes and pulls his hair. His heart is pounding in his chest. "I can't believe this is happening."

"OK, let's stay calm, Luca," Roberto implores him. "We got to keep a cool head now. This could be serious."

"I will be over at your place in 30 minutes," Luca states. "Meanwhile you call whoever you can to locate them or find some kind of trace. Where did they come from? When did they leave there? How did they travel? Find the driver who picked them up. Do whatever." He loses his temper.

"Yes, Luca. I will do whatever is in my power. Maybe by the time you get here I will have more information or hopefully they will show up meanwhile."

Luca rushes back to the table.

"Kataryna and Francesco are missing. I have to leave to meet with Roberto to see what we can do to find them."

"Oh my God! Let me know if there's anything I can do," his father offers before Luca runs off.

Luca arrives at Roberto's home. "What did you find out meanwhile?" He charges through the door.

Roberto motions him to take a seat.

"According to Ernesto, Kataryna had left a message for him to tell him that the company's driver had called to let her know that he would send another car to pick them up because his car had broken down. Ernesto said he has been trying to reach the driver to find out whom he sent there in his place but so far he did not return Ernesto's call."

"Is that all we know?"

"I called their hotel in Manaus to see if they had any information. The concierge said that Kataryna had asked him how long the ride to the manufacturing company's address would take and he had told her about 35 minutes from the hotel depending on traffic."

Luca is holding his chest. "What else did he say?"

"He mentioned that shortly thereafter he overheard Francesco telling Kataryna that their car service was outside. They left the hotel and got into the car. That's all he knows."

"And that was how long ago?"

"About three hours ago." Roberto runs his hand through his hair nervously. "Obviously that is not a good sign, Luca."

"Well, you know the area. What could have happened? Where could they be?" Luca raises his voice.

Roberto looks at him with a pain-stricken face. "At this point we have to prepare for anything."

TEN

Kataryna glances at Francesco. "We have been on the road for over an hour. Does this guy know where he is going?" she whispers.

Francesco shrugs his shoulders. "Excuse me, driver," he tries to get his attention, "how much longer until we arrive?"

The driver doesn't respond. Francesco taps him lightly on the shoulder. "Did you hear me?"

The car pulls into a gas station and stops.

"I think he is lost," Kataryna mouths to Francesco when both back doors fling open simultaneously and two armed men get into the car flanking Kataryna and Francesco.

"Who are you?" she asks terrified. "What do want? Money?" She reaches for her bag. One of the men grabs her arm to stop her.

"Senhora, Senhor, listen closely," he starts in a rough tone and broken English. "You are under our control now. Sit back and don't try anything stupid."

"OK," Francesco remains calm. "What is this about?"

"No more questions!" he is instructed sternly.

Kataryna stares at the guns the two men hold in their laps. This is serious. Her heart is racing. Realizing they have just been kidnapped her thoughts go immediately to Luca. He will go crazy once he finds out and he will blame himself for letting her go on this trip. Luca's worried face appears in front of her. She won't even have a chance to say goodbye and tell him one last time how much she loves him if she and Francesco don't survive this ordeal. She should have been more vigilant. What was she thinking not questioning that the car Ernesto sent for them broke down? Luca had warned about the dangers of this trip. A deep sadness comes over her imagining Luca, Patrizia and their other family members finding out about their demise. The thought that she and Francesco may not survive this abduction is a real possibility.

Francesco puts his arms around her. He gives her a faint smile. "Think positive, Kataryna," he whispers in her ear in German. "We'll figure something out."

The car stops at a small airport in a remote area. The driver leaves the car and speaks briefly with the pilot of the small plane parked on the tarmac. The two armed men proceed to board Kataryna and Francesco onto the jet and discuss the flight plan with the pilot. Kataryna grabs the opportunity to talk to Francesco.

"Francesco. I have something very important to tell you," she whispers holding on to his arm with both hands. "You will be terribly confused but I need you to know because we may not survive this."

"Please Kataryna, let's not think that way." He tries to reassure her, seeing her panic-stricken face.

"Listen to me. I recently learned that I have a brother who my parents gave up for adoption at birth but they told Aleksandra and me he had died during childbirth. My father came out with the truth in November last year when I visited him. I hired a lawyer to search for my brother and I got the paperwork identifying him in March."

"Wow, Kataryna. That's incredible. Have you located him yet?"

"Yes." She pauses for a moment to compose herself. "You are my biological brother, Francesco."

"What are you talking about? You are not making any sense. You know my parents." He looks at her worried.

"No, these are not your biological parents. Your father was informed already. Luca talked to him about it. He wanted to wait until your adoptive mother was in a better condition health-wise before telling you. I can prove it. I have the papers at home in Italy. You are undoubtedly my brother."

Francesco stares at her silently then buries his face in his hands. "What is happening here?"

"I know this is a shock," she takes his hand in hers, "but under these circumstances I had to tell you now because I don't want us to go to our grave without at least having a few hours together as brother and sister. I have been wanting to tell you for a long time." She starts crying. "Whenever I saw you I wanted to shout it out, however, I promised your father and Luca that I would be patient until Sylvia got better. But what is happening here right now supersedes everything. It may be the last chance I have to let you know."

After a long pause Francesco deals with the situation at hand.

"Well, I am still dumbfounded but if I am honest, I have been wondering for some time why I have this deep connection with you and also felt so close to Aleksandra immediately when I met her at Christmas. The mystery has been solved, I guess." He hugs her tightly.

"Thank you for telling me. Wow! I can't believe I have two sisters. Did our father explain why they give me up?"

"Our parents' marriage wasn't the best and our father was trying to built up a new business at that time. In addition, our father was pretty tough to live with and I can only imagine that our mother wasn't strong enough to raise another child under these circumstances. It must have been pretty bad otherwise she would have never given up her child. She was the best mother in the world, and now I understand why she always cried on a certain day in May. Your birthday, Francesco. And on Christmas Eve she was always so sad. Every year there was an extra Christmas gift under the tree. When I asked her whom that gift was for she just said 'for your brother in heaven'. Can you imagine the burden she carried for keeping such a secret all her life?"

"Must have been extremely difficult. Does our father know yet that I am his son?"

"No, only Aleksandra, Luca and your father know. Well, actually I had to tell Dr. de Angelis the other day. When the lab did our blood work, they found that we had the DNA of related persons. Dr. de Angelis thought that his staff had messed up the tests big time and he spoke to me about it before you joined us. He wanted to start a huge investigation and fire the staff member who had done the tests. So I had to come out with this information but told him he could not reveal it to anyone until we had spoken to you."

"I was just going to suggest that we get a DNA test when we get back to make sure."

"If we survive this kidnapping, we will have a huge celebration. I am so relieved this is out in the open now. I even forgot our dire situation for a moment."

Francesco sighs. "I wonder who these people are and what they want with us. If it's money, I am sure Luca and Patrizia will pay whatever amount to get us back home."

"I am certain of that but can you imagine what these two must be going through? They will know by now that we are missing. It's been at least four hours that no one has heard from us. Do you think Ernesto will be looking for us?"

"I would hope so. I still can't believe that you are my sister. What a twist of fate. I will have to get over the fact that I was never told that I was adopted but it couldn't have turned out any better than this."

They hear the plane door close. The two kidnappers seat themselves opposite of Kataryna and Francesco.

"Put your seatbelt on," one of them demands.

"Why don't you tell us what you want from us?" Francesco questions the men.

"We don't know. We are just delivering you to the place we were told to. So shut up."

As soon as they are airborne the two men head for the cockpit.

Kataryna turns to Francesco. "So this is not a random kidnapping. Someone planned this, but who and why?"

"I am telling you, they want money," Francesco murmurs. "Most likely someone we met at Ernesto's welcome party in Rio is behind this. They know we have money."

Kataryna stares at her handbag, which together with Francesco's briefcase was placed on a seat near them.

"If I could only get to my phone. I am sure Luca left me a thousand messages meanwhile."

"Even if we could get to our phones, who would we call and what could we tell them? We have no idea where we are or where we are going."

"I would call Luca, of course. He would move heaven and earth to help us."

"I don't doubt that for one second but he would need to know where we are to send help. Why don't you tell me a little more about our parents and how you grew up. We have a lot to catch up on."

◆◆◆

"Let's call Larissa," Luca says. "She asked me to meet with her yesterday. She acted kind of strange and didn't want to tell me on the phone why she wanted to see me. Maybe she knows something."

"She's been acting quite strange for a while," Roberto responds dialing her number.

"In what way?"

"I ran into her the other night at a restaurant. First of all, she totally changed her appearance and then... I don't know. It was just weird."

Larissa answers her phone after the second ring.

"Hello, Roberto. What a pleasant surprise." Her tone seems to suggest a big smile on her face.

"Hello. I am here with Luca. You are on speakerphone. Kataryna and Francesco are missing. We can't get hold of either one of them. I spoke to Ernesto Oliveiro earlier and he told me that the driver who was supposed to pick them up from the hotel broke down and apparently sent another one to get them but they never arrived at the manufacturing plant in Manaus."

"What? Really?" Larissa sounds genuinely concerned.

"Yeah, we are worried. Maybe you could call your brother in Manaus and ask him what he can suggest to help us find them?"

"Yes, of course."

"Thanks for your help, Larissa."

Roberto's phone rings. "Hello Ernesto, let me put you on speakerphone. Kataryna's fiancé is here with me."

"I don't have any good news," Ernesto starts. "I got a call from the Manaus police. They found our company driver dead, somewhere along a road on the outskirts of the city but there are no leads on Kataryna and Francesco."

Luca buries his face in his hands. He is sick to his stomach. His chest is aching. He can hardly sit up straight. "Please God, no," he utters quietly.

"Thank you for the update, Ernesto. Any idea of what might have happened?" Roberto asks solemnly keeping an eye on Luca.

"Sorry, my friend. At this point the police have no idea but I will not rest until I find out what happened to them. I will call you as soon as I know more. We are all in shock. We never had anything like that happen before."

"Luca," Roberto approaches him calmly, "with your permission, I am offering to go over there to look for them. I know my way around there. I will take my friend Sergio with me. He and I have been on dangerous missions before. We are good together when things get tough. We also have some local buddies there who can help us."

"I am coming with you," Luca responds. "Let me get the jet ready."

"No Luca, you are too emotional right now. I don't need another casualty I would have to rescue in a special operation like this. Please let me do this for you."

"And what about your emotions? I know you love her," Luca opposes him. "Can you operate under these conditions knowing what is at stake?"

"Better me than you, Luca. I know that she loves you deeply and I had to make peace with that as you know. Does it hurt? Yes, if I want to be totally honest but I have accepted that there will never be a Kataryna and me. All I want now is for her to be happy spending her life with you. Let me redeem myself for what I did in Venice. It will help me getting past this guilt I am still feeling and you will hopefully get the love of your life back. If I don't make it back alive, so be it."

Luca looks at him holding back tears. His hands are trembling. "I am trusting you with the most precious thing in my life, Roberto. Don't even think about trying anything like in Venice again or you will see a side of me you wish had never come out."

"Thank you for trusting me, Luca. It means a lot. I will do everything in my power to get her back to you. Let's just hope it's not too late. If I had gone with them to Brazil right away, this may not...."

Luca raises his hand gesturing him to stop talking.

"Please don't lecture me, Roberto. I feel guilty enough as it is. You have no idea what is going through my mind right now. I will never forgive myself if I don't get her and Francesco back here in one piece. I am well aware that I might have been able to prevent this if I had let you go with them right away but I just didn't trust you with her away from me."

"I didn't mean to lecture you, Luca. It just slipped out," Roberto replies, "and yes, I can understand why you didn't want me to go with them. I might have reacted the same way had I been in your place."

"Thank you for understanding. This is between you and me, Roberto. We will not tell anyone what is going on, especially not Patrizia. She would fall apart. I am going to stall her trying to contact Francesco. I will tell her that they are in a remote area where cellphones don't work. Please remind Larissa not to say anything to anyone about them having disappeared. So far only my father knows and I want to keep it that way."

"Are you sure you want to do this, Luca? What about Carlotta?"

"No, I don't want her to know either because it will upset her. She is pregnant, remember?"

"Not even Francesco's parents?"

"No one!"

"OK. Covert mission it is."

Roberto calls Sergio while Luca gets in touch with the company's pilot.

"Please get the jet ready and file a flight plan to Rio de Janeiro. Two passengers. Roberto Silvestri and Sergio de Angelis."

◆ ◆ ◆

"We are going back to Rio," Kataryna whispers to Francesco. I can see the Christ statue in the distance. What a beautiful view. If only we weren't in this uncertain situation."

"Yeah, looks great with all these lights at night," he agrees. "I wish you, Luca, Patrizia and me were on a sightseeing trip here instead of in the hands of some thugs who have God-knows-what planned for us."

"I can't see the statue anymore," Kataryna says a few moments later, "it's pitch black outside."

One of the men comes toward them. "Hey, if you have to use the toilet, you better do it now. We are landing soon and we will have another hour to travel by car."

Kataryna gets up to rush to the bathroom. She grabs her bag. Surprisingly no one stops her. A flicker of hope runs through her. She locks the lavatory door and quickly retrieves her cellphone. Various email messages from Luca pop up. She speed dials his number hastily. Damn, no connection. Wiping the sweat from her forehead she tries to send him an email.

Help us, Luca. We have been kidnapped. We are somewhere in the Rio area on a private plane and are landing shortly and then will be brought somewhere an hour from where we land. We don't know who these people are and what they want. I am scared. I love you. I am so sorry. Please forgive me for putting you through this.

She pushes send. "Please God let this go through," she prays when a loud knock scares the living daylights out of her.

"Are you still alive?" she hears one of the men ask, banging on the door.

"I will be done in a minute," she manages to respond calmly, flushing the toilet and dialing the Rio emergency number for the Policia Civil she had stored in her phone.

170

"Precisamos de ajuda," she whispers into the phone hoping that someone can hear her on the other end. She lets the water run to make some noise. "Ajuda, ajuda, I am Kataryna Taylor." She continues to give her cellphone number. "We have been kidnapped in Manaus and are now being brought to somewhere in the Rio area," she continues in English. She hears a crackling sound but nothing else. Sliding the phone in her underwear she grabs a paper towel and opens the door to exit.

"Sit down quickly and put the seatbelt on," one of the kidnappers orders her sharply.

"I did my best, Francesco," she whispers.

The plane makes a rough landing bouncing up and down a couple of times before it comes to a full stop. One of the men starts cursing.

"Yeah, that's exactly how I feel," Kataryna says out loud.

When the pilot emerges from the cockpit the three men open the aircraft door.

They get a signal from the men to disembark. Once outside, they are ushered into an SUV, which had been waiting for them on the remote airstrip. Surrounded by wilderness, they are traveling on a dark deserted road lined with lush vegetation.

Kataryna attempts to calm herself. She closes her eyes, takes a couple of deep breaths and imagines herself and Francesco surrounded by a golden light inside of a beach ball. This protective exercise usually helps her through difficult situations, however, the severity of what is happening right now is something she has never experienced before. Francesco is trying to scan the area. No signs of life anywhere. He figures they are in some rain forest. No one will ever find them here, he reckons. A little further down the road he spots a sign saying Ilha Grande. He recalls having seen that name when he had researched the Rio area online for some sightseeing ideas before their trip. That means they should be about 1 ½ to 2 hours from Rio de Janeiro, off the beaten path. The uncertainty of why they are being brought here sends a chill down his spine. Who are these people? A drug cartel maybe?

An hour later they turn onto a hidden sand road leading to a secluded house. The driver parks the car in an adjacent garage. Two men approach and open the back door to let Kataryna and Francesco get out. They lead them into the house where another man walks up to greet them. Kataryna recognizes him. He was one of the guests at the welcome party in Ernesto Oliveiro's house a few days ago.

"Good evening and welcome," he greets them with a sinister grin. "I hope you had a nice trip."

"What is this about?" Kataryna charges at him. "Why are we being brought here? We missed a business meeting and need to urgently call Ernesto to let him know where we are."

"I am afraid that won't be possible, Senhora. I am Mario. We met at your welcome party at Ernesto's house the other day." He extends his hand.

"Why not?" she challenges him without shaking his hand.

"Very simple. You will be my guests until my clients, who can't wait to meet you, arrive," Mario responds coolly.

"We are not interested in meeting your clients," Kataryna submits impatiently.

"But they want to meet you."

"We want to leave immediately and return to Rio."

He signals his men. "Bring them to their room."

He turns to Kataryna. "You just took a long trip. You must be very tired. Get some rest. You will feel better in the morning."

Francesco's patience wears off. "Look, we think that we deserve an explanation of why we were snatched in Manaus on our way to a business meeting and brought to this deserted location here. You can't hold us here against our will. This is kidnapping."

"I would say that I am in the better position to decide what I can and cannot do," Mario contends with an air of superiority. "I recommend that you go to your room now and rest. We will speak again tomorrow."

He gives them a cold stare signaling his men to take them away.

Francesco and Kataryna, both uneasy, look at each other as the door to their room is locked behind them.

"Let's get out of here," she whispers heading for the window.

"Wait!" he stops her. "Let's think this through. We have no idea where we are and we know there was nothing on the way up here we can escape to. We would be wandering through some kind of wilderness not knowing what to expect out there."

"Better than staying in here not knowing what happens to us tomorrow," she responds.

"No, Kataryna. Once they find out we are gone, they will be looking for us and they are much better equipped than we are. We are screwed either way."

"I say we leave while we still can," she asserts.

"Do you really think that they haven't secured the windows somehow to prevent us from leaving?"

He hugs her. "Let's sit down and rest for a moment. I am exhausted. We need our strength. How about you tell me a little more about our mother. She must have been awesome. I wish she was still alive so I could meet her."

"I am sorry, Francesco. My mind is too preoccupied trying to find a way out of here. I have a really bad feeling about this."

"What can I do to make you feel better?" he asks still holding her.

She shakes her head. "There is nothing you can do. My intuition tells me we are in a grave situation."

"Luca will pay any amount of money to get you back. I am sure of that."

"If I was sure that all they want is money, I might be able to feel a little better but I don't think so. I am afraid we are in the hands of human traffickers."

He looks at her contemplating how to calm her while his heart is racing at that horrendous thought. He can't let her sense his fear. He has to be strong for his sister.

"If that is what's going on here, Francesco, please promise me that you will kill me. Don't let them take me to a place where I will be a sex slave for the rest of my life."

Francesco eyes well up. "Oh God, please don't make me do this. How can I kill my own sister?"

"If you love me, you'll do it. Consider the alternative for me."

Francesco is shaken. "Can life be that cruel? I just found out that I have two sisters and now one of them and I may die together."

The door opens and a young woman enters carrying towels and clothes, which she places on the bed. Kataryna grabs her by the arm.

"Please help us escape from here. We will pay you a lot of money if you do. You will never have to work again. Please help us!"

"Eu não falo inglês," the woman says in Portuguese when one of the men appears with food and water for them.

Mario and his men sit around a table drinking.

"So when will your clients arrive here?" one of the men asks him.

Mario makes a face. "Not before tomorrow evening the earliest."

"What are you going to do with the guy in there?"

"Well, Pedro, I was thinking we will ask for some kind of ransom from his family. I am sure they will pay a nice sum to get him back."

"So, you want to sell the woman to these clients from Colombia for how much?" Pedro probes further.

"They said somewhere around a million dollars but they want to see her in person first," Mario responds.

"Hmm, what if her family pays more than a million dollars to get her back?"

"Yeah, the thought crossed my mind but I promised these guys I would sell her to them. I don't want to upset these people. You can't mess with these guys. They need fresh material, so to speak," he chuckles. "Besides I may be able to get more for her. She is not only beautiful but also smart. That should count for something. She can actually have an intelligent conversation with whomever she ends up with. At least that's how I am going to spin this to get more money out of them. Selling her back to her family is too risky with the money drop to be arranged."

"Aren't you taking the same risk when you sell the guy back to his family?"

"Most likely, that's why I have to think about how to do it without being exposed. If it appears too dangerous for us we may have to dispose of him somehow without cashing in. Would be a shame, though. I'd rather have the money. We'll see. I am not in a rush with this one."

"Maybe the Colombian guys will buy him, too? They can use his organs if they don't want to deal with him alive," Pedro suggests.

"Not a bad idea, Pedro. You are not as stupid as you look." Mario bursts into laughter patting him on the back.

◆ ◆ ◆

"You want us to go to Brazil tonight?" Sergio asks astonished.

"Yeah, urgent and confidential matter. Bring our usual equipment," Roberto responds.

"Everything?"

"Yes, everything and bring some medical supplies, too. This could be one of our most exhilarating but also most dangerous missions."

"Are you going to tell me what we will be doing there risking our lives and why we have to leave tonight?"

"I'll tell you when I see you. Get the stuff and meet me at the Romano corporate jet hangar."

"Did you say Romano? I thought your relationship with that family is strained at best."

"I'll explain later."

"OK. I'll be there in about an hour. Gisella is not going to be happy but you can count on me."

"Thank you, Sergio. If I ever needed you it is now."

Roberto hangs up the phone and walks over to Luca.

"All set. I got to pack some things. Try to calm down, Luca. I will be in touch as soon as I have something for you."

Luca is holding his chest. "Please check in with me after you have landed and let me know where you are headed. Do you have a plan?"

"I sent an email to a couple of people I know in the Rio area and asked them to try to find out what may have happened in Manaus. They have a lot of contacts. Ernesto Oliveiro is expecting us at his house after we arrive. We'll go from there unless there are new developments when we get there."

"Why isn't Larissa calling us back?" Luca sighs.

Roberto dials her number. Her voice mail comes on.

"Larissa, please call us ASAP!" He hangs up.

"I am going to take a quick shower and get a few things I need together," Roberto says.

Luca nods. "I will take you to the airport when you are ready."

"Let me take a cab. I don't want you to drive in this condition, Luca."

"No, I am going to drive you. I can't sleep anyway."

Roberto throws up his arms and disappears in the bathroom.

The doorbell rings. Luca picks up the intercom.

"Roberto?" he hears a woman's voice ask.

"No, Roberto is not available at the moment. Who is this?"

"It's Larissa. Can you buzz me in please?"

Luca presses the buzzer to let her in.

"What are you doing here?" he asks her when she enters the apartment.

"I thought I'd come over for some morale support," she replies.

"You were supposed to get hold of your brother." He sounds testy.

"I couldn't reach him."

"Did you leave a message telling him how urgent this is?" Luca asks impatiently.

"Yeah." She nonchalantly shrugs her shoulders when Roberto walks out of the bathroom with just a towel wrapped around him.

"Hi Roberto." She moves toward him with a dreamy smile as her desire for him reaches its peak. She wants to tear off that towel and be ravished by him. God, this man is gorgeous. Too bad Luca is here. She contemplates how she can get rid of him fast.

"What the hell is this?" Roberto blasts out when he sees her coming closer to him. "What are you doing here?"

177

Luca motions him to calm down. "She came over to offer morale support," he explains his lips pursed. "She hasn't reached her brother yet."

"This is getting crazier by the minute," Roberto yells at her seeing her dreamy grin. This woman makes him uncomfortable like no one before. "You are the last thing I need here right now." Furious he turns around and leaves the room to get dressed.

Larissa stares after him in disbelief. The stark reality that he has no feelings for her whatsoever sinks in.

"Thank you for your concern, Larissa. Why don't you go back home. We are leaving in a few minutes anyway."

Luca attempts to offset the air of hostility Roberto just left behind.

Larissa looks at him teary-eyed. "Why is he so mean to me? I am just trying to help. I would expect you to be upset and angry that Kataryna is missing but why him?"

Luca sighs, realizing that this woman is deeply in love with Roberto. He doesn't want to put more fuel into that fire.

"Look, Larissa, Roberto and I are in bad shape right now trying to find out what happened. So we have a short fuse."

"You are nice to me, although it is your fiancée who is missing. That's what I mean. Why can't he be as courteous with me as you are? I tell you why. They are having an affair behind your back."

"You don't know what you are talking about, Larissa. You better stop right here," Luca comes at her sharply. "We don't need more drama right now. You can air your displeasure with him when he gets back but right now I need him composed and alert."

"Gets back from where?"

"From Rio, to look for Kataryna and Francesco."

"No, Luca! Please! You can't let him go there. They probably planned this together. That's why I called you yesterday, to tell you," she yells out just as Roberto enters the room fully dressed.

"Who planned what together?" he asks puzzled looking at Luca who just shakes his head hoping to stop the potential drama unfolding.

Luca takes Larissa gently by her arm prompting her to leave.

"Try to reach your brother, please, if you really want to help us." He closes the door behind her.

"What was that all about?" Roberto asks irked. "Is she insane or what?"

"Yeah, she is insanely in love with you to the extent that she tried to convince me that you and Kataryna are having an affair and have planned her disappearance in Brazil together."

"I don't know if I can handle this. This is over the top crazy. She has got to go."

"Well, you heard the saying. What goes around comes around. This is where you were a few months ago. Pursuing Kataryna relentlessly, although she told you over and over that she wants to be with me. Now you are getting a taste of what it's like to be on the other side. So in a way it's probably a good thing that you are getting out of here and away from Larissa. She must be totally infatuated with you if she comes up with something like that in the middle of this serious situation."

"Thank you for not believing her, Luca. I want to strangle her, that's how angry I am right now."

"To be totally honest, I was wavering for a moment when she came out with that accusation but then I was quickly reminded that Kataryna would never do it that way. She would tell me if she fell out of love with me. Not to mention that Francesco disappeared with her. I doubt he would deceive me like that."

"You got that right, Luca. Let's get going now, the sooner I get to Rio, the better. I will try to call Larissa's brother myself. I don't want her involved anymore. It would be best if her employment would be terminated immediately."

"How? The Chairman and CEO of the company are both missing. Oh my God! It just hit me. We have to call Kataryna's partner Stephen and let him know what happened. What time is it in New York?" Luca checks his watch. Let's call him quickly."

Luca's phone rings. "Speaking of the devil. Stephen is calling me." He answers the call.

"Ciao Luca," Stephen greets him cheerfully. "Can you tell your fiancée please to give me a call. I haven't been able to get in touch with her. I am curious how the meetings in Brazil are going."

Luca takes a deep breath and holds his head. "Believe it or not, I was just going to call you, Stephen. Let me put you on speakerphone. I am at Roberto's place. We have a couple of very serious developments." Luca turns on the speaker.

"Hi Roberto, what's going on? Should I be worried?"

Luca glances at Roberto and gives him a sign to talk.

"Hi Stephen. We have some really bad news. I'll come right out with it. Kataryna and Francesco are missing and the driver who was supposed to take them to a business meeting was found dead."

"You can't be serious!" Stephen sounds shaken to the core.

"That's all we know for now. I have been in touch with Ernesto in Brazil. He is doing all he can to find out what happened to them," Roberto explains.

"I am going to call the U.S. embassy after we hang up and report Kataryna missing," Stephen says.

"OK. Stephen. I am flying over there to see if I can find them. Luca and I were just leaving for the airport when you called."

"Both of you are going?"

"No, just me and my friend Sergio. Luca would only be in the way. He is too emotional right now as you can imagine. Sergio and I have been on many daring trips before and we are both former Special Forces military. We also have the appropriate equipment for such a mission. As soon as we find out where they are, we will be laser-focused to get them out of there. I have already mobilized a couple of buddies of mine in Brazil who we need to assist us. They are kick-ass guys and are already putting their underworld feelers out to get a head start in the search."

"Holy God," Stephen breathes heavily, "so you think Kataryna and Francesco are being held somewhere for ransom?"

"As bad as that may sound, Stephen, that would be the best case scenario. I would hate to assume the alternative."

"Oh for God's sake, Roberto. I don't want to think these kind of thoughts." Stephen sounds devastated. "If it's money they want, we will arrange for it to get them back."

Luca's hands are still trembling when he picks up the phone. "I don't want to assume the worst either, Stephen. You have no idea what I am going through. I want to scream from the top of my lungs but I don't even have the strength for that. As far as money is concerned, I will pay any price to get her back."

"There's not a doubt in my mind that you would, Luca. Has anyone contacted Kataryna's sister yet?"

"No. Should we wait until we actually know more?"

Stephen swallows hard. "I don't think so. We can't keep this from her. I will call her after I hang up with you."

"I don't want my sisters to know yet," Luca explains. "Please make sure that Aleksandra doesn't call them."

"OK Luca. Let me make the calls to the U.S. embassy and Aleksandra now. Oh God, I dread this call to her sister. Hey Roberto, this is a great thing you are doing. I wish you and Sergio the best of luck. God's speed my friend."

"Before we hang up, Stephen, there is one more thing," Roberto pauses for a moment glancing at Luca.

"Sure, what I can do for you?"

"You need to terminate Larissa Dos Santos' employment with BioMedyca."

"Why? I thought she was a great hire."

"Let me give you the short version for now. It appears that I have become her love interest and she gets bolder every day to make something happen. God knows how far she will take that. I can't subject the company or myself to that kind of liability. In addition, she just tried to convince Luca that Kataryna and I are having an affair and that we concocted her disappearance so we could be together."

"That's insane," Stephen exclaims.

"Exactly. I can't continue to work with her under these circumstances. It's too risky and I feel very uncomfortable around her."

"I get your point but don't we still need her? With Kataryna and Francesco missing and you heading to Brazil we need someone at the helm of company. I have to sleep over it before taking that step, Roberto."

"Let me offer this," Luca injects, "I still own ten percent of BioMedyca and Kataryna signed a Power of Attorney before she left, just in case. So if we let Larissa go, I can manage this together with you Stephen for the time being."

"Thanks Luca. I'll alert HR and get back to you on that. Have a safe trip, Roberto and please keep us posted on the developments in Brazil. Ciao."

"Will do, Stephen. Ciao."

As soon as they end the call, Luca and Roberto head out to the airport. Sergio is already waiting for them by the jet.

"I can't thank you two enough for doing this," Luca says shaking hands with Roberto and Sergio. "Please keep in close contact with me."

The two men pat him on the back and head up the gangway to board the plane.

On the way home Luca calls the family's priest.

"I hope I didn't wake you, Father Antonio. May I come and see you?"

"Yes, of course. You sound distressed, Luca. Are you alright?"

"No, I am not. I need someone to talk to."

ELEVEN

Patrizia is staring at her phone for the fifth time in ten minutes. No return calls, texts or emails from Francesco since yesterday. "This is outrageous," she fumes. She calls her brother.

"Buongiorno Luca. I haven't heard from Francesco since yesterday. Can you tell Kataryna please to let him know that I would really like to speak with him?"

Luca wipes his eyes to check what time it is. 10 a.m.

"Be patient. They are on the road, Patrizia. The reception for cellphones may not be that good in that area." He yawns.

"Did I wake you?" she asks alarmed.

"Yeah, I had a long night. Didn't get much sleep. I won't be in the office today."

"I see. You sound exhausted. That acquisition must be doing a number on you. Anyway according to Francesco's travel itinerary they are in Manaus. Why would there be a cellphone reception problem? He called me from there the day before yesterday."

"I recall Kataryna saying that they would be in the outskirts of Manaus today, so expect not to reach him." He feels terrible lying to his sister.

"That's kind of strange," she comes back with. "Aren't you worried?"

"Let me call you back later, Patrizia." He hangs up on her, puts his head back on the pillow and closes his eyes. Nothing feels right. His body seems to be disconnected from him. It feels heavy like a ton of lead. He has trouble moving and focusing. A deep sadness fills the room when he imagines Kataryna's beautiful face in front of him not knowing if she is dead or alive. The mental exhaustion lets him eventually drift off.

Patrizia dials her sister's office number.

"Ciao Carlotta. Do you have a moment?"

"Sure. You sound stressed. Are you okay?"

"No. I am so upset I could cry. I haven't heard from Francesco since yesterday so I called Luca to see if he can get Kataryna to give him a message from me. He was totally out of it. I think he is killing himself with this acquisition. He said Kataryna and Francesco are in a remote area and may have a cellphone reception problem, and then he pretty much hung up on me."

"Really?" Carlotta responds kind of amused. "Calm down. I know it's the first time Francesco is that far away from you but you have to understand that this comes with his new CEO position. This is not going to be the last overseas trip for him. As he becomes more experienced, Kataryna will let him handle most of BioMedyca's business in the future. So, you better get used to it. Let me see what's going on. Based on what you just told me, I am more concerned about Luca, though. I'll call you right back."

Carlotta dials Roberto's number. She leaves a voice mail for him when he doesn't pick up. "Please call me when you get this message."

The persistent ring of his phone tears Luca out of his sleep. He checks who is calling him before he answers.

"Ciao Luca," Father Antonio greets him in a gentle voice. "Please allow me to give you my thoughts about our conversation earlier."

"Go ahead, Father."

"You should tell your sisters what's going on. You three need to stick together now and support each other.

Each one of you has something huge at stake. Your future wife is missing along with your sister's future husband and the father of Carlotta's unborn child is putting himself in great danger right now to find them. The extra burden of you keeping this information from them is going to make it more difficult for you, Luca."

"I appreciate your concern for me, Father. I admit this is the toughest situation I have ever gone through, however, I don't want to put my sisters through this torment right now. Maybe Roberto can save the day and we can tell them after the fact what happened."

"You are not thinking clearly, Luca. How long do you think you can keep up this façade? For you it means another layer of guilt on top of the guilt you are already dealing with letting your fiancée go on this trip and preventing Roberto from going with her and Francesco immediately, like she had suggested."

"This is something I will have to live with for the rest of my life if I don't get her back. I might as well shoot myself because I know I will never ever get over the fact that I could possibly have prevented this."

"I am praying that you will not have to deal with this for the rest of your life, Luca but for now please reconsider and let your sisters in on what is going on. I suggest we meet tonight and tell them together."

Luca weighs the option before he responds.

"OK. I will arrange for us to meet at Carlotta's for dinner tonight," he agrees. "I can't believe that all three of us are basically in the same position."

"Have faith, Luca. I will see you and your sisters tonight."

Late afternoon Carlotta places another call to Roberto, which goes to voicemail again. She hangs up without leaving a message and calls Luca.

"Ciao Carlotta. I was just going to call you, too."

"Oh? Do you feel better?"

"Who said I wasn't feeling well?" he asks.

"Patrizia said she called you this morning and you sounded out of it and even hung up on her abruptly."

"Yes, I did. I slept maybe two hours last night. I was drained and not coherent when her phone call woke me up."

"I guess anyone can have a bad day or, as in your case, a bad night. I am just wondering if the acquisition deal you are working on might be too much for you to handle on your own. If there's anything I can do to help you, please let me know and I'll do it."

"Thank you. I need to talk with you and Patrizia. Can we have dinner at your place tonight?"

"Sure, that sounds great. I'll call Patrizia to let her know."

"Perfect. I will bring Father Antonio if it's alright with you."

"Absolutely. Before we hang up. Can you please ask Kataryna to have Francesco call Patrizia or at least send her text message? She is getting kind of antsy not having received a call or message from him since the day before yesterday."

"I'll see what I can do. Father Antonio and I will be at your place around 8 p.m."

"OK. We will expect you then. By the way, I meant to tell you that I had dinner with Roberto the other night. We had a nice evening and talked about the baby and our relationship as parents going forward, etcetera."

"I got to go, Carlotta," he cuts her off. "Let's talk tonight."

"See you later." Carlotta hangs up shaking her head. She has an eerie feeling.

Luca is nauseated. He checks the time. Roberto and Sergio should be in Rio by now. He calls Roberto's cellphone.

"I was just going to call you, Luca," Roberto comes on immediately. "We are at Ernesto's house. He received a call from the Policia Civil. We might have a lead. The police said that they received some kind of distress call last night from a woman speaking English but the connection was so bad that they couldn't make out what exactly was said. The call was short, fading in and out. Apparently some tech guys will attempt to improve the quality of the recording. In any event, the call came into their emergency center somewhere outside of Rio."

"Rio? Kataryna and Francesco were in Manaus last, which is about 1800 miles from Rio." Luca is at a complete loss.

"Yeah, that's why we are not sure if it really is a lead for us. Ernesto suggested that we drive out there and listen to this recording to see if we recognize her voice. I am just afraid that since we all want it to be her, we will read something into it and potentially follow a wrong lead and waste precious time."

Luca lets out a scream. "God, I feel so helpless at a time when she needs me the most."

"Just try to stay calm, Luca. I am still waiting on some report from my buddies here. We may head out to Manaus tomorrow."

"You do what you have to. The jet is at your disposal. The pilot has my permission to take you wherever you need to go."

"Thank you. That's helpful. By the way, I saw that Carlotta tried to reach me on my Italian cellphone earlier. I am not answering her calls because I don't want to lie to her. As a matter of fact, I have a cell with a Brazilian number for over here. Let me give you that number, just in case."

Luca jots down the number.

"I have decided to tell my sisters the truth tonight. It's going to be a tough one. I wish I had more information. Please call me soon with an update, Roberto."

"You'll be the first one I'll call, Luca."

Patrizia arrives at Carlotta's apartment at 7:30 p.m.

"What can I do to help?" she asks her sister.

"Just have a seat and relax. Would you like a glass of Prosecco while we are waiting for Luca and Father Antonio to arrive?"

"Excellent idea," Patrizia says taking the glass Carlotta hands her. "I really need a drink. I am so mad at Francesco, you have no idea."

Carlotta pours herself a glass of sparkling water.

"You better not become a nagging wife, Patrizia. Give him a break. He is on a very important mission. Here's to us," she clinks glasses with her sister. "I had dinner with Roberto the other night. We had a really nice evening talking about our baby and how to share certain responsibilities."

"I am glad to hear that," Patrizia smiles at her sister happily. "Maybe you two will end up together after all."

Carlotta shrugs her shoulders. "Maybe. We also talked a bit about him working as a consultant with Kataryna's firm. I asked him point blank if he was really over her."

"You didn't. You really went there? What did he say?"

"He said it has sunk in that she loves Luca. His obsessive behavior in Venice and realizing that he could have killed Luca shook him up pretty good. He explained what he went through when he met Kataryna in person for the first time. Apparently he had never experienced such an immediate deep connection of mind, body and soul with anyone before her. He was drawn to her like a magnet. He also believed at that time that if he had met her alone first that she would have started a relationship with him instead of Luca. The loss of this opportunity drove him to the brink of insanity."

"I hope he finds his happiness with you one day."

"Aww. Thank you, Patrizia. Speaking of Roberto, I tried to call him earlier to see if he can assist with getting Francesco to call you. I didn't reach him but I left a voice mail. Unfortunately he hasn't returned my call yet."

"Thank you for trying. I hope Francesco will call me later when he is done with his business for the day. It's not like him to leave me hanging like this."

"I am sure he'll call you as soon as he can. Please don't give him a hard time when he calls. I just thought earlier how lucky we are. You and Luca getting married to the love of your lives, and me, well, I am looking forward to raising this child with Roberto and if I am really lucky we may also end up together in the future. Let's count our blessings."

"You bet, and what a nice surprise that Father Antonio is joining us for dinner tonight. He can bless us some more."

The two break out into hysterical laughter when the doorbell rings.

"Welcome Father Antonio," Carlotta greets him. "We are so happy that you are joining us. Patrizia and I just talked about counting our blessings because everything is going so well for the Romano family. We have only happy occasions to look forward to. Two weddings and the birth of a child."

Father Antonio nods not showing any emotions. He glances at Luca who looks pale and worn out. They gather in the living room for an aperitif.

"Luca, you look terrible," Carlotta looks at her brother shaking her head. "It's time that Kataryna gets back to give you some TLC as well as a pep talk about working these long hours."

"Despite your displeasure with my working hours, could you please turn on the TV before we sit down to eat. I need to get the latest news from Wall Street real quick."

"Sure."

Carlotta turns on the U.S. financial news station. The latest stock market information flashes in front of them. The commentator delivers his report when the station suddenly switches to a breaking news announcement.

"We interrupt our regular programming to bring you these important breaking news. Our station just learned that Kataryna Taylor the Co-Chairman of Adryana Investment LP and Francesco Barone, the CEO of BioMedyca, her recently acquired company, have been missing since yesterday morning in Brazil. They were last seen when a car service picked them up from their hotel in Manaus, the capital of Amazonas. The driver of the company who was dispatched to pick them up was found dead yesterday on the outskirts of Manaus. There is no trace of the two executives who went to Brazil to complete the due diligence in connection with the proposed acquisition of a Brazilian company. We will get more details to you as soon as they become available. A press conference with Stephen Wagner, Ms. Taylor's business partner here in New York, is scheduled for 5 p.m. We have been informed that the management of BioMedyca in Milan, Italy has been turned over to the existing minority shareholder Luca Romano for the time being." A stock photo of Kataryna and Francesco appears on the screen.

Patrizia's face turns ashen. Her glass drops to the floor.

"NO!" she screams before she collapses on the couch hyperventilating and crying uncontrollably.

Father Antonio sits next to her trying to comfort her.

"You knew all along that they disappeared and didn't tell us? Why? What's the matter with you?" Carlotta charges at Luca. "You practically crucified Kataryna and me for keeping secrets after what happened in Venice. We have two future family members missing and you hide that from us? I can't believe you would do this to us."

Luca struggles to answer her. "Please hear me out, Carlotta. I swear that is why Father Antonio and I came over tonight. To tell you the terrible news. I am devastated. I have hardly slept or gotten any food down since I found out. I thought I could spare you this news. There is nothing you could have done for them anyway."

"I can vouch for that," Father Antonio states calmly. "Luca came to me last night and explained what had happened. When we spoke earlier today we planned to meet you two tonight to break it to you gently. I am here to help you through this and pray for the safe return of Kataryna, Francesco and Roberto."

"Roberto?" Carlotta shouts out. "What does Roberto have to do with this? He didn't go with them."

"He and his friend Sergio went over to Brazil last night to look for them and hopefully bring them back," Luca explains.

Carlotta holds her stomach trying to compose herself. All kinds of thoughts are racing through her head. She fears the worst. There goes her hope for a happy ending with the father of her child. Major setbacks seem to be a regular guest in her life. Patrizia is still crying on the priest's shoulder. Carlotta gently takes her hand. The priest leads them into a prayer but neither of them can focus on his voice while attempting to deal with the uncertainty of ever seeing their loved ones alive again.

◆◆◆

"What did you find out?" Sergio asks when Roberto gets off his phone.

"I am not sure if I like what I heard," Roberto states. "My guys heard some rumors from the underworld about a foreign woman and a man having been captured by some human traffickers. If it's true and it's them at least we would know that they are still alive."

"That is one way to look at it. However, we don't know where they are and for how much longer," Sergio concludes.

"Let's drive to the Policia Civil station and listen to that recording. If we recognize her voice that would be a sign that they are in the Rio area," Roberto responds.

"They were in Manaus when they disappeared. That's about a four-hour flight from here," Sergio opposes him.

"Yeah, but they could have been brought here. I am sure whoever kidnapped them hasn't done this for the first time. They probably have a private plane at their disposal."

Roberto opens up a map of the area on his iPad. "If they are anywhere in this region here," he marks the area, "finding them would be like a needle in a haystack. This territory has some pretty good hiding places between the dense forest, the waterfalls and the mountains. They could be anywhere."

"Looks like a mission impossible to me," Sergio replies concerned. "We also have the time factor against us. They might be out of the country already."

"We have to step it up a notch," Roberto answers. "Let's start by listening to that call."

When they arrive at the police station they are escorted to a room where the recording is played for them. Roberto closes his eyes to focus on the voice. At first all he hears is a humming sound like the inside of an airplane in flight. Then a crackling noise and water running, it appears, after which a woman's voice in a whisper comes on. Her first words are unintelligible and don't sound like English either. But then he hears "I am Kata...," when the connection goes bad again. He strains to listen to the rest of the recording. It sounds as if the person said something like kid and Rio before everything breaks down.

"I need to listen to this again," he tells the policeman.

He turns to Sergio after the second listen. "It's her. I heard her trying to say her name. She said 'I am Kata' but then it breaks off. However, toward the end I heard the word 'kid', she probably said kidnapped, and Rio. So she or hopefully both of them are in this area." He runs his hands through his hair and lets out a deep sigh. "The only question is where?"

Roberto is still shaken when they leave the police station. He is trying to imagine what situation Kataryna is in, which makes his chest tighten up again. A familiar feeling. He takes a deep breath to relieve the tension.

"So shall we call Luca and tell him?" Sergio asks.

"No way! He will have heart failure. It was tough for me already. Her voice sounded desperate. We got to find her, Sergio. I am going to call my guys here to see if they have any clue where they could have taken them."

Sergio raises his eyebrows. "At what point are you going to tell Luca?"

"When I know for sure where they are and we are on our way to get them out."

"OK, guys," Roberto says when he gets his Brazilian friends on the phone, "it appears that they have been kidnapped in Manaus and are now somewhere in the Rio area. Any ideas where they could hide them?"

◆ ◆ ◆

Kataryna and Francesco start eating their food.

"Oh my God," Kataryna jumps up. "I forgot I put my phone in my underwear." She quickly retrieves it and dials

Luca's number seeing the low battery indicator appear. Her heart is racing waiting for him to answer the call.

"Where are you?" Luca screams into the phone when he picks up. "God, tell me you are okay."

"Listen, Luca please stay calm. We were kidnapped in Manaus and brought back to the Rio area. We are probably about two hours from Rio in some god-forsaken wilderness. Francesco saw a sign with Ilha Grande when we were driven here. We are in a remote area with nothing but tropical vegetation around us. We went off a hidden sand road, which leads to a house where we are kept in a locked room. I think our kidnappers are human traffickers. I am so sorry to put you through this. Please help us get out of here."

Beep, beep-- the low battery indicator comes on.

"Roberto is in Rio to find you," she hears him say. "I will call him right away. You know that I'll do anything in my power to help you. Did anyone hurt…," the phone shuts off mid sentence.

She clutches the phone to her chest, tears streaming down her face.

"His voice, he sounds terrified," she utters sobbing. "He said Roberto is in Rio trying to find us. Before the battery gave out I heard him say he will call him."

A trace of a smile appears on her face. "You have no idea, Francesco what it means to me to have heard his voice. I have renewed strength now. I need to survive this for him. He is the best thing that ever happened to me. In case I don't survive this and you do, please tell him that I have never loved anyone like him and that he was on my mind when I took my last breath."

Francesco embraces her tightly. "I can't lose you. You are the sister I always wanted to have. I refuse to give up on us having a life as brother and sister together."

"Me, too. Let's just hope that Roberto finds us in time."

Luca is shaking as he dials Roberto's number.

"Ciao Luca," Roberto answers rolling his eyes at Sergio. "I don't have anything for you yet."

"She just called me," Luca interrupts him.

"WHAT?" Roberto shouts out. "How? What did she say? Are they okay?"

"No. They have been kidnapped. They are in some remote area about two hours from Rio in a secluded house off the beaten path. Francesco saw a sign with Ilha Grande when they drove to where they are kept now. So it must be on the way to that island. She thinks human traffickers have captured them. Please hurry up and get them out of there."

"What else did she tell you?"

"Nothing. The phone shut off. I guess the battery was empty or someone caught her with the phone."

"You must have been shocked when you saw her number on your screen."

"My anxiety level is through the roof. I am coming over there."

"Luca, no, don't ..."

"Save your breath, Roberto," Luca interrupts him. "Nothing can keep me over here right now."

"OK. Sergio and I will be heading toward that area. I will get some of my Brazilian friends to join us."

"Thank you. You have to look for a secluded house off a hidden sand road. If you pull this off I will be forever in your debt."

"No Luca, let's just say we are even then. I will be in touch. Ciao."

TWELVE

Larissa is pacing her living room impatiently. She is an emotional wreck. Roberto went to Brazil to find Kataryna. That wasn't supposed to happen. But does it even matter? She recalls his outburst and the disgusted look he gave her yesterday. It's very clear now that he despises her. So all was in vain.

"I am all packed." Manuela joins her in the living room. "I hate to leave you here like this. I hope you'll get back to normal soon, Larissa. It hurts me to see you go through this unrequited love drama. It's time to move on."

"Who would have thought that I would fall that deeply for a man? Just a short while ago I had zero interest in meeting anyone but when Roberto appeared on the scene, it was love at first sight. Anyway, he was not very nice to me yesterday. He would never have reacted that way if he had any feelings for me."

"Do you need me to stay a little longer so you have someone to talk to?"

"No, thank you, Manuela. Actually, I have to make some urgent phone calls now. Have a safe trip home. Thanks for everything. We'll talk soon."

Manuela exits the apartment. Larissa closes the door behind her and immediately picks up the phone to make an important call.

"Olá," the man on the other side answers.

"Olá, Carlos. Things are not turning out the way I thought, so you can let these two go now."

There is silence on the other end.

"Carlos? Did you hear me?"

"Something really terrible happened, Larissa."

"What?"

"The guy I had asked to help me keep them occupied for a while took them. He wants to sell the woman to some guy from Colombia for a million dollars."

"WHAT? NO! NO! Are you out of your mind? I told you to just keep her out of my way for a little bit so I can get closer to this man I am in love with, not to sell her to anyone. You were supposed to make this look like you all got lost on a sightseeing trip to the rain forest." She stomps her feet in a desperate rage.

"I know, I know. I had no idea that this guy was into something like that. He took both of them and said I would get some money once he sold them. I told him that this wasn't the deal. He was just to help me hide them for a while because he has an ideal place for that. He laughed and said that he is doing it his way now and if I say anything to anyone, he would have me taken care of. I am sorry, Larissa. I feel really bad but these guys are well connected. I have no way of getting these two back. I don't even know if I am safe anymore."

Larissa is wailing. Her stomach is in knots. She drops to the floor. "Oh my God, what have I done? Carlos, please help me get them back. Please, I am begging you."

"There is nothing I can do. I swear. I feel so guilty myself that I wasn't more careful but I trusted this guy."

"Do you know where he is keeping them?" she asks sobbing.

"Yeah. I think I know."

"Can you at least help someone find them?" Her voice is quivering.

"I am scared they would know that I helped, Larissa. This is not an easy place to find unless you know where you are going."

"Well, you don't have a choice, you stupid coward," she yells into the phone angrily now. "You either help me find them or I will turn you over to some other merciless people. I will hunt you down. You will never be safe again for the rest of your miserable life."

"OK. I will tell you where I think they are but I am not talking to anyone else."

"Tell me already," she screams frantically.

"Remember where we used to go on the mainland close to Ilha Grande? Somewhere around there this guy Mario, who took them, has a hiding place. I am pretty sure they are there. They wanted them out of Manaus because they figured everybody would be looking for them there once they found out that these two were missing."

Larissa slams down the phone and then dials Luca's number. Before she can even greet him he barks at her.

"Listen Larissa, I neither have the time nor the nerves to deal with you right now."

"I know where Kataryna is," she states calmly. "If you want to save her you will listen to me."

"How would you know?" Luca asks tensely.

"That's not important right now and there is no time to waste. She is in great danger. The people who have her want to sell her for a million dollars to a guy from Colombia. I will email you a description of the general area close to Ilha Grande."

Ilha Grande, that's a place Kataryna mentioned in her distress call, instantly flashes through his mind.

"Send it to me right now," he orders her sharply. "You better pray that she is alright and Roberto finds her alive."

"Here you go," she presses the send key and hangs up.

Luca stares at the map with Larissa's remarks. Holy God, this is in the middle of nowhere. He sends it on to Roberto and then places a call to him.

Roberto opens Luca's email. "What the hell is this?" he curses when Luca calls him. "Why did you send me this map?"

"This is where Kataryna and Francesco are supposedly being kept."

"Says who?"

"Larissa. She just called to tell me that she knows where they are and said they are in great danger. They are in the hands of human traffickers who want to sell Kataryna for a million dollars."

"Can we trust her, Luca? Or is this a figment of her imagination to make herself important? You know what I am thinking. She's got a screw loose. Hell, she might even be on some kind of hallucinating drug."

"That was my first reaction, Roberto, but look at the map. It shows Ilha Grande and Kataryna mentioned that they drove by a sign with that name."

Roberto lets out a loud whistle. "You know what I am thinking now, don't you? How in the world does she know this? What a lunatic."

"I asked her. She said it wasn't important right now."

"Hell, yeah, it's important if I am to trust this. We got one shot here to get this right. If we miss the target, they might be gone forever."

"I understand but my gut feeling tells me that this is where they are. Please try to find this place. At this point it is our only real lead. I have chartered a private jet. I am leaving as soon as we can take off. I also asked Dr. de Angelis to join me in case these two need any kind of medical attention if you find them. I am not taking any chances."

"We are on our way over there, Luca. Wish us luck."

Roberto's adrenaline is rising up high as he, Sergio and the two Brazilian friends discuss their strategy.

"OK guys. This is how this is going to go down. We take a helicopter and chute out of there into the targeted area with all our stuff. One of you has to drive out there to pick us up. Once we have rescued these two we need to drive back to where the helicopter is parked and get out of there fast. Luca and your father, Sergio, will be leaving Milan any moment. When they get to Rio in about 12 hours I want to have Kataryna and Francesco in our hands and in tip top shape. Clear?"

The four fist-pump indicating a go of the plan. Sergio reinforces it with the sign of the cross. "We really could use some divine intervention," he murmurs.

◆ ◆ ◆

Mario slams his phone down. "This is bullshit! These freaking people have no idea what kind of a production this whole kidnapping thing is."

"What happened?" Pedro asks.

"My client's client refuses to come here to pick them up. He insists that we bring them back to the Amazon region."

"They can't be serious. We have to drive with these two back to the airstrip and fly them out there?"

"Yes, what else you idiot." Mario smashes his hand against the wall regretting it instantly.

The three men look at each other confused.

"And when is that supposed to happen?" one of them asks, expecting a tirade from Mario.

"We will leave as soon as it gets dark."

"Tonight?" Pedro questions the plan.

Mario looks at him and explodes. "No, a week from now so we all can get arrested, you moron."

"OK, OK, Mario. Calm down. It's not the end of the world. I am tired of sitting around here anyway."

Mario ignores him and gulps down a beer. "Let's get them ready to go. I want to get rid of them fast."

A full moon shines some light on the otherwise dark and bumpy road when the SUV with Kataryna and Francesco on board leaves the area.

Roberto and Sergio, camouflaged and heavily armed wearing night-vision goggles, approach the secluded house. One of Roberto's friends follows them slowly, watching the house, which shows no signs of life from the outside. Skillfully Roberto opens one of the windows, which lets them enter a dark room. Sergio flashes a light to get his bearings. Spotting an open door he signals Roberto to continue on. Quietly they move from room to room. The house is empty. Not a soul anywhere.

"Either they were never here or we are too late," Roberto kicks one of the doors in a mad rage. "That nut job Larissa probably sent us on a wild goose chase."

They send a message to one of their friends outside and then proceed to head back when Roberto spots a leather portfolio. He opens it and lets out a sentence laced with profanity.

"They were here," he declares fuming, holding up Francesco's business cards. "Holy crap. In a couple of hours we'll have to face Luca with this piece of news."

Dismayed he tries to imagine what kind of horrific situation Kataryna may be stuck in.

"One thing is for sure, Sergio," he vows, "I will look for her for the rest of my life and whoever harmed her will not die an easy death."

Sergio nods. "I figured as much."

◆ ◆ ◆

Larissa picks up an incoming call.

"Olá Carlos," she answers, surprised to hear him call.

"I called this guy Mario again. I told him that I know for sure that the family would pay more than what he is expecting to get. I even offered to pick up the money and take these two back to make the exchange."

"Muito obrigado, Carlos. I will call her fiancé right away to arrange for it. How much do they want?"

"He didn't go for it. He told me that they have already been taken back to the Amazon region. He is expecting this client from Colombia to pick them up from there any day now, or at least the woman."

"Oh God, no! What a nightmare." Larissa is sobbing again. "Please, please help them, Carlos," she begs.

"I don't know how to help them but I think I know where they might have taken them," he says.

"Where?"

"It's close to the Colombian border. I am pretty sure that they went to this location to make it easier for the client to pick them up from there."

"Send me an email immediately how to get there."

"It's on the way. I hope it's not too late."

"NO! Tell me this is not happening!" Luca screams at his phone when he reads Larissa's email. He quickly forwards the message to Roberto.

"Please relax, Luca." Dr. de Angelis tries to reverse his meltdown. "What happened?"

"They moved Kataryna and Francesco from the Rio location to an area near Colombia. This is at least a four-hour flight. We are racing against the clock here."

"Look at the positive side, Luca. They are alive and we know where they are going. Don't give up hope."

Luca takes a labored breath. "I guess hope is all I have at this point." He leans back burying his face in his hands in desperation.

Roberto opens the email he received from Luca.

"Holy Mother of God," he yells out, "we just got a new lead. They apparently are back in the Amazonas region. How does this woman have this information? She must be involved in their disappearance. I knew all along that there was something wrong with her. Luca already informed the pilot that he has to take us as close as possible to that location immediately. He also changed his flight route to Manaus."

Sergio and the two Brazilian friends glance at each other puzzled while Roberto prepares a response to Luca:

On our way. How is Larissa involved, I wonder, and who is this Carlos guy the original email came from?

Luca responds: *No idea. We'll deal with that later. We need her cooperation right now. Finding Kataryna and Francesco has priority over anything!*

"It's ironic, but this is close to the area where the plant fields are that Francesco and I were supposed to visit in a couple of days," Roberto says, taking a closer look at the directions in the email.

"This whole thing is crazy," Sergio responds. "So you think that Larissa, who apparently is after you, has something to do with this kidnapping?"

"Well, look at the facts. She is the one who told Luca about the first location close to Rio they were kept at, and she apparently knows where Kataryna and Francesco have been brought to now. She must be behind this."

"Yup. That's highly suspicious," Sergio agrees.

"Listen to this. She came over to my place right before I took off for Brazil and tried to convince Luca that Kataryna and I have been having an affair insinuating that we concocted her disappearance so we could be together. I just don't understand yet what her reason for doing something so irrational could be," Roberto says.

"The first question in my mind is why does she think that you and Kataryna are having an affair?" Sergio asks.

"There is something seriously wrong with her," Roberto concludes. "She has been acting strange for a while."

"I guess jealousy could be a motive if she really believes that. Maybe she wanted Kataryna out of the way so you would be free for her?" Sergio suggests.

"I shudder to think that she could be that calculating and cruel to put Kataryna in this kind of danger. But if she did, God help her once I get back to Italy." Roberto rubs his eyes. "Let's get some rest now for the next four hours, guys. We need to have all our energy for this mission. Did you guys make sure that we have a helicopter when we land there?"

The two Brazilian guys nod. "All taken care of, Roberto. We also asked a couple of our buddies to head to that location and do some reconnaissance. If all went well they should be in place soon, and they will try to engage if they see any movement."

"You guys are awesome." Roberto pats them on the shoulder. "Luca will feel better knowing that someone is looking out for them."

"Yeah, but we don't know what the situation there is, Roberto."

◆ ◆ ◆

"We've got to do something, Francesco." Kataryna is anxious and paces the room they've been locked in.

"Look outside, sis. There's only wilderness around us. I think we are close to Ernesto's plants, though."

"If we can get out of here somehow we can try to make it to the plant fields. We know that the company has some employees there who, I am sure, will help us."

"Yeah, I don't think we can count on Roberto finding us anymore. If he ever made it to our first location, I can just imagine his mood when he didn't find us there. He wouldn't know that we have been brought to this area now."

She nods. "Yeah, we are on our own now. So listen to your big sister. I say we try to get hold of a phone when someone brings us food. Maybe we can overpower that person together. Then call Luca to tell him where we are and try to escape from this hell. I'd rather be eaten by a wild animal than fall into the hands of human traffickers."

"Let's see what comes our way and then capitalize on that." Francesco suggests.

"I hear voices outside." Kataryna gets excited. "Hide behind the door. Here, take one of my shoes and hit whoever comes in hard right on the top of the head with the heel."

The door opens.

"So Rico. Let's have a look at the lovely lady I found for you," she hears Mario say as he enters the room with another man.

Francesco abandons the plan they discussed, seeing two men coming into the room. No chance to pull it off. He moves to stand next to Kataryna.

"And this is the young man, I mentioned," Mario informs Rico pointing at Francesco.

Rico stands close to Kataryna. He reaches out to touch her. Francesco steps in front of her. "Leave her alone!"

Rico's fist hits Francesco's face with violent force. He drops to the floor, his nose bleeding profusely.

"You animal," Kataryna spits in Rico's face. "Don't you have any value for human life?"

Rico laughs glancing at Mario. "A feisty one. I like it. You can keep the guy. I have no use for him."

Mario makes another attempt. "I'll throw him in for free. Hey, you may be able to use his organs. He looks healthy."

"Let's talk price for the princess," Rico says, grinning at Kataryna, his hand tracing her silhouette.

She takes a step back to escape his unwelcome touch.

"I actually may keep her for myself for a little while until I turn her over for more cash." He moves closer to her, inspecting her body. He reaches out to open her blouse.

"Don't touch me!" she screams, moving her arms violently to get his hands off her.

He grabs her throat with one hand and her bra with the other. "The more you fight, the more I want you. I can hardly wait to tame you." His hand slides down her body.

"You can't have her yet," Mario steps in. "You have to pay up first. We discussed a million on the phone but I think she is worth more."

"I am not paying a million. I give you 500,000 US Dollars and take the guy off your hands. I can use him for an experiment. I am gonna let one of the spiders bite him to see if it really causes a four-hour erection like I've heard." His loud wicked laugh fills the room.

Mario looks at him disgusted. "500,000? No way! Look at her. She's worth more than that. Hell, her family would pay millions to get her back. I am giving you a bargain already only asking for one million."

"You drive a hard bargain, amigo. You sure, you want to go down that road with me?" Rico's voice sounds sinister as he faces off with Mario.

"Let's have a drink and go over it." Mario tries to turn the situation around sensing danger.

"I'll take that drink, amigo and after we seal the deal I want to have her. I need to check if she is good for the troops, you know what I mean? A seller has to be able to describe his product benefits in great detail," he smirks cynically still staring at her intensely his arousal becoming obvious.

Kataryna rushes to take care of Francesco as soon as the two men are gone.

"How are you doing? You shouldn't have done that. These people are brutal. Let me get a wet towel. Tilt your head back and pinch your nose."

"I am not watching while they fondle my sister," Francesco responds.

Kataryna returns with towels from the adjacent bathroom. She wipes the blood from Francesco's face and puts a cold wet towel on his nose.

"Did you hear what they said? We've got to get out of here, Francesco. We would not survive what's in store for us anyway."

He agrees grimacing with pain. "I really don't want to go through that experiment with the spider."

Kataryna starts crying. "How did everything go so wrong? A few days ago we were so happy having dinner in Milan looking forward to our weddings and now we are facing torture and our demise. Luca and Patrizia will die a little bit every day, and so will the rest of our families. It will be unbearable for them. I know I will be dying here today. When this criminal comes back to rape me, I will be fighting him with everything I got. He will have no choice but to kill me unless I can somehow kill him first."

A loud noise goes off in the house.

"What was that?" Kataryna asks, her eyes wide in fear.

"Maybe these two criminals killed each other over the price for you," Francesco replies. "That would be the best outcome we could hope for in this situation."

A sudden blast shakes the entire house and smashes the windows. Pieces of glass fly all over the place. Francesco and Kataryna go quickly for cover.

"I smell smoke," Kataryna says. "Let's try to get out through the window."

"Wait!" Francesco holds her back forcefully. With the bedspread wrapped around his hand and arm, he cleans up the remaining glass particles in the window frame.

"Let me go first, so I can help you climb out."

He arranges the bedspread on the frame and lets himself out slowly, then grabs his sister's arms to carry her outside. They carefully inspect the area. No one seems to be outside to stop them. They sneak around some plants toward the driveway leaving the house full of thick smoke behind them.

Kataryna shrieks loudly as a hand grabs her from behind and drags her into a nearby bush. Francesco ends up captured next to her. They struggle to get free from the tight grip to no avail.

"Stop fighting," the man having his arm around her neck and chest orders her in broken English. "We are with Roberto and Sergio to get you out of here."

Kataryna relaxes. "Where are they?"

"Inside the house, trying to break you out."

"Oh no! Can you let them know we are outside already?"

One of the men sneers. "They might be a little bit busy at the moment. We were just about to go in there to assist them. You two stay right here and out of sight. We will get you when we come back out."

"Please hurry," Kataryna pleads as the two men rush toward the burning house.

Roberto kicks in the door and finds an empty room. He glances at Sergio. "Not again. They must be here. Keep searching."

Not a soul in the next room either. They hear footsteps coming closer prompting them to hide behind a door with weapons drawn.

"Roberto," one of his friends calls him. "Let's get out of here. We have your people outside."

The four jump out of a window and sprint toward Kataryna and Francesco. A hail of bullets coming their way hits one of the men. He just barely manages to get behind the bushes with the others, blood oozing out of his leg.

"Can you walk?" Roberto asks him.

"I'll give it a shot," he says wincing, attempting to stand up.

"Let me take a look," Sergio inspects the wound and administers first aid. He hands him a pill. "Take this for the pain so we can get out of here. We will have a closer look when we get to the helicopter."

Roberto takes a look at Kataryna's shoes. "Not the ideal shoes to walk through this wilderness here but we have to make the best of it."

Kataryna hugs him first and then moves over to Sergio.

"Thank you. How in the world did you find us?"

"No time for that right now," Roberto rushes them to start walking. "We've got to get some distance between us and these savages if we want to make it out alive."

"Can we call Luca and tell him we are safe?" Kataryna glances a Roberto.

"First of all, we are not safe yet. We have quite some ways to go to reach the helicopter and your kidnappers might still follow us. They've got an arsenal of weapons in the house and might be able to get some of their guys to meet us in the rain forest, which we still have to manage. We are on dangerous territory. And second, I think getting a connection here is out of the question. So let's get going now." He sounds impatient. "I want to be far away from here when it gets dark."

"Is there a car somewhere to pick us up?" Kataryna asks.

"Do you see a road here where a car can travel?" Roberto responds. "We jumped from a helicopter, which we have to meet again to get to Manaus. We didn't have much time to plan anything else. When we arrived at the first place you were kept at, you were gone. Once we found out where you had been taken we had to move our butts to get here. Looks like we just made it. A few more minutes and you may have been on the way to Colombia and that would have been it."

"How did you find out where we were in the first place?"

"Brace yourself for this piece of news. From Larissa. She contacted Luca."

"Larissa? How did she know?"

"Well, that's a good question. I believe that she was not only involved in your kidnapping but actually the driving force behind it."

Kataryna is stunned. "Why? That doesn't make any sense. We are the hands that feed her."

Francesco offers her his arm when he sees her struggle walking the treacherous path.

Roberto takes a deep breath. "Long story short. She fell in love with me and became obsessed. For some reason, she believed that you and I are having an affair behind Luca's back. I think she wanted you out of the way so I would be free for her."

Francesco's and Kataryna's mouths drop open in disbelief. They pause their hike.

"Don't stop walking," Roberto admonishes them, "we are too slow. It's going to get dark soon." He grabs the other side of her to give her more stability.

"By the way, maybe I can make you pick up speed if I tell you that Luca is in Manaus with Sergio's father."

Kataryna flashes a huge smile and starts walking faster despite the blisters on her feet.

"That'll do it, Roberto. Let's run. Maybe I should take off these shoes?"

"No way!" he shouts. "If you step on one of those spiders or some other nasty insect, we will have a huge problem on our hands." He picks her up. "I'll carry you for a little while."

The closeness of his face and breath on her reminds her of their dramatic encounter in Venice but she has no heart feelings. She puts her arms tightly around his neck and her head over his shoulder realizing that this man has risked his life in order to save hers and her brother's.

"Let me take her for a while," Francesco offers.

"You are in no better shape either," Roberto replies refusing to hand her over to him. "But I think we should take a short break and drink some water. This humidity is going to drain us fast."

He puts her down and sits next to her holding her against him so she won't fall over. Her body has reached its limit. She closes her eyes with her head on his shoulder. He positions the water bottle on her lips and lets her drink. Sergio takes a look at Francesco's swollen face.

"Uh, that doesn't look good, Francesco. I wish we had some ice for your swollen eye. Can you see properly?"

"Not really, it's a challenge and it throbs like hell."

Sergio takes a vial with capsules out of his pocket. "Here take one of these. At least the pain should go away somewhat."

"Thanks. How much longer until we get to the helicopter?" Francesco asks.

"If we pick up the tempo, probably about 30 minutes but look, Kataryna is totally out of it. That'll slow us down."

Roberto's two Brazilian friends catch up with them.

"How are you doing?" Sergio asks the injured one.

"I'll live," he answers grimacing.

"I got you, buddy," the other guy pats him on the shoulder. "Hey, it could be worse. We could all be dead."

"Don't praise the day before the evening has come," Roberto chimes in. "We still have a good chunk of road ahead of us and the sun is setting."

"Watch out, Roberto!" Francesco shouts out when a snake creeps up behind them close enough to strike him and Kataryna.

"Shit," Roberto jumps up taking Kataryna with him. He shoots the snake. The sound echoes through the jungle.

"As I said earlier, we are far from safe," he lectures everyone. "Don't be complacent. Let's move on."

A loud crackling sound alerts them of imminent danger. Roberto and Sergio look around worried. What is coming at them next? A leopard or some human predators? Neither one would be good for them. They quickly take cover behind a couple of dense trees. The men put on some goggles to improve their vision and signal each other. Some code language Francesco and Kataryna don't understand. Tension is building as the four men walk toward the sound with weapons drawn ready to engage whatever comes their way. Kataryna and Francesco hold onto each other terrified when they hear a burst of shots being fired.

"We got to go fast," Roberto tenses up. "We have been followed by some guys. I suspect they are your kidnappers. I don't know if we hit them but regardless, let's roll." He gives the two Brazilian guys some instructions.

Kataryna can hardly stand up straight but she makes a huge effort to continue, imagining herself in Luca's arms once they reach Manaus. The intense feeling of soon being safe with him gives her the strength to walk briskly toward her goal. She can see him and taste him already but the blisters on her feet are unbearable. She stops to take a closer look removing one of her shoes.

Sergio hands her a bandage. "Put this on, so you have a bit of a cushion." He makes a face seeing the raw blisters.

"Auhhhhh," Kataryna screams out in pain when an angry spider appearing out of nowhere bites her on the foot.

"Holy crap, Roberto, she got bitten by a spider."

Everything starts spinning around her. She collapses into Sergio's arms. He looks at her in sheer horror.

"Get out the syringe from my backpack," Sergio yells out. "Hurry."

He jams it into her chest and then attends to the bite trying to get the venom out of the wound.

"Sergio, please do something. Don't let my sister die," Francesco cries out frantically.

Roberto moves him aside. "Step back, Francesco. You are not in your right mind. You don't have a sister, remember?"

"This may sound crazy but I just found out that Kataryna is my biological sister."

"OK. Francesco. Just stay calm, please. We have enough stuff going on here."

Roberto and Sergio glance at each other rolling their eyes, appeasing Francesco for the moment. Sergio works on Kataryna.

"Her pulse is weak," he explains. "We've got to get her more meds fast otherwise we are going to lose her. Time is of the essence."

THIRTEEN

"I am going insane, Salvatore," Luca says. "I don't know if she is dead or alive or what is happening. This silence is deafening."

"I know how you feel, Luca. My son is at risk too. I don't want to lose him either."

"Of course. I am extremely grateful to your son risking his life for my fiancée and her brother."

Salvatore looks up astonished. "Did you know that I know that they are siblings or was that a slip up?"

"Kataryna told me that she had to confide in you after you had the issue with the DNA tests."

"It's a small world, Luca. I am just glad that you didn't turn out to be her brother."

"That would have been tragic. I don't think I could have survived that. Well, we don't have to worry about that but I really need to find out what is going on otherwise I will explode from the inside out."

"You have to relax. I don't want you to get a heart attack over this." He checks Luca's pulse. "Let me give you a mild sedative."

He hands him a pill. Luca takes it reluctantly.

"I really have to wonder why all these awful things are happening to Kataryna and me. We have barely recovered from Roberto's assault in Venice and now we have to deal with this terrifying situation. Why?"

"You two have overcome an enormous amount of drama in a short period of time but there is a silver lining in every cloud. I think it will make your relationship even stronger, Luca. You two will never take each other for granted. Every moment of your life together will be precious and meaningful from here on."

Luca manages a smile. "That was a great explanation, Salvatore. You are a wise man. I am glad you are here with me."

Salvatore grins reassuringly. "Glad to be here. Let me ask you, is there a chance that you will reconcile with Roberto if he brings her back to you?"

"I will be forever in his debt if he saves her."

"He wouldn't want that. Just let bygones be bygones and forgive him for his trespassing in Venice. Roberto is a good man. He is not a malicious character. His problem was falling in love so deeply with Kataryna and not knowing when to let go or seek help. We all make mistakes."

"I'll take it under advisement," Luca murmurs. "I kind of feel sorry for him but let's not forget that he could have killed me."

Salvatore nods. "Sure, but that wasn't his intention. He just wanted you out of the way for a little while to see if she had the same feelings for him. I know it's irrational but considering all the drugs and alcohol he ingested, he wasn't thinking clearly anymore. These are powerful chemicals."

"As far as I know she told him several times that she loves me. He should have gone with that and left us alone."

"How is Carlotta? Isn't she due in September, around the time you and Kataryna are getting married? That will be an exciting month for the Romano family."

"Carlotta is holding up okay under the circumstances. Needless to say, she is very worried now because of Roberto's mission over here."

"I don't blame her. He is putting himself in great danger."

"Yeah, for Kataryna. I wonder how Carlotta feels about that. As far as September is concerned, I think I am going to make a change. I will move my wedding up to

July. Life is short and if anything else happens at least we are married."

"Haha. Good luck, Luca. You know how women are when it comes to weddings. They want everything just perfect."

"It will be. What could be more perfect than Kataryna and I married? All we need is our friends and family to show up. I am not budging on that. I already mentioned it to Father Antonio. He is prepared to marry us whenever we want."

Luca's cellphone rings. He immediately answers the call expecting Roberto.

"Ciao Luca. Did you forget about us?" Carlotta is calling him.

"We have no idea yet what is going on. So, all three of us are in the same position. Waiting for a call, which will either make us deliriously happy or extremely sad and suffering for the rest of our lives."

"How did you find out where Kataryna and Francesco are?" Carlotta asks.

"From Larissa."

"Larissa? How did she know?" Carlotta is totally taken aback.

"We will deal with that when we are back but it appears that she is the force behind this kidnapping. All I know for now is that she fell in love with Roberto and for some reason thought that Kataryna and he are having an affair behind my back."

"That is the last thing I would have expected," Carlotta replies flabbergasted. "I just recently told her that Roberto is the father of my child and that we are getting closer again. Does Roberto know about her apparent falling in love with him?"

"Oh yes. That's why he asked Stephen to fire her from BioMedyca. He told him that she had become a liability because of her feelings for him. So I agreed to manage the company in the meantime. It's also ironic that in a way Roberto is the reason why Kataryna and Francesco are in this grave situation."

"In a remote sense," Carlotta objects. "If Larissa fell in love with him so deeply that she would resort to something criminal in order to get his affection, then she is the sole guilty party. Roberto is an innocent bystander in this case."

"Of course. Don't get me wrong, Carlotta. I am extremely grateful that Roberto is risking his own life to save Kataryna's and Francesco's. I don't know what else we could have done. I just hope we hear something positive soon. This uncertainty is driving me over the edge."

"Me, too. Just make sure you let us know the minute you hear something. Regardless if it's good or bad news. Patrizia is really scared and can't stop crying. I am not much better off either. Even if Roberto and I don't have the kind of relationship you and Patrizia have with Kataryna and Francesco, he still is the father of my child and we made great progress recently. You might as well know that I still have very strong feelings for him."

"I understand. I promise I will call you as soon as I know something," Luca responds calmly as the sedative is kicking in full force now making it impossible for him to stay awake.

"Why don't you lie down, Luca," Salvatore suggests when he sees Luca getting drowsy.

Luca follows his advice without resistance and is soon fast asleep. Salvatore stares at his phone for a while and then dials his son's number. After the third attempt Sergio answers.

"Sergio, where are you? What is going on?"

"Papá," Sergio yells into the phone. "We got them out but we are being followed by the kidnappers. Kataryna is unconscious. She was bitten by one of these poisonous spiders. I administered one of the syringes with the antidote you gave me but she is not responding. Her pulse is weak. I need to give her more but the rest of the meds are in the helicopter we are trying to get back to. Francesco is not coherent. He got beaten up before we got them out. His face is badly swollen and he may have a concussion. He is hallucinating. He thinks Kataryna is his sister. One of Roberto's Brazilian friends got shot in the leg. It looks like the bullet only grazed the leg but he also needs medical attention to avoid an infection. I am not sure we are going to make it. We are facing so many obstacles right now."

"Please think positive, son. You have been in sticky situations before. I have faith in you. First of all, Francesco is not hallucinating. Kataryna really is his sister. I will explain when I see you. Just focus on her now. Did you try to get all the venom out of the wound?"

"Yes, of course. But there is a swelling where she got bitten. Her immune system was already down before. She could hardly walk and her feet are full of blisters."

"How much longer until you reach the helicopter?"

"Under normal circumstances about 15 minutes but we have to carry her through this dense forest now, so I don't know how fast we can get there." Sergio sounds distressed.

"I brought more medical supplies with me, Sergio. If you can stabilize her, I might be able to save her. Try to give her plenty of water if she comes to."

"We don't have that much water left. We are all dehydrated. Is Luca with you?"

"Yes, but he fell asleep after I gave him a sedative. I dread to tell him about his fiancée's condition now that I managed to get him somewhat calm. I am afraid it will agitate him again. Let me know when you think you will arrive at the Manaus airport. Luca's jet has been equipped with medical monitors and the necessary supplies I need for a potential emergency. Just get her here as fast as you can. This is crucial if she remains unconscious."

"That was my father," Sergio explains after he ends the call. "Good to know that our phones work again. We must be close to the helicopter. He said we have to stabilize Kataryna and get her to him fast."

"Easier said than done," Roberto snarls. "Was Luca with him?"

"Yes, but he was sleeping. My father had given him a sedative."

"Good. I wouldn't want to alarm him with what's going on here."

"I am sure my father will tell him at the appropriate time."

"Shush. Can you hear that?" Roberto asks. "Sounds like we are near water. Let's see if we can catch a break and take a quick dip and cool our overheated bodies down. Truth be told, I am pretty wiped out from this heat."

Roberto puts Kataryna's lifeless body over his shoulder.

"Thank God she doesn't weigh that much," he smirks lightening up the mood a bit with some humor.

"I see water," Francesco yells out elated. Soaked in sweat from the humidity he runs toward it.

"What is---?" Francesco stops cold, staring at a group of indigenous tribesmen with arrows pointing straight at them. Overcome by the heat and shock, Francesco collapses at their feet. One of the natives bends down to take a closer look at him.

Roberto turns to one of his Brazilian friends. "Now what? Are we doomed?"

"Let me try to communicate with them," one of Roberto's friends says quietly while approaching the group slowly. He talks to them in one of the many tribe languages hoping that they understand him.

"We are sorry if we intruded on your territory," he starts out, getting a reaction from one of them indicating he speaks that language. "We have two sick people here," he points to Francesco and Kataryna. "They need urgent medical treatment. A poisonous spider bit the woman. She is unconscious. The man at your feet appears to have a heat stroke and concussion. We are all overheated. Please let us take a quick dip in the water. We promise to leave immediately thereafter."

Two of the natives shake their head and move forward in a defensive position. "No! Don't come any closer."

"Please," Roberto pleads with them. "We need to save this woman's life. We don't mean any harm."

"Give us the woman," the native says in broken English, grabbing Kataryna's legs.

"No, no, please let her be. She is very sick," Roberto responds trying to move away from them with Kataryna.

Sergio steps in front of them. "Take me instead."

The tribesmen look at each other baffled. Roberto's friend continues speaking to them in their language again to diffuse the tense situation. After an exchange of several sentences, he turns around to Roberto.

"They said they want to help her. Put her down and let them look at the bite."

Sergio and Roberto glance at each other. "Can we trust them?" Roberto murmurs.

He slowly puts Kataryna down holding on to her while two natives inspect her badly swollen foot. One of them cleans the area of the bite and then applies a powdery substance to the wound while a third one appears with water to moisten her lips and face. He then hands the water to Roberto. Relieved he drinks it.

"Where are we?" Francesco regains consciousness holding his head.

Sergio hands him some of the water. "Here, drink this quickly. We have to bring your temperature down. Can you get up?"

Francesco attempts to get up. He is shaky. "I need to go into the water. I am burning up."

"No! You can't go into this water," the English-speaking tribesman warns him sternly, holding him back with his spear.

"Why not?"

"This water has candiru fish. You can't see them. They are tiny. They would get inside of you and feed on your blood through your genitals. The pain would be excruciating and you will die of shock. There is no remedy."

Roberto is holding his head. "We got water right in front of us but can't go in. Let's move on. We've got to get to the helicopter fast."

"Let us carry the woman," the native says. They assemble a couple of pieces of wood, tie them together and put Kataryna on it gently.

"Thank you," Roberto extends his hand. I wish we could reciprocate."

"Maybe you can. Bring awareness so people will leave our rain forest alone," the native suggests. "There is illegal trade of our animals, endangered species, to laboratories in Europe and North America. They pay a good price for the animals. More than what people here can earn in a year. Why do humans have to destroy our territory? Everything is taken from us. Our only chance to slow this destruction down is the research on medicinal plants to protect the Amazon rain forest. Maybe that will stop the ongoing deforestation."

"I will do everything in my power to help with that," Roberto responds. "As a matter of fact, our company in Italy wants to acquire a medicinal plant field here, and, given the viability, we would develop this area for that purpose. But right now I have to get this woman to a safe location so she can get the medical treatment she needs and hopefully survive this."

"We will escort you to the location you have to reach. I have applied a special remedy to her foot. It should at least delay the spreading of the poison from the bite."

"We are very grateful for your help," Roberto says humbly. "I would like to stay in touch with you regarding the medicinal plants we are looking to acquire and work with you toward a common goal in the future."

"I am hopeful we may be able to help each other," the tribesman responds.

◆ ◆ ◆

Luca is rubbing his eyes. "How long have I been out?"

"A good two hours and you needed it badly," Salvatore responds.

"Two hours and no word yet from anyone? This doesn't look good."

"I spoke to Sergio about an hour ago," Salvatore states as calmly as possible.

Luca sits up straight, instantly wide awake. "What did he say?"

"The good news is they got them out."

"Thank God," Luca lets out a long sigh of relief. "So where are they?" A trace of a smile is on his face.

"Once they reach the helicopter, they should be in Manaus in about three hours. They have a tough road behind them and a tough road still ahead. One of Roberto's friends got shot during the rescue mission."

"Oh my God. Is he dead?"

"No, but he needs medical attention."

"What about Kataryna?"

Salvatore takes a deep breath.

"What's wrong with her?" Luca's face turns to stone.

"Let's just say, she could be better."

"What happened?" His heart is pounding in his chest.

"She's unconscious. She got bitten by a poisonous spider. Sergio gave her an injection immediately but she has not come to and her pulse remains weak. I did some research on the Internet. The bite of the Brazilian wandering spider causes inflammation of the throat and lungs, potential paralysis of the respiratory system and a lot of pain. Since she is unconscious, she most likely isn't suffering."

"Most likely?" Luca can't help being sarcastic. "What does all that mean, Salvatore? Please don't sugar coat it."

"Luca, nothing in medicine is for sure. Everyone reacts differently depending on a person's overall health. Kataryna was in good health when I examined her a few weeks ago. The fact that she is unconscious could be an advantage. Sometimes extreme pain can make the situation worse because the body has to deal with that on top of the other symptoms. I read that over the last year only about 10 people have died from the wandering spider bite."

"So she could die?" Luca shakes his head in disbelief, an ice-cold chill running down his spine. "God, what have I done that I am being punished like this?" He yells out looking up to the ceiling.

Salvatore tries to reassure him. "Please don't give up hope. Let me give you another sedative."

"No! I want to be awake for this regardless how painful it is. There will be plenty of time for tranquilizers if she dies. So where are they now?"

"When I spoke to Sergio, they were about 15 minutes from the helicopter they need to reach to bring them to Manaus. Sergio has more meds in the helicopter. Once they get there he can give her another antidote."

"What about Francesco?"

"I understand he is pretty beaten up. He has a swollen face and a possible concussion. One of the kidnappers hit him badly before Roberto and Sergio got them out."

"So his life is not in danger?"

"It wasn't when I spoke to Sergio. I don't know what happened meanwhile, though. Oh, by the way, Francesco knows that Kataryna is his sister. She must have told him when they were captured."

"I guess she figured they wouldn't survive this," Luca murmurs. "Well, based on what you just told me, she may not, so it's good that they had some time together as brother and sister."

Salvatore's phone rings. "It's my son," he tells Luca after seeing the caller id.

"Sergio, I will put you on speakerphone. What is the latest?"

"We made it to the helicopter with the help of some natives. Kataryna is shaking violently. Looks like she has convulsions. Should I still give her the shot?"

"Seems like her body is trying to fight the toxins. Put her on her side and wrap her in a blanket or something soft. Let it pass before giving her anything. Monitor her vitals. How much longer until you get to Manaus?"

"About two hours. We don't have a blanket. Roberto and Francesco are cushioning her."

"Let me talk to her," Luca grabs the phone.

"She can't talk, Luca. She is unconscious." Sergio explains.

"Just hold the phone to her ear, please," Luca requests.

Sergio hands the phone to Roberto who holds it against Kataryna's ear.

"Hello Principessa," Luca says calmly, "I need you to get well. Can you do that for me? I can't lose you. Please, I am begging you. If you don't want me to suffer for the rest of my life, you will give it all you can and fight this. I will be at the airport when you get there. Dr. de Angelis is with me, too. We have everything ready for you. All you have to do is pull through now. I love you more than anything else. You promised to marry me and have two children with me. I am holding you to that promise."

"Keep talking, Luca. She stopped shaking."

Francesco takes her hand. "I don't want to lose you either. We still have to catch up for all the time we lost as brother and sister. I know you are a fighter. Don't give up."

He puts a cold compress on her forehead, which Sergio handed him. Sergio inspects the bite on her foot. He applies some more of the powdery medicine the tribesmen gave him on the wound and covers it with gauze.

"We got to analyze that stuff when we are back home," he says to Roberto. "Her foot looks much better than before. The swelling seems to have subsided. Maybe this is some kind of natural miracle drug."

"How are you doing, Francesco?" Luca asks

"My head and face hurt but I'll be okay. I just want Kataryna to wake up."

"You and me both," Luca sighs. "Please take good care of your sister. She really needs you now."

"I'll be here for her," Francesco vows.

FOURTEEN

"I know that you are behind Kataryna's kidnapping," Carlotta greets Larissa coolly after she answers her call. "Why? What made you do something so heinous? She was your biggest supporter."

"I feel so bad, Carlotta. Please hear me out. This wasn't supposed to happen. I swear. I can't believe how this turned out. Do you have any information how the search is going?"

"Why should I even tell you? I don't trust you as far as I can throw you."

"I deserve that Carlotta, but please believe me, I have never done anything like this in my entire life. I know that your family will never forgive me if they don't get Kataryna and Francesco back alive."

"That's putting it mildly, Larissa. Do you even realize the magnitude of this situation? My brother and sister are hurting badly. I don't even want to imagine what would happen if they don't make it back here alive and well."

"I am so ashamed that I wasn't able to bring my feelings for Roberto under control. He just touched me like no one ever has." Larissa sobs.

"I don't get it. Why did you think that letting Kataryna disappear would get you any closer to Roberto? I am the one who carries his child. How was Kataryna in your way?"

"It doesn't matter anymore."

"It matters to me. I want to know."

"Because I thought they were having an affair."

"You are so wrong. Kataryna is not that kind of a woman. She loves my brother. She would never betray him like that. How did you come up with that idea?"

"I have seen photos of them on his phone, which show them embracing and being very close. I always sensed that there was more between them than a business relationship. I don't know how else to explain it. My intuition told me there was some kind of bond between them even before I saw the photos."

"I have heard enough, Larissa. Prepare for the worst when Luca is back. You won't get away with this. You have no idea what my brother is capable of when someone screws with any of our family members or close friends. He will become your worst nightmare if he loses Kataryna or if any harm comes to her. As far as I am concerned, after today I don't want to talk to you or see you again. And one more thing, tell your daughter to stop pursuing my son. I already told you Enrico has a girlfriend and she comes from a family with integrity. He will not speak to your daughter anymore. So save her the embarrassment."

As soon as Carlotta ends this call her phone rings.

"Luca. How are you? Any news?"

"Roberto and Sergio rescued Kataryna and Francesco from dangerous international human traffickers."

"Thank God," Carlotta exhales.

"I understand this played out like an action movie. They even have some footage on their phones to show us how the rescue mission went down. It wasn't easy but they managed to do it. We owe them a lot."

"I am so relieved that this will have a happy ending," she says.

"I wasn't done yet. Here is the sad part. They had to walk quite a while through the Amazon rain forest to get back to the helicopter waiting for them to bring them to Manaus. A poisonous wandering spider on the way bit Kataryna. She is unconscious and in bad shape."

"Oh, no, Luca! This is terrible news. I pray that Dr. de Angelis will be able to help her."

"That's the only hope I have right now. I am glad that I asked him to come along." Luca chokes up. "I wouldn't know how to go on without her. This is so heartbreaking."

"I know what you are going through, Luca. I wish there was something I could do. What about Francesco?"

"He got hit hard in the face. Other than the swelling and pain, though, he seems to be okay. Let's hope nothing adverse happens until they get here."

"I don't think I can take any more bad news."

"There is something else you and Patrizia need to know. I will give you the short version for now."

"What else? You are scaring me, Luca. Is something wrong with Roberto?"

"No, don't worry. Other than being dehydrated like all of them, he is in good health and so is Dr. de Angelis' son Sergio who has been taking excellent care of Kataryna and Francesco."

Carlotta is relieved. "Good. So what else is going on?"

"Last November, Kataryna found out that her parents had a son who they had been given up for adoption right after he was born. So Kataryna made it her life mission to find her brother. She hired an attorney in Berlin to assist her in that mission. He sent her the paperwork recently showing the name of the adoptive parents and birth details about the boy. Here comes the incredible part. It turned out that Francesco is her biological brother."

"This is unbelievable. How is that even possible? What did the Barones have to say about that?"

"Vincente Barone is in shock that it came out. He hasn't told his wife yet because she is quite sick."

"I can understand that. I wouldn't say anything either unless I was really sure."

"They are sure. In connection with their medical exams for their trip to Brazil, Kataryna and Francesco also had certain genetic tests done to get that out of the way when we want to start a family. Dr. de Angelis' lab ran the necessary DNA tests and discovered by accident that these two are a match. At first the doctors thought that the lab had made a terrible mistake. But the second closely supervised test showed that it wasn't an error. So Kataryna revealed to Dr. de Angelis in confidence that she had proof that Francesco is her brother."

"Wow!" Carlotta is blown away.

"Please call Patrizia and our parents and update them on everything I just told you."

"I will do it right away. Have a safe trip home. I can't wait for you all to be back here. Oh, by the way, Larissa called me. I told her that you will pursue this legally and that I didn't want her to contact me anymore."

"I don't know if this was a smart thing to do, Carlotta. At this point she has nothing to lose. Stephen Wagner has terminated her employment with BioMedyca and his lawyer is standing by to sue her once he has all the facts for a case."

"Wow, she really messed up her life. How sad for her daughter," Carlotta responds.

"I would feel better if she was in custody. So please be careful."

"Don't worry about me Luca. Just focus on Kataryna now. Ciao."

◆ ◆ ◆

"God willing, we will arrive in about 30 minutes in Manaus," the helicopter pilot advises Sergio.

Roberto looks at Kataryna, still holding her close to him. Her shaking has stopped. He touches her forehead and looks questioningly at Sergio.

"She is totally dehydrated," Sergio explains. "I don't like what I am seeing here. I am sure my father brought an intravenous line so he can give her what her body needs. But first we have to get there."

"You did a great job so far, Sergio," Francesco says.

"Thank you," Sergio responds. "I am a medical doctor. I just don't want to practice it on a daily basis, although my father tried to talk me into it more than once."

"Will you take over his clinic one day?"

"Yes, but I will just manage the clinic in an administrative position. I will leave the medical part up to the physicians on staff."

"Same with me," Francesco says. "I also became a doctor to do my father a favor but then decided it wasn't for me. With what I recently found out, it kind of explains it."

"Can you talk about it?"

"I found out that I was adopted. I tried to tell you guys earlier that Kataryna turned out to be my biological sister. I think you didn't believe me, though."

"True, we thought you were losing it but my father confirmed it when I spoke with him earlier," Sergio replies.

"You never mentioned before that you were adopted," Roberto says. "Congratulations, Francesco. So you actually have two sisters now."

"I didn't know I was adopted until a few days ago. Yeah, I have two fabulous sisters and nieces. I am really happy about that. I just have no idea why my adoptive parents kept this from me."

He strokes Kataryna's hand softly. "We will be safe soon and get you more help. Just hold on a little longer, please."

Luca paces up and down the jet. "Where are they? They said half an hour."

"It's just been 35 minutes, Luca. I am sure they will be here soon."

Salvatore tries to calm him, although deep down he is anxious himself. The huge task ahead of him as soon as he takes Kataryna under his care is weighing heavy on him. What a responsibility and emotional undertaking with her fiancé and brother standing by hoping that he can perform some kind of miracle.

"Luca, I need you to manage your expectations. Even though Sergio was able to prep Kataryna somewhat with the emergency supplies, I don't know what I will find once I examine her more closely. We may have to admit her to a local hospital in the worst case scenario."

"I know you will do your best, Salvatore."

Luca jumps up. "I just heard a helicopter." He rushes to the plane's door."

A helicopter approaches the airfield and slowly sets down close to the jet. Luca clutches his chest when the door opens and he sees Roberto carrying Kataryna to the jet. Sergio and Francesco follow them closely. Luca runs down the stairs to meet them.

"Please hurry, Roberto. Put her on the bed we put up in the jet."

Roberto nods and races up the steps with Kataryna.

"Hi Principessa," Luca kisses her softly on the cheek and takes her hand in his after Roberto puts her carefully on the bed.

Salvatore immediately puts an IV line into Kataryna's arm. He screens her vitals with a portable device and pricks her finger to get some blood.

"Luca, I need you to step back for a moment while I am examining her," he urges him.

Luca hesitantly lets go of Kataryna's hand. He turns to Roberto and Sergio. "I can't thank you enough. Please let me know if there is anything I can do for you."

"Don't worry about it, Luca. We are just glad we made it in time to get them out of there. She most likely wouldn't have survived this," Roberto says.

"I know she wouldn't have," Francesco says. "She begged me to kill her rather than letting them take her."

"Did they harm her in any way?" Luca asks him.

"No, but she came close. When the man, who wanted to buy her, started touching her, I stepped in to prevent him to go any further and promptly got hit in the face. Of course in true Kataryna fashion she took care of me then."

"Thank you, Francesco." Luca pats him on the shoulder. "I can just imagine how she reacted."

"She was pretty fearless but she wouldn't have had a chance. Thank God she was spared the worst when Roberto and Sergio busted in there to get us out."

"Put this on your face, Francesco." Sergio hands him an icepack and gets cold water for him and the others.

"Why don't you guys eat something. We brought some food for you," Luca says.

"Thanks. We are starved." Sergio and Francesco take off to the galley.

Roberto and Luca stare at each other for a moment, both subdued and close to tears.

"You must be exhausted," Luca finally says.

"I am but I didn't realize it until a few minutes ago. I guess the rush of adrenaline kept me going until now. In hindsight I can truly say that this was one of the most difficult things I ever had to go through. Mostly because of the uncertainty of what we would find once we were inside the house. I still can't believe we all made it back here alive. If it wasn't for my two Brazilian friends we might not have been so lucky. They were remarkable."

"I will definitely do something for them," Luca assures him. "Were are they?"

"They went on to the hospital. One of the guys got shot in the leg. Nothing life-threatening but he needs some medical care."

"I will take care of his medical bills," Luca says. "I am also deep in your debt, Roberto. I am fully aware this was not a run-of-the-mill favor. You and Sergio put your lives on the line."

"I had to do it. Not only for you but also for myself and for Kataryna, of course. I know what I did to you two a couple of months ago was despicable. In my defense, though, I have to say that I was not myself then. My feelings for her and what I thought was a missed opportunity brought out the worst in me. I still can't believe how messed up I was in my head."

"I know she forgave you. I have been dealing with it as best as I can," Luca admits. "What I am going through right now, not knowing if she will come out of this and be well, is tough to handle. I am a non-violent person but I am sure I would have been capable of killing the criminals who kidnapped her. I can't imagine my life without her. So I can somewhat comprehend now what you were going through at that time with me standing in the way of your happiness."

"I went through a difficult phase. If you love someone that strongly nothing can make you not love that person from one moment to another. I guess every human being hopes to find that kind of love one day."

"Sure. The minute she stepped into my office, I knew that she was the one for me. I was not about to let anyone derail that. Let me ask you this. Would you be emotionally able to attend our wedding or would that be too painful for you?"

A series of loud beeps interrupts their conversation and makes them jump out of their seats in shock.

"She is crashing! Sergio, get the defibrillator, stat," Salvatore screams out pressing hard on Kataryna's chest.

Luca, Roberto and Francesco rush over to Kataryna's bedside.

"No! Salvatore, bring her back," Luca cries out. He lunges forward and grabs her by the shoulders shaking her violently. "Come back! Please! You can't do this to me!"

"Luca, get out of the way!" Salvatore yells at him with the defibrillator ready to hit Kataryna's chest.

Roberto rushes to Salvatore's aid. He intercepts Luca from shaking her any further.

"Luca, please let the doctor do his job." Roberto is fighting tears trying to restrain Luca at the same time.

"Kataryna, please don't leave us," Francesco implores his lifeless sister, putting himself in front of Luca to keep him away from her.

"Clear," Salvatore shouts out as he charges the paddles and then presses them onto Kataryna's chest making her body jolt up in the air like a rag doll.

Luca, Roberto and Francesco watch in horror when she remains flat lined after the doctor's attempt to revive her. Luca tries to free himself.

"Stay back, Luca or I will have to sedate you," Sergio comes at him with a syringe. "You are not helping her. Let my father do what he needs to do."

They succeed in getting Luca to sit down on the nearby couch. Roberto and Francesco bury their heads in their hands while Kataryna gets shocked again with the life-saving equipment.

"What is happening to her?" Luca cries out.

He doesn't get a response. Salvatore and Sergio focus frantically on bringing Kataryna back to life.

Francesco embraces Luca. "She's been through a lot. She is dehydrated, her blood sugar is probably low and the poison from the spider bite on top of it," he sobs.

"What about the remedy the natives gave you for her?" Luca asks. "Could that have done some harm?"

"I don't think so. Her foot was swollen and now it looks almost normal. I think these natives know what they are doing when it comes to natural remedies. That's why we want to acquire the plants, which come with this acquisition. She is just too weak from all the other factors," Francesco rationalizes. "I was also unconscious for a while.

I didn't tell anyone that I felt faint the whole time we walked through the rain forest because I didn't want to slow us down."

The paddles are hitting Kataryna's chest with full force as Salvatore slams them down in a final attempt, sweat breaking out on his forehead.

"Come on Kataryna, get back here," he calls out to her.

"I can't take this. I want to die with her," Luca says quietly.

He makes an attempt to compose himself but when he closes his eyes and Kataryna's face smiling at him sweetly appears in front of him, he lets out an emotional cry.

"She's back!" Salvatore exclaims, extinguishing the impending chaos. He exhales relieved, wiping the sweat from his face.

Luca hurries to her side. Roberto and Francesco follow him closely. He takes her hand and holds it to his face. Tears of relief stream down his face as he watches the monitor showing Kataryna's heartbeat. When she finally opens her eyes, she takes a deep breath and looks around.

"I must have died and gone to heaven," she says after a period of silence, managing a weak smile. "I have five extremely good-looking men standing next to me catering to my every need. Wow! Lucky me."

"You have no idea how close to heaven you came," Luca says wiping the tears from his eyes.

"I am in heaven when you are next to me," she responds looking at Luca, caressing his face. "Thank you for coming all this way to pick me up. Let's just not make a big deal out of this, okay? I know I should have been more careful."

"We'll talk later," he responds kissing her hand.

"I am sure we will," Kataryna rolls her eyes.

She reaches for Roberto with her other hand.

"I really don't know how to thank you for risking your life to get us out of this hell of a situation. Wow! You and

Sergio deserve a medal of honor. I hope Luca showed you his gratitude already because without you, Francesco and I wouldn't be here right now."

Roberto nods and smiles at her reassuringly, holding her hand. "I am just glad we made it in time."

They will never have a closer moment than this one right now, he thinks, reminding him to realize the true value of a moment. This is the second time he risked his life for her, and he would do it again in a heartbeat.

"Francesco, my dear brother, you look very colorful," she says. "This guy did a bang up job when he hit you in the face. Are you in pain?"

"A little, but it looks worse than it is. Patrizia will probably freak out when she sees me. I better call her now. I am sure she is on needles and pins."

The pilot comes on the intercom. "What shall I tell Air Traffic Control? Any idea when we can take off?"

Luca glances at Salvatore for an answer. "Is it safe for Kataryna to fly?"

"Looks like she is stable. I'll keep the IV line open in case I have to give her something else on the way," Salvatore replies. "How do you feel, Kataryna? Is there any way I can make you more comfortable?"

"I am a little hungry and I would like to know how I got here. I don't remember what happened after I got bitten by this nasty spider."

Francesco chuckles. "For starters, Roberto carried you after you fainted and then, well, that's another story. We ran into some native tribesmen, which was quite adventurous because at first we didn't know if they were friend or foe. I think we will leave that story for later when we are back home, together with a nice meal and a good bottle of wine. You won't believe what happened."

Luca returns with some food from the galley. "My turn to feed you, Principessa. Let me just go talk to the pilot first so we can leave here soon."

"So what did the tribesmen do?" Kataryna asks.

"After an initial misunderstanding, they were quite helpful," Roberto explains. "They gave us some natural remedy for your bite, which we need to analyze as soon as we are back in Italy. I think they can be helpful to us in the future when BioMedyca owns that medicinal plant field. They asked us to tell the world to stop destroying the rain forests."

"Really?" Kataryna says astonished. "I am sorry I missed all that. I definitely want to make saving the rain forests one of our causes."

"Are you talking business?" Luca's voice sounds concerned when he returns from the cockpit. "I think there will be plenty of time for that once we are back and you have completely recovered."

"Yes, darling, you are right. How about some food now?"

Luca starts feeding her. "We will be taking off in 15 minutes. Arrivederci Brazil."

FIFTEEN

"Francesco! Where are you?" Patrizia starts crying when she hears his voice on the phone.

"I am fine. Please don't cry. We are taking off from Manaus in a few minutes."

"How is Kataryna?"

"She seems good now. It was touch and go for a while. I'll explain when I am back home."

"I can't believe she is your sister. What are the odds of something like that happening?"

"I am dumbfounded myself. Please don't say anything to my parents yet. I need to talk to them first."

"Of course I won't. Luca explained it to Carlotta the other day and she told me. The rest is up to you."

"As happy as I am that I have two wonderful sisters, it's a strange feeling that my parents are not really my parents, and I still have to face my biological father in Berlin. It will be an emotional time for me, especially since I will never meet my biological mother. Kataryna said she was a wonderful and loving person."

"I will help you through it, and so will Kataryna and your other sister Aleksandra."

"Now I understand why Kataryna so easily agreed to give us the ten percent shares of BioMedyca as a wedding gift."

"It all makes sense now," Patrizia agrees.

"I just got a signal we are ready for takeoff. I love you. See you soon. Can you do us a favor please and call Carlotta and tell her that Kataryna is doing well and that we are on our way home?"

"I'll call her right away. She was so upset and worried about Kataryna's condition. These two have gotten very close. Is Roberto okay?"

"Yes. Exhausted, of course, but otherwise in good shape. What he and Sergio de Angelis did for us is incredible."

"I agree. I am so grateful to them. In my book Roberto has redeemed himself in a big way."

"He sure did. See you soon. Ciao."

"All's well that ends well," Luca sighs happily checking on Kataryna to make sure she is strapped in tightly for takeoff.

"Please prepare for departure," the pilot's voice comes on via the intercom, "we received a green light from Air Traffic Control."

◆ ◆ ◆

"What are you doing here?" Carlotta hisses when she opens the door. "I told you I never want to see you again."

"Please, Carlotta," Larissa pleads. "I need to get this off my chest. I never meant to bring any harm to Kataryna and Francesco."

Carlotta reluctantly motions her to enter. "You need professional help, Larissa. When someone becomes so infatuated with a person, as you have, and goes to great lengths to force a relationship, there is something terribly wrong. I am sure my brother will not let this go easily. He almost lost the woman he loves more than anything in this world. As a matter of fact, my entire family has been going through some kind of hell including me."

"I know this is no excuse but so have I, Carlotta. I didn't recognize myself anymore. My love and desire for Roberto robbed me of all my senses," she sobs piercingly. "I don't know how to go on and where to go from here. I lost my job, my reputation and the respect of people I so admire. I am honestly considering killing myself but I needed to talk to you first to ask for your forgiveness."

Carlotta struggles to keep her emotions in check, recalling Roberto's desperate actions in Venice when he couldn't let go of his feelings for Kataryna and almost killed her brother because of it. The man she loves so deeply is the common denominator of two near tragedies.

"Please think about your daughter, Larissa and get professional help. Suicide is not the answer. You will hurt your loved ones and they don't deserve that kind of pain. I forgive you just like I have forgiven someone else recently in a similar situation but I can't speak for my brother."

"I am sorry, Carlotta. I didn't mean to upset you like this. Thank you for hearing me out." She kisses her lightly on the cheek. "I won't bother you again."

"Just for the record, Larissa. I know exactly how painful unrequited love is. I have been going through this myself with Roberto but other than being extremely sad, I didn't do any harm to myself or other people. You will get over this with the appropriate therapy and support from your friends and family. I wish you well."

Carlotta closes the door and lets Larissa's emotional visit sink in. The ringing of her phone interrupts her sad thoughts.

"Pronto," she answers shaky.

"What's going on, Carlotta?" Patrizia asks alarmed. "You haven't answered your phone for hours."

"Larissa came by to see me," she responds with a tentative voice.

"WHAT?" "How dare she? Are you alright?"

"She is gone. I am fine, Patrizia but I am not sure about her. She is suicidal."

"What happened? Talk to me."

"She feels extremely guilty and said she wants to kill herself."

"She should have thought about that before she initiated Kataryna's and Francesco's senseless kidnapping. I almost lost my fiancé and Luca his. I couldn't eat or sleep for days. I am still not 100 percent until Francesco stands in front of me."

"I understand, Patrizia and I felt the same at first. We could have lost Kataryna, Francesco and Roberto if things had gone really bad. I don't know if our family would have recovered from that kind of tragedy. To be honest, I feel kind of sorry for her. I can't help thinking about how Roberto had lost control of his senses in Venice when he drugged Luca because he was obsessed with Kataryna. He should have gotten professional help before letting it go that far. I think the same happened to Larissa. She was totally infatuated with Roberto. We just don't know enough about these kinds of psychological conditions and what they can do to people."

"No, we don't," Patrizia agrees, "but if Luca had not survived Roberto's assault, we would not have forgiven him."

"Suffice it to say that in both cases we were lucky to get our loved ones back alive. I have forgiven both of them."

"I am not there yet with Larissa," Patrizia admits, "but I have forgiven Roberto, especially after what he just accomplished. Getting Kataryna and Francesco out of the hands of these ruthless human traffickers is a heroic deed. He risked his life to save theirs."

"Which brings up the question if he did it because he still loves Kataryna and that love gave him the strength to pull it off. I understand they have some dramatic footage of how he and Sergio stormed the building to get Kataryna and Francesco out of there in the nick of time."

"Don't go there, Carlotta. He not only saved Kataryna's life but also Francesco's, for which I will be eternally grateful. Not to mention that his friend Sergio also risked his life and he didn't do it because he is in love with Kataryna."

Carlotta chuckles. "No, probably not but he may have done it for his best friend who loves her."

"So what are you saying? You think he is not over her yet?"

"Well, I am not over him so I have to wonder if he can really be over her. He admitted that he loved her deeply when he went through therapy."

"Only he and his therapist know that for sure, I guess. Are you still hoping for a relationship with him?"

"That would be my dream ending. Roberto, me, our son and Enrico together as a family but I have to be realistic."

"I wish that for you, Carlotta but would Luca be happy with that outcome?"

"I think after what Roberto just did for him, he would not stand in our way."

"True. Wouldn't it be ironic if the woman who was the catalyst for their friendship ending so abruptly could also be the reason for them to rekindle it?"

"All in the spirit of love. For now I am living in the moment, Patrizia. The past is history and the future is unpredictable. Why worry about it?"

"Exactly. Speaking of the future, are you up to joining me next week for the final fitting of my wedding dress?"

"I wouldn't miss it for the world, my dear."

"I will do the same for you if….."

"Let's not fantasize, Patrizia. I have to keep it real."

"OK. Let's get some rest now so we are ready when our guys arrive here from Brazil. I have prepared everything for a wildly romantic night with Francesco."

"Hahaha," Carlotta laughs out loud. "The poor guy. After the ordeal he just went through."

"He has about 12 hours to rest on the plane," Patrizia responds enthusiastically. "I am sure he will rise to the occasion."

◆ ◆ ◆

"Welcome home to bella Italia," the pilot announces as the jet touches down in Milan.

"How are you doing, Kataryna?" Dr. de Angelis asks her.

"Never better," she responds smiling. "Just get these straps off me, please." She impatiently tries to open them herself.

"Whoa. Hold your horses." Luca opens the door to the plane and summons two men to come up with a wheelchair.

"Here comes your coach, Principessa. Just enjoy the ride."

"Really? Do I have to go on there?"

"Some people would kill for a royal treatment like this but not my sister, of course," Francesco jokes.

"I wish someone would carry me down the stairs," Sergio says. "I am aching all over. I need a really good massage."

"You and me, both," Roberto chimes in.

They head down the stairs where two cars are waiting for them on the tarmac. Luca positions Kataryna into the back seat of one of the cars.

"We will have a welcome and thank you party soon for all of you," Luca says hugging Salvatore, Sergio and Roberto. "There are no words strong enough to express how grateful I am to each one of you." He looks at Roberto to make a point.

Kataryna waves at her rescuers. "You guys rock, all of you. She throws them a kiss. "Love you. See you soon."

Roberto smiles at her. Love you more, he thinks as Luca and Francesco get into the car with her and close the doors.

"I will be home in about 40 minutes," Francesco calls his fiancée as they are leaving the airport. "I am sorry to report, though, that I didn't get a chance to buy you a gift this time," he jokes. "I was a bit busy trying to stay alive."

"Just get here fast," Patrizia responds happily.

"Did we just experience the most insane event of our lives? Francesco asks, looking at his sister.

"Yep," Kataryna nods, "and lived to tell about it. What doesn't kill you makes you stronger, though."

"I only regret that we didn't have a chance to see more of Brazil. It's an amazing country. Well, when we go back to finalize the due diligence we can make up for it."

Kataryna looks at him sideways. "You really are my brother. I was just thinking the same."

"Ah, excuse me," Luca voices sarcastically, "are you two trying to kill me?" He gives Kataryna an intense look. "I am not going through this again, darling. This was the ultimate torture. Let's recover from this ordeal first and get our lives back to normal before anyone goes anywhere."

"Of course," Kataryna agrees with him softly.

"By the way, I have moved our wedding up so that will have to be your first priority now."

"Moved it up to when?" she asks.

"Beginning of July. Not negotiable."

Kataryna looks at him seductively. "You really are seriously sexy when you take charge, Luca. I will be yours in July, then."

Luca smiles shaking his head. "You just disarmed me, once again."

"I am always a step ahead of you, Luca Romano."

"Remains to be seen," he counters with a cute grin. "I think I am catching up with you fast."

"Ooh, you are getting uppity with me," Kataryna remarks.

"This can't end well. You two need to be alone now. Let me out of here," Francesco says laughing when the driver stops the car in front of his apartment building. The door flings open and Patrizia lets out a loud scream.

"Oh my God. What happened to your face?"

"I told you. I had a minor collision with a fist," he responds laughing.

"Welcome home, everyone." She hugs and kisses Francesco first and then greets her brother and Kataryna with a long hug. "Do you want to come in for a moment?"

"No, thanks," Luca says. "I need to get Kataryna home to Lake Como. Let's meet in Bellagio for a family get-together in the next few days."

"Need to or want to get me home?" Kataryna challenges him again.

"Both," he responds. "What's with the interrogation?"

"Take it as my version of foreplay today," Kataryna responds affectionately.

Mariya runs toward the car as it pulls into the villa's driveway. "Mamma mia," she exclaims, "grazie a Dio, Signora, you are safe now. I went to church everyday to pray for you." Tears of joy streaming down her face.

"Grazie, Mariya," Kataryna also in tears, embraces her. "The prospect of never being able to eat your delicious meals again was the worst of the ordeal."

"Oh, Signora, that was so sweet," Mariya responds to Kataryna's cute white lie.

Luca watches the two women hugging and crying, suppressing tears himself. He takes a relieved breath looking at Lake Como recalling Kataryna's first time there and all the amazing moments they shared at his villa since then. "That was a close one," he says quietly. "I will never let that happen again."

After one of Mariya's sumptuous meals, Luca and Kataryna take a walk along the lake.

"I swear this lake gets more beautiful every time I look at it," Kataryna marvels.

"And so are you, Principessa. I don't even want to think about what I would have done if you had disappeared forever."

"I wouldn't have just disappeared, darling. I knew what would be at stake for me if they had succeeded in putting me into sex slavery. That's not a world that I wanted to experience. So I made a pact with Francesco to kill me before they could transfer me to some god-forsaken area."

"And he agreed to kill his sister?"

"Not at first. He said he couldn't do it but when I begged him and painted a picture for him of what it would be like for me to be abused like that, he reluctantly agreed. If he hadn't, I would have killed myself. I wanted to die with the knowledge that you were the last one who had the pleasure of having me like this, and then I would have become your guardian angel. I would have brought you another woman to love so you could have a happy life until we met again."

"While I believe in many of your powers, Principessa, that is one thing you couldn't have done. There could never be another woman to make me as happy as you do. This would also have been the end of my life. Thank God, it turned out in our favor. However, that means that from now on I may be somewhat overprotective. I hope you will understand and remember why when that happens."

"I will do my very best not to put us into any position like that again but some things maybe out of my control."

"Let me handle the things out of your control."

"I put my life in your hands, darling."

"Good. Now that we settled that how about you get some rest?"

"I was unconscious for days and rested. I don't want to close my eyes. I am afraid I won't wake up again."

"OK. Here's another idea. Would you like to rest together with me with eyes open?"

"That is a much more appealing version of resting, darling. I need to feel alive after what I have been through."

"As always, your wish is my command, Principessa. I will make you come alive. Pun intended."

Kataryna leads Luca into the master bathroom. "How about our famous bath for starters?"

"I was just thinking the same. Maybe tonight we can create even more memories. I'll get a nice drink for us to relax with."

"Hurry back." She kisses him softly.

Kataryna gets comfortable in the hot water. Leaning back she lets the bubbles cradle her body while listening to the beautiful music Luca put on, grateful to be back home in one piece in her perfect life. A burst of tears escapes her eyes, realizing how close she came to death.

"Let it all out, darling. You are safe now," Luca says returning with the drinks.

"I know I am. I felt safe with you from the first day we met. What a great feeling to know you always have my back."

"This time having your back wasn't enough, though. I had to rely on some other people to help me to get you out of that mess."

"I can't believe how many people risked their lives to save mine. I am so grateful that everyone came out of this unharmed."

"Me, too, darling. We'll do something appropriate for all of them. For starters, tomorrow we'll make a donation to organizations working on stopping human trafficking. I also want to contribute to Salvatore's research project at his clinic, and Roberto mentioned some native tribes in Brazil who are looking for support to preserve the rain forests. We'll look into all that, too while working on completing your acquisition over there. Now let's get back to us and think some happy thoughts."

"Yes, let's. In case I haven't told you yet, you are the most amazing person I have ever met in my entire life. I thank the universe every day for bringing you to me."

Luca smiles at her. "And here I thought the universe brought you to me. Hmm, I wonder what really happened?"

"I think we both got it right. The universe just knew we needed each other."

"Speaking about needs…," he murmurs.

"Yeah. I am ready for you," she whispers, letting her hand slide down his body under the warm water.

SIXTEEN

"Ciao Carlotta. When can we get together to talk?" Roberto calls her a few days after his return from Brazil.

"I have been waiting for your call. When and where would you like to meet?"

"Sorry for not calling sooner. I had to reflect on a few things first. I am pretty flexible except for tomorrow afternoon when I have an appointment with my therapist. I think it's important to get everything out in the open. We will need some privacy, so can we meet at either my home or yours?"

"Would you like to come over to my place for dinner after your therapy session tomorrow?"

"That would be good if it fits your schedule."

"I don't have much of a schedule these days, Roberto. I am pregnant. So other than my work, regular doctor's visits and seeing my family, I am usually at home."

"What time would you like me there?" he asks.

"Whenever you are done with your appointment. By the way, Larissa came to see me a few days ago."

"What did she want? She didn't threaten you, did she?"

"No. She asked for my forgiveness."

"She should ask for Kataryna's and Francesco's forgiveness. They almost died because of her."

"They were on the plane with you coming back from Brazil. So she came to see me. I guess to test the waters. She is suicidal. I advised her to think of her daughter and go for therapy."

"Well, since I am a major cause for her situation, I will discuss it with Dr. Giordano tomorrow."

"Are you saying that you feel guilty about what she did?"

"Maybe in a way. I have to sort it out yet."

"Why would you feel this way? That would be as if Kataryna felt guilty about what you did to her and Luca but your obsession with her wasn't their fault."

"I could have handled it differently, I believe. I may have triggered her insane actions. Unfortunately I ignored the early warning signs."

"Well, as far as I know this all started after she found some photos on your phone and concluded that you and Kataryna were having an affair. May I ask why you still kept these photos? I would think after all that happened in Venice you would have deleted them. They, at the time, definitely made me believe that Kataryna and you were having an affair."

"Dr. Giordano and I are using these photos for my therapy. He wants to see how I react to them as time goes by. We can talk about that tomorrow."

"OK. See you then. Ciao."

Carlotta calls her sister after she hangs up with Roberto. "Do you have a moment to talk?"

"Sure. Is everything okay?"

"Roberto just called me. He wants to get together to talk."

"Talk about what?"

"He didn't exactly say about what. Just that we need to talk."

"Ooh. Interesting," Patrizia says.

"I wouldn't read anything into it. He is going to a therapy session tomorrow and wants to discuss Larissa with his psychiatrist. It appears he feels guilty about how he treated her. He thinks he could have triggered her actions."

"Really? This is getting complicated if he feels like that."

"Yeah, I also asked him why he still has the photos of him and Kataryna on his phone. He said his doctor is using them in their therapy sessions to see how he reacts to them. Obviously, there must still be lingering feelings if the psychiatrist wants to use them in his treatment. Honestly, it kind of rattled me. I just needed to talk to someone about it."

"Yeah, yeah, no problem, Carlotta. Just wait to hear what he has to say tomorrow. I hope all turns out well. Francesco just mailed him an invitation to our wedding next month. Hopefully he can be your date."

Carlotta lightens up. "Nice thought, little sister. Let's see what he comes up with tomorrow. How is Francesco?"

"He just left to see his parents to discuss his adoption and how to go about communicating it to their extended family. Thereafter Kataryna will tell her father that she found her brother and reveal his identity.

"My goodness. I can't believe all these changes we are going through right now. I got to go. Thanks for listening. Ciao."

◆◆◆

Roberto arrives at Dr. Giordano's office.

"Ciao Roberto," the doctor greets him. "Well, you've become quite a hero. I am so proud of you."

Roberto signals him to stop. "I just did what anyone else would have done to help out a friend in a desperate situation."

"Why are you playing this down? Most people, including me, wouldn't and couldn't do what you just did. You saved two people's lives. They wouldn't be here today without you. What part of that don't you understand?"

"I saved some lives but I also ruined some."

"Go on," the doctor prompts him.

"Carlotta Romano and Larissa Dos Santos are both seriously unhappy because of me and one is suicidal."

"Which one?"

"Larissa. She went to see Carlotta a few days ago and apparently told her she wants to kill herself because of what she has done. I guess she is facing an indictment of some sort once the prosecutor has all the facts and can bring a suit against her. I am pretty sure Luca wants to bring her to justice and I don't blame him."

"That's not your fault, Roberto. You did not encourage her feelings for you. So get off the guilt trip."

"The idea that my behavior might have triggered her to have suicidal thoughts is tough to digest."

"You were in a similar situation with Kataryna at one time. Your controlled substance abuse at that time was the way your body reacted to scream for help. You may not have consciously determined to commit suicide but you were in a depressive state and the signs were there. Honestly, with all these pills and the alcohol on top of it you could easily have killed yourself."

"Yeah. I completely lost control, that's for sure and I didn't care if I lived or died. That was a dark time. I don't ever want to go through something like this again."

"Let me ask you this. How did you feel when you rescued Kataryna Taylor?"

"I don't even know how to answer this question. There are so many parts to that."

"OK. Then answer this. Would you have done that for any other person? For instance for Carlotta?"

"The short answer is yes."

"I would like to hear the long version."

"Yes, but for different reasons."

"You are evasive, Roberto. Please elaborate."

"For Carlotta because she feels like part of my family. For Kataryna because she is everything I ever wanted in a woman. If something bad had happened to her, I would have been capable of killing the responsible person without giving it another thought. Don't worry. I understand that I will never have a romantic relationship with her."

"I am glad you qualified that, Roberto."

"I am working on myself but I have a long way to go. I often wonder why she came into my life when I can't have her. It's a bit cruel, don't you think?"

"We'll get you where you need to be in due time. Please come see me again in a week. Meanwhile hold your head up high and be proud of what you accomplished."

"Thanks, Dottore. One question. Is it possible for a person to romantically love two people equally at the same time?"

"I had a couple of cases where people claimed to have loved two people the same way but once they chose the one to be with they were fully committed to that person. However, this is not an exact science and there are many variables. Why do you ask?"

"Just curious. See you next week."

"Or sooner if you feel the need," the doctor offers.

◆ ◆ ◆

"Come in, Roberto. How was your day?" Carlotta greets him.

"Good, considering what I just went through. The Brazilian police asked me to review the footage of our rescue mission again to see if I could find any more clues about the human traffickers."

"I would like to see the footage, too."

"Here you go." He hands her his phone.

"Oh my God! This looks like a war zone. I can't believe you are alive." She gasps for air.

He takes the phone from her. "This wasn't a good idea in your present state."

"Wait, I didn't see the end yet." She reaches out to take the phone back.

"Let it go, Carlotta."

"OK, Roberto. You wanted to talk."

"Yes. Here's what I need you to know. I am going to help Kataryna and Francesco complete the acquisition of the Brazilian company. Thereafter I will leave Italy for a while to reflect on my personal life and my future."

Carlotta looks at him sadly. "Where will you go?"

"Far enough away from here so I won't run into anyone connected to the mess I made. I am trying to regain equilibrium. I suppose Kataryna was the catalyst for me to become a better person."

"I wish I could have been that person. What about your therapy?"

"Dr. Giordano agreed to do it via video call."

He sees the sadness in her eyes. "I am sorry, Carlotta. In my present state there is no way I could lead a normal personal life with anyone."

"Except with Kataryna, I guess," she states, her voice faltering.

He ponders his response for a moment. "I am sure that I would not pursue her again or do anything to harm Luca. I made peace with the fact that these two are meant to be together. Dr. Giordano did an incredible job bringing me out of the dark I lived in a few months ago. What he cannot do, though, is eliminate my feelings for her. You can't erase that kind of love with a magic wand. It will take time to heal. That's why I can't offer you, or any woman for that matter, a romantic relationship right now."

"I didn't expect that anyway," Carlotta says recovering from the initial disappointment. "If anyone, I should be the person to understand what you are feeling because I feel the same for a man who is unattainable to me."

"I guess we have something in common then," he says.

"Yeah, and you know what they say. Misery loves company. Maybe you and I should open up a lonely hearts club."

Roberto takes her hand. "Thank you for understanding. We will get through it somehow. Meanwhile I asked my lawyer to open up a trust account for our son once he is born. I will be back for the birth in September."

"Thank you. It would be nice to have his father there for his birth. Ready to have some dinner?"

"I am. I feel so much better now with this conversation out of the way. Somehow a huge burden has been lifted off my shoulders."

"If there's anything you need, Roberto, I will be here for you and I promise I won't tell anyone where you are if that is what you want."

"Good to know I have a friend I can trust."

◆ ◆ ◆

"Ciao, Kataryna, would you have some time to meet with me this morning?" Roberto calls her the first day back at the office.

"Yes, of course. I was just going to call you. Larissa's brother has removed himself as our attorney so we will be working with one of the other partners of the firm."

"Good."

"Yeah. It's for the best. Larissa tried to call me but needless to say, I can't talk to her under the circumstances, apart from the fact that Luca wouldn't stand for it anyway. See you in a few minutes."

Kataryna's assistant escorts Roberto to her office.

"I still can't believe what you did for us." She greets him with a hug.

The scent of her perfume triggers a flashback of his assault on her in Venice. He tries to shake it off quickly. She motions him to take a seat on the couch.

"How can I ever thank you? Well, I might have an idea."

He smiles. "I didn't do this to get something in return. This was a matter of life and death for two people I admire and respect. Not to mention that I needed to redeem myself with you."

"And you did, Roberto, by taking such a huge risk. Luca and I watched the footage of the rescue mission. We were in awe of how you and Sergio charged in there. It looked like a scene out of an extremely thrilling action movie. Only, this was real."

"Here's an idea, Kataryna. Why don't you write a book about your ordeal and then sell it to a Hollywood film producer."

"Not a bad idea." Kataryna is all excited. "You are on to something. You can help me write the action part how you broke us out of there and what you went through in the process. We can be co-authors. I can see the credits rolling already. Based on a true-life story written by Kataryna Taylor and Roberto Silvestri. Hehe."

"By the time we finish that book, it would be Kataryna Romano, I believe, or are you keeping your current last name?"

"Oh no, of course I am taking Luca's last name."

"Why don't we table the thought about writing a book for later?" Roberto suggests.

"Absolutely. I am actually going to start on it in my free time. That was a genius idea, Roberto. I predict that you and I will be famous one day."

"I love your energy and enthusiasm. You make me feel alive."

"Listen, I would like to make you an offer," she starts.

"I am intrigued." He looks at her raising his eyebrows.

"How would you like to take the position of CEO at our new Brazilian company after we complete the acquisition? You can work out of Milan but you would have to travel over there several times a year."

"Wow! I didn't expect that one." He runs his hands through his hair, stalling for time.

"Please say you'll do it. I need you, Roberto."

His emotions are all over the place. "I... I don't know what to say, Kataryna."

"Luca is on board with that idea. He didn't even hesitate when I asked him."

"I came over here because I wanted to tell you that once we have completed the acquisition, I will leave Italy for a while."

"Fine with me if you want to work out of Brazil instead."

He sighs. "This is not about wanting to be in another country. This is about you and my feelings for you. I can't be that close to you for now. Not because I would do anything to you or Luca but rather to protect myself so I can heal and resolve these feelings for you. It would be like an alcoholic having a bottle of booze constantly within reach."

"Yeah, but didn't you tell me that you know you can't have that bottle and are moving on?"

"Knowing that is one thing, but how does it make me feel? I've got to be at a safe distance for now."

"I am sorry to hear that. I thought this was over."

"It is over as far as me not being a danger to you two or anyone else but I can't just wish these feelings away or make them disappear on command. So obviously being around you would not be therapeutic for me, rather the opposite. For that reason, I have to decline that offer regardless how attractive it sounds. At any other time I would have been thrilled to take this position and work with you to make this a phenomenal success."

"I have to respect your decision under these circumstances but I am enormously disappointed. It's also painful to know what you are going through. If there is anything I can do to make it easier for you, please, by all means, let me know." Her face turns sad.

"I am afraid it's up to me to find a way to deal with that. While we are on the subject, I better let you know that I explained it to Carlotta already so she understands why I can't offer her a relationship, although she is pregnant with my child."

"I still have to process all this." Kataryna shakes her head in disbelief. "I am not going to fill this position for now in the hope that you will take it in the not too distant future. I wouldn't know whom else to offer it to anyway. There is no one out there with your credentials or whom I trust to take on this enormous challenge. Meanwhile, Francesco will have to act as CEO for both companies. I am also going to ask Ernesto Oliveira to stay on a bit longer than anticipated to bridge the gap."

"That's a good plan, Kataryna. As always you've got everything under control."

"I don't have a choice right now, Roberto, but I will revisit my original plan with you at the helm down the road."

"I can't think that far into the future. I have to stay in the present now. Once I leave here, I am going to have to cut contact with all of you, so I can focus on my new life."

"What about Carlotta?"

"I will be loosely in touch with her but we agreed that we would never bring up the subject of you or anything related. I intend to be back in September for the birth of my son."

"Did Carlotta tell you that she wants me to be your son's godmother?"

"Yes, and I would be very happy to see Luca as the godfather."

"OK. Just remember the Brazilian CEO position will be open for you whenever you want to take it."

"Thanks. You trusting me to work with you means a lot. Are you talking to Salvatore de Angelis regarding the development of the medicinal plants?"

"Yes, we are in advanced discussions to form a joint venture in that area."

"Maybe Sergio would be a good prospect to approach for the Brazilian CEO job?"

She shrugs her shoulders. "It's something to consider as plan B."

"I am going to head over to Francesco's office now to finalize some paperwork. Hopefully we can close this deal soon."

"Are you in such a hurry to get out of here?" Kataryna jokes.

"I am sure you can understand that I would like to get started on my new life as soon as possible."

"I do and I wish you well."

◆ ◆ ◆

"Looks like you are in deep thought," Luca enters Kataryna's office finding her staring into the room.

"I may have to rethink my management plan. Roberto has decided to leave Italy for a while."

"It will be good for him to get away from here to get a new perspective. I just hope that it doesn't rattle Carlotta too much."

"He told her already that he will be leaving after we closed the Brazilian acquisition. Apparently she took it well. However, I am not sure how she really feels deep down inside. I think she still had some hope that they might have a life together as a family."

"Maybe you can have a talk with her?"

"I will, but I have to be honest, Luca. I am struggling myself knowing what he is going through because of me."

"Look, we have to be realistic. There will always be a big hole in his heart because of what happened. So maybe it's for the best if he isn't around us for some time."

"Do you think that makes it any easier for me?" she asks. "He will not get over this ever. The best we can hope for is that he will learn to live with it and hopefully find peace and a person he loves to share his life with. However, he will never again be the person he used to be."

"I know it doesn't make it easier for you. I'll just have to do my very best to distract you from thinking about it. So why don't we start by focusing on our wedding now? Have you told your family and friends yet that we have moved our wedding date up to July?"

"No, I wanted to wait until we were sure when we will have it."

"We are sure," Luca smiles. "You can go ahead and alert the media."

"Hey, speaking of media," Kataryna spurts out in a lighter tone, "Roberto had a great idea earlier. He suggested that I should write a book about my ordeal."

"Do you really want to go back to that experience?" Luca is skeptical.

"I always wanted to write a book about certain of my life experiences and with what I have been through just now it would be a real thriller. It may even become a movie."

"I see. Will Roberto be in it?"

"I don't see how I can leave him out of it, but you, my darling, would be the star, of course."

"I'd rather be your star in real life, Principessa and I really don't want to relive the Venice incident either."

"I understand but I have been bitten by the writing bug now. So I will just write the book for myself and not show it to anyone. At least for now."

"Go ahead. As long as it doesn't stir you up or make you unhappy."

"I think it would be therapeutic for me."

Francesco walks into her office. "You wanted to see me, Kataryna?"

"Yes, I thought we should call --," she is interrupted by her phone ringing. She looks at the screen.

"It's my, I mean our father. I was just going to suggest we call him and let him know."

"Hallo Papa," Kataryna answers putting him on speakerphone. "I had planned to call you too in a moment. Is everything okay?"

"Yes. I am just calling to see how you are doing and to talk about my trip to Italy for Francesco's and Patrizia's wedding."

"Yeah, about that..." Kataryna pauses glancing at Francesco.

"What about it? Did something happen?" he asks alarmed.

"Yes, but something good. First of all, I need you to know that Luca and I will get married in the beginning of July instead of September. So you will have to attend two weddings within a month or so, and I would like to introduce you to your son before you get here."

"Are you saying you found your brother?"

"Yes, and you are not going to believe who it is."

"You mean I know him? Is he someone famous?"

"Famous? Not yet," she laughs, "but you have met him at my engagement party. Say hello to your son and my brother, Francesco Barone."

She hears her father take a deep breath. "Oh my God. "Are you sure?"

"Yes, no doubt. I got the paperwork and DNA to prove it."

"Does he know?"

She signals Francesco to speak.

"Hallo Papa," Francesco greets him. "How about joining me for my 33rd birthday party and make up for lost time?"

Dear Readers,

Thank you very much for purchasing my book. I hope you enjoyed reading it as much as I loved writing it for your entertainment.

If you liked this story, the favor of a review is requested on the site where you purchased this book and any other review site, like Goodreads, you wish to post your review to.

I would also appreciate it if you would share your opinion on your social media channels.

If you would like to connect with me on social media, you can do so on these sites:

Twitter: @Karynne_Summars
Facebook Fan Pages:
Desperate Pursuit in Venice
Desperate Pursuit in Rio de Janeiro
Karynne Summars

My blog: http://ksny25.wordpress.com

Please sign up with your email address via my official website: www.karynnesummars.com for updates on future books. Your email address will not be shared or sold to anyone.

All the best,

Karynne Summars

Karynne Summars

The author of the drama romance thriller novels Desperate Pursuit in Venice and Desperate Pursuit in Rio de Janeiro was born and raised in Berlin, Germany. She currently lives in New York and Marbella, Spain. The winner of the 2014 MARSocial Author-of-the-Year Award and an Executive Producer of the psychological thriller / mystery feature film Disturbed (2015) was named one of the winners in the 2014 "50 Great Writers You Should Be Reading" contest.

Website: www.karynnesummars.com